CONTENTS

The Chequered History of This Book	5
Chapter 1	13
Chapter 2	18
Chapter 3	28
Chapter 4	33
Chapter 5	37
Chapter 6	43
Chapter 7	48
Chapter 8	54
Chapter 9	56
Chapter 10	62
Chapter 11	65
Chapter 12	71
Chapter 13	83
Chapter 14	86
Chapter 15	92
Chapter 16	97
Chapter 17	112
Chapter 18	124
Chapter 19	130
Chapter 20	139

Chapter 21	144
Chapter 22	152
Chapter 23	156
Chapter 24	169
Chapter 25	180
Chapter 26	183
Chapter 27	196
Chapter 28	201
Chapter 29	207
Chapter 30	214
Chapter 31	221
Chapter 32	226
Chapter 33	232
Chapter 34	241
Chapter 35	249
Chapter 36	265

CHARLES TOWNSEND

Charles Townsend is a member of The Magic Circle and particularly enjoys devising new magic tricks. He is now retired from a long career running companies. In 2012 he took over a pub with his eldest son and has since built a brewery and distillery in the pub's outbuildings. He lives with his wife Hayley in an historic house in old Harwich and has five children.

CHARLES TOWNSEND

The Magician's Secret
Charles Townsend

Book 1 of Illusions of Power

The Magician's Secret
All rights reserved

No part of this book may be reproduced in any form by photocopying or any electronic mechanical means, including information storage or retrieval systems, without permission in writing from the copyright owner and publisher of the book.

All characters are fictional. Any similarity to any actual person is purely coincidental.

© Charles Townsend 2021

Published by

Charles Townsend

West Street

Harwich

THE CHEQUERED HISTORY OF THIS BOOK

The Magician's Secret was originally written over 25 years ago. When it was first written it was entitled 'Magic of the Mind', but as with many new novels, it failed to find a publisher

A series of disasters then struck. My wife died of cancer and I was left working full time and bringing up my two youngest children. This did not leave much time for pursuing a writing career and 'Magic of the Mind' was consigned to the bottom drawer of my desk. In 2011 the house two doors away caught fire. The fire spread in both directions and five houses were burnt down including mine. The house was largely destroyed and it took two years to rebuild. My desk was badly burned but I managed to retrieve some of its contents including most of 'Magic of the Mind', although it was singed and soaked in water. I was not able to dry it properly since there were many other things that needed attention. It was placed in a plastic carton and stored with the other items I had rescued.

During the covid lockdown I decided to look at it again. So I got out the carton. Some of the pages had been burned and many more were stuck together. But by prising the pages apart, and where necessary turning to an earlier draft, I was able to read it. I was pleasantly surprised and decided it was worth developing. The original title did not inspire, so I retitled it 'The Magician's Secret', edited it, tidied the plot and published it.

THE MAGICIAN'S SECRET

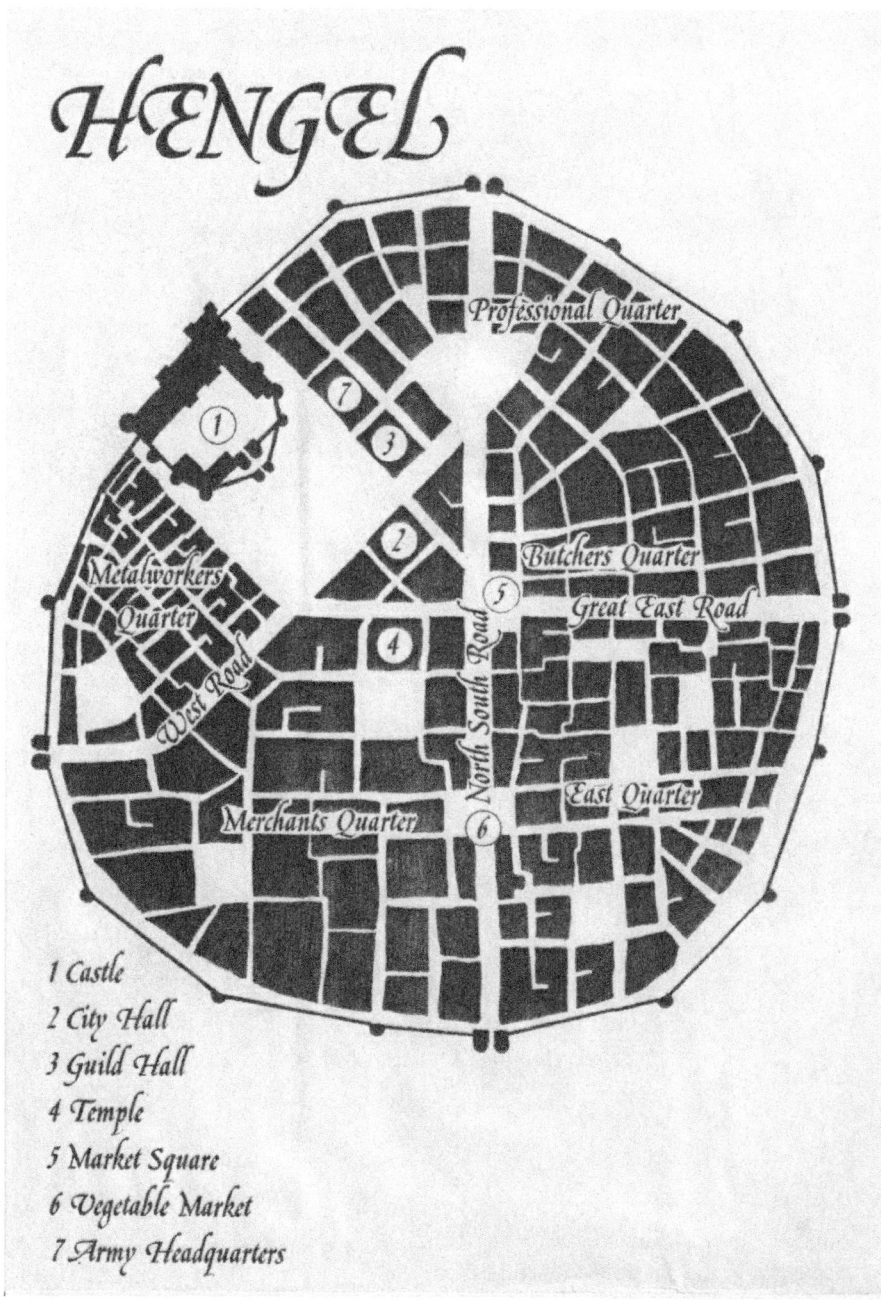

1 Castle
2 City Hall
3 Guild Hall
4 Temple
5 Market Square
6 Vegetable Market
7 Army Headquarters

HENGEL CASTLE

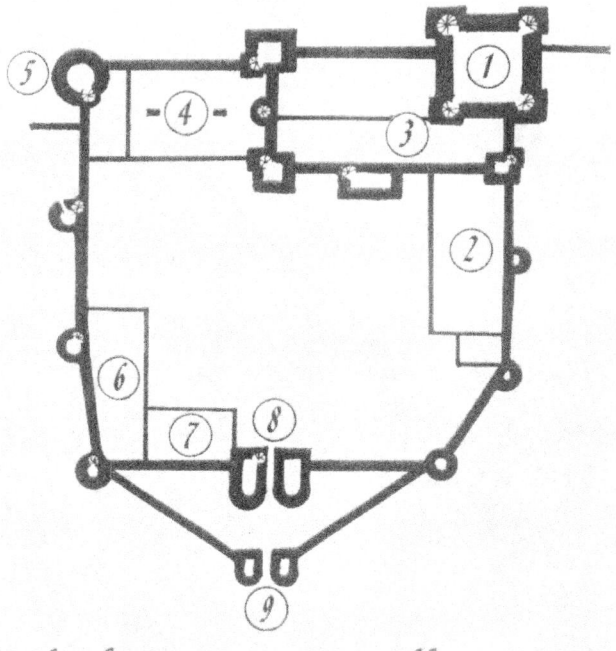

1 Hengel's Keep
2 Great Hall
3 Rooms of State
4 Kitchen and Offices
5 Lyles Tower
6 Stables
7 Servants' Wing
8 Great Gate
9 Barbican

THE MAGICIAN'S SECRET

HENGEL CASTLE

Ground Floor 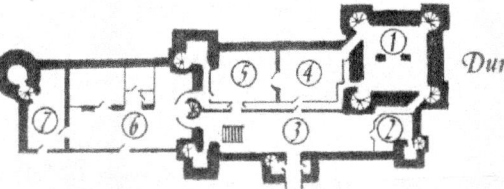 Dungeons below

1 Armoury
2 Court
3 Grand Hall and Stair
4 Blue Drawing Room
5 Royal Dining Room
6 Kitchen
7 Servants' Hall

First Floor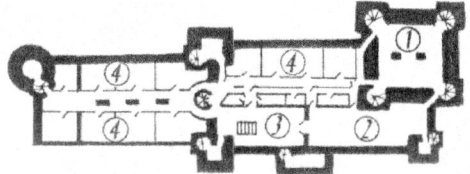

1 Guard Room
2 Throne Room
3 Lobby
4 Offices of State

Second Floor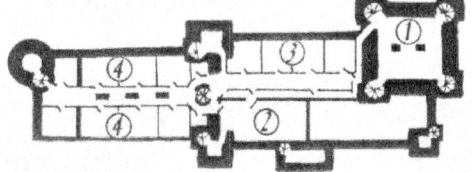

1 Duke's Drawing Room
2 Library
3 Royal Bedchambers
4 Bedchambers

Third Floor

1 Duke's Bedchamber

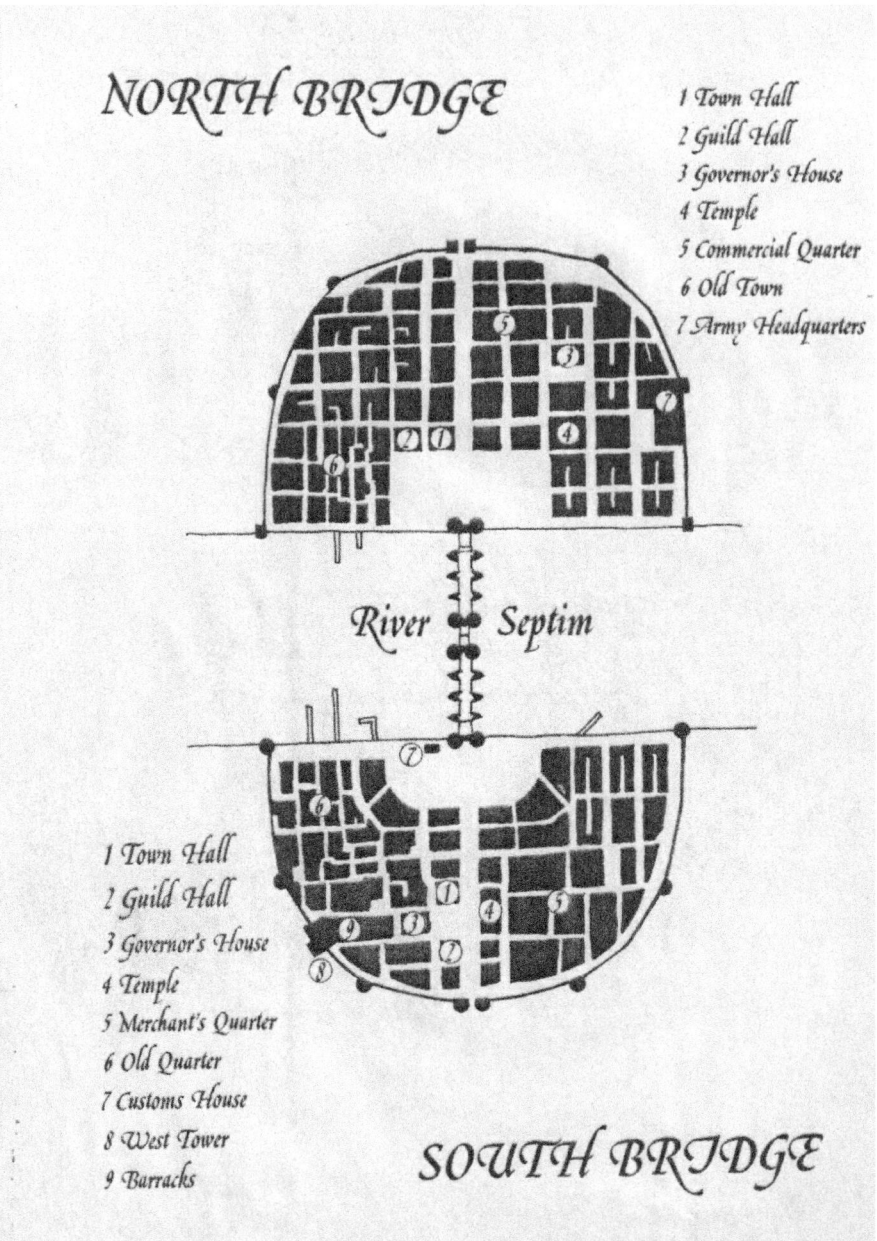

THE MAGICIAN'S SECRET

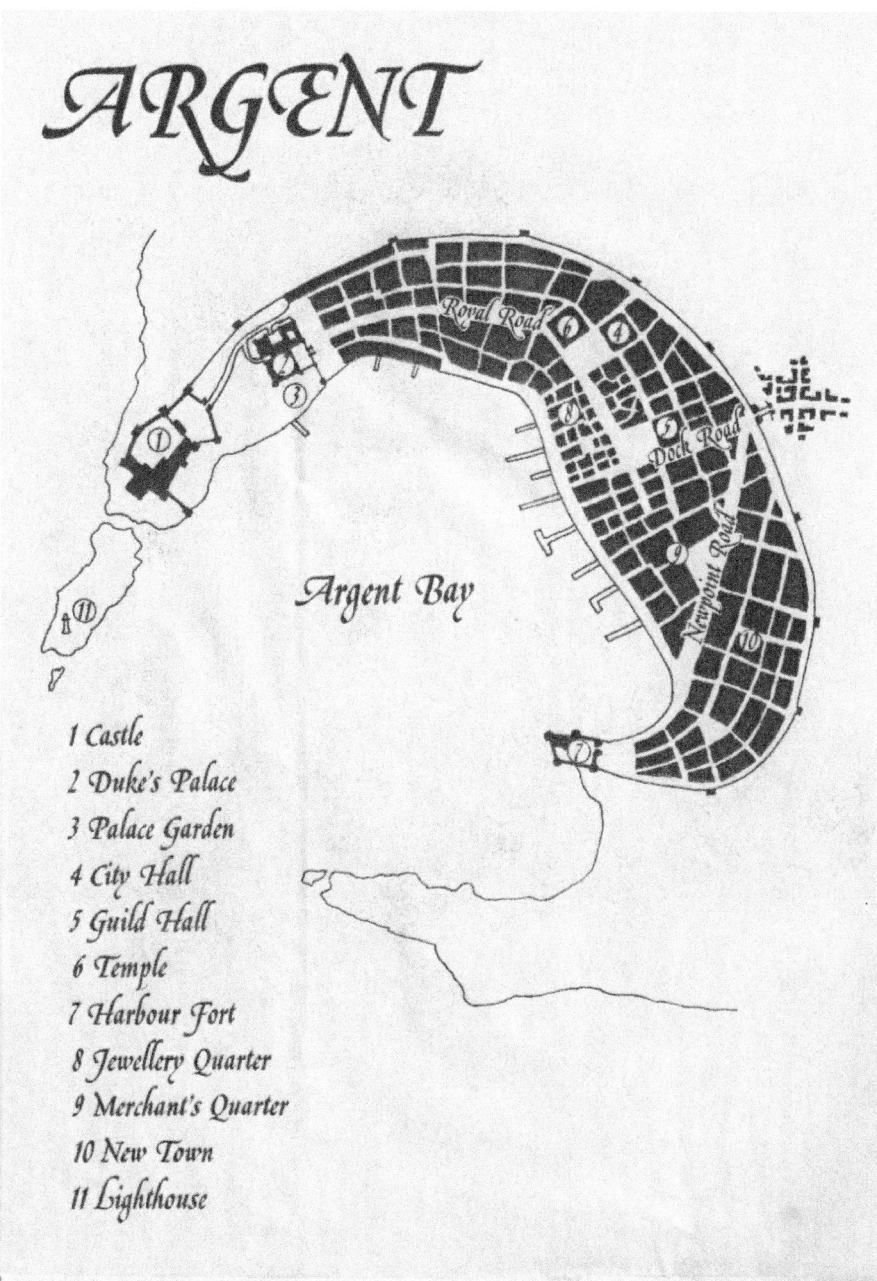

ARGENT

Argent Bay

1 Castle
2 Duke's Palace
3 Palace Garden
4 City Hall
5 Guild Hall
6 Temple
7 Harbour Fort
8 Jewellery Quarter
9 Merchant's Quarter
10 New Town
11 Lighthouse

CHARLES TOWNSEND

CHAPTER 1

Delvin stood looking down at the bundle of rags in the corner. Where was he? His mind was a complete blank.

"Murderer!"

Delvin spun round towards the voice. A black clad figure was pointing at him accusingly.

"You've murdered him!... Landlord! Landlord!" the figure shouted. "Landlord… Come quickly…There's been a murder!"

Delvin looked around him in growing panic. The room looked a wreck, and for some reason he could not remember he was holding a chair leg in his hand.

He looked again at the pile of rags, and with a sudden shock realised it was a person. He stepped closer, and felt the blood run from his face as he saw in horror that it was his friend Borlock the travelling magician. Borlock's red robe was ripped open, a knife was protruding from his chest, and blood was welling from the wound.

There was the sound of running outside, and the door burst open.

Delvin turned towards the door and through tears in his eyes saw the sturdy figure of Berman, the Ploughman's Inn's landlord, charge into the room with a cudgel in his hand and one of the kitchen boys following closely behind.

"Help him," pleaded Delvin. "We must help Borlock."

"What's all this?" demanded Berman.

"It's Borlock. Someone's stabbed Borlock," gasped Delvin.

"You stabbed him. You're a murderer!"

They all turned to the black figure still pointing his accusing finger at Delvin.

"You must be mistaken sir," began Berman. "I know Delvin. He and Borlock were great…" A sudden glazed look came over the landlord's eyes. "Drop that chair leg my lad and move away from the body." He had raised his cudgel and was advancing menacingly on Delvin.

"I didn't do it," said Delvin desperately.

"Drop that chair leg and come out slowly."

Delvin let go of the chair leg and slowly moved into the centre of the room. He had not had a chance to have a proper look around him before, but now realised he was in Borlock's room in the Ploughman's Inn. Pieces of broken chair and washstand lay around the room, and Borlock's small chest was smashed open, its contents spread about. The figure in black stood by the window with his arms folded and a satisfied smile on his face.

Berman grabbed Delvin's right arm and twisted it up his back. "Right young man, we'll lock you in the cellar and then see what the elders are going to do with you."

"I haven't done anything," said Delvin desperately as he was hauled towards the door. "Listen, please listen! I haven't done anything."

Berman turned to the kitchen boy. "Get the elders, then get Meril to tidy this place up."

Delvin glanced around desperately as Berman yanked him out of the room. "Borlock may not be dead, we must help him. Please…Please! Don't leave Borlock with that man."

Berman hesitated, and looked back towards the black figure still standing by the window. "Come with us please. You'll be needed to give evidence." He nodded to the kitchen boy. "Get Meril to check he's dead. Right, come on."

It was a strange procession that moved through the inn. The kitchen boy ran ahead, calling out to Berman's wife Meril, as he went. Delvin followed his arm still twisted up his back by Berman. The black clad man walked silently behind.

A small crowd had gathered at the bottom of the stairs. They were all faces Delvin knew. Hambil the baker, Korren who worked on the farm with him and seven or eight others.

"What's going on?" asked Korren.

"Will Borlock be telling any more fortunes tonight?" asked another voice.

"Not tonight," growled Berman. "Delvin's murdered him!"

There was instant shocked silence.

"No," said a voice from the crowd.

"I don't believe it."

"Not Delvin."

"You've got that wrong Ber…" The black clad figure had come into view, and there was a moment's silence as he fixed the crowd with a silent stare. The crowd's mood suddenly changed.

"Murdered him, he'll hang!"

"The little…"

"Let me get him."

They had reached the bottom of the stairs, and hands grabbed at Delvin.

"Let him be lads, he must be put before the elders." Berman tried to force a path through. A kick landed on Delvin's shin, and he doubled up in pain, so a punch aimed for his face caught him on the top of the head.

"Lads, we must do this properly," yelled Berman.

"Let's lynch him," came a voice.

More blows and kicks rained in. With his right arm twisted up his back Delvin could not fend them off. Berman suddenly let go of Delvin's arm and swung his cudgel over his head. With the release of his wrist Delvin pitched forward and fell on the floor. A boot thudded into his back and another into his thigh.

"Stop!" yelled Berman. "I said we must do this properly."

The crowd hesitated in the face of Berman's authority.

"Get back to the common room, all of you. We are calling the elders."

There were murmurings and mutterings then the door to the stables suddenly burst open, and a young man with a shock of unruly sandy hair burst in.

"What's happening?" gasped the newcomer.

"Greg, about time," growled Berman. "Help me get these gentlemen back to the common room."

Greg moved forward purposefully, and the crowd began to move back.

"What's going on?" asked Greg again.

"Delvin's killed Borlock," replied Berman grimly.

"He can't have," said Greg incredulously.

"I know you and Delvin are friends but it looks bad, I've called the elders."

"You know Delvin," said Greg. "He wouldn't do that. Come on Berman, he wouldn't kill Borlock. He lived for when Borlock came here. You know he's been teaching him magic. Borlock even said he might take him on as an assistant. He wouldn't kill him... Come on... You saw them talking in the common room after the show today. Delvin had made some charms that he was showing him. He wouldn't kill Borlock. He just wouldn't."

"He's been accused," said Berman glancing towards Greg.

The crowd had moved back to the common room, and Delvin began to carefully pick himself up off the floor, gingerly feeling the lumps and bruises from the fists and boots.

"Right," said Berman turning back to Delvin. "You're going in the cellar until the elders get here."

"But...," started Greg.

"No buts Greg. We do this properly."

Berman opened a door off the passage that led to the cellar. There was no light in the cellar, but with the passage door open Delvin could just see the steps going down. By the time they had reached the bottom of the stairs it was pitch black. Berman knew exactly what he was doing, and from the dark Delvin heard the scrape of a bolt and the squeak of hinges.

"Right, in there."

A hand pushed Delvin, and he stumbled into the blackness. There was a squeak from behind, a clank, and the sound of the bolt being pushed to. The thick storeroom door that now imprisoned him cut off most of the sound from outside, but he heard the faintest sound of steps on the stairs and the clank from above as the cellar door was finally closed and bolted above him.

CHAPTER 2

Delvin felt around himself in the dark. There were stacks of barrels and a pile of boxes and what felt like sacks with lumpy things in. There was a scurrying as some small animal ran across the floor.

He leant back against the barrels and tried to make sense of what had happened. He couldn't believe it. Why couldn't he remember anything? He wouldn't have murdered Borlock. Why had his friends turned against him? He tried to think what was the last thing he could remember.

He had been milking the cows when he had heard that Borlock had come. He had got off work early to go and see Borlock's show. The show was the same one Borlock always did for the children when he visited the village of Byford.

There was the trick with the three cups and several balls, that was the first trick that Borlock had taught him. A lump came to Delvin's throat as he remembered how he had stayed behind after one of Borlock's shows years before, desperate to be taught how it was done. How Borlock had sensed the interest in him and taught him that trick. Delvin pulled his thoughts back.

There was the trick where he made the handkerchiefs disappear which then reappeared on his back.

Then there was the final trick, the genie's palace. That was the way Borlock always ended his show. The children waggling their finger trying to magic away the genie. Then when the palace was lifted, rather than a genie, there was a rabbit.

Delvin started up. The figure in black who had accused him of murder had been there at the back of the crowd. Delvin had noticed him because he didn't seem to laugh when everyone else laughed. It was as though he knew what would happen next. Delvin shivered.

What had happened then? After the show he had helped Borlock pack his things back onto his cart and then driven it through to the stable yard. Greg had come and offered to stable the horse for them. He and Borlock had gone to the common room where he had shown Borlock the trick with the rope he had been learning, and a new charm that he had made out of a piece of glass and some wire. When the first customers for Borlock's fortune telling had come, he had gone to get his supper.

He had returned after supper and looked for Borlock in the common room. There had been no sign of him there, just three or four people looking slightly nervous and bored, probably waiting to get their fortunes told. He had asked the barman where Borlock was. The barman said he had gone upstairs with a stranger. He had decided to follow him upstairs. He remembered hearing shouting.

"You know the penalty for not obeying the Guild."

"Get out of here I want nothing to do with them."

Then there was nothing. A blank until he was in the room with a chair leg in his hand. How had he got there? What had happened?

He was still desperately trying to figure it out, when there was a scrape of bolts from above and the faint sound of feet on the stairs. Delvin's heart seemed to come into his mouth as he realised that they had come to get him.

The bolt on the storeroom door squeaked and crashed open, and light flooded in from a burning torch held by Berman. The flickering flame leant strange shadows to the faces of the three men standing outside the door.

"Out of there," commanded Berman.

Two pairs of hands grabbed Delvin's arms and he was hauled out of the storeroom and up the steps to the inn's main passage.

The door from the passage to the common room was open, and Delvin could see the room had been transformed. The tables and benches were no longer around the walls but had been set in rows facing a table, behind which sat the three village elders. The room was packed. All the benches were filled, and a crowd stood behind. Delvin knew almost every person there. He could see his parents looking worried at one side and Greg pushing forward to try to get himself a better position.

As he was marched in a sudden hush came over the room, and all eyes turned towards him. The chief elder was a bald sallow faced man with a hooked nose. He had never liked Delvin, after Delvin as a joke, had removed the pins from the hinges on his gate, so when he tried to open it, the gate fell off. He now looked Delvin up and down distastefully.

"Delvin Farmhand, you have been accused of murdering the magician Borlock. Did you do it?"

"No!" gasped Delvin.

The chief elder turned towards someone on the other side.

"What have you to say?"

With a sudden chill of fear, Delvin saw the man he had turned to was the stranger in black.

"I saw him stab the magician. It was an unprovoked attack." A rumble of disbelief came from the crowd.

"He wouldn't have."

"Who are you anyway?"

The stranger in black turned to the packed benches, and the noise died away. One of the elders opened his mouth as if to say something, but a look from the stranger stopped him.

The chief elder turned back to Delvin.

"Have you anything to say?"

"I didn't do it," started Delvin. "I don't know what happened. I can't seem to remember anything. I came back to see Borlock after he had finished his fortune telling. I went upstairs. I remember shouting, they said..." Delvin's mind suddenly went blank.

"Well, what did they say?" asked the chief elder irritably.

"I can't seem to remember," whispered Devin, tears beginning to well up in his eyes.

The cold voice of the black figure cut in. "Lost your memory?

How very convenient."

Delvin turned desperately to the chief elder. "Is Borlock dead? I didn't have time to look. Is he dead?"

The chief elder opened his mouth to reply when the cold voice cut in again.

"It is immaterial. The intent to kill him was there."

The chief elder glanced at the black figure then back to Delvin. "Attempted murder carries the same penalty as murder."

"It's not the penalty I am worried about," pleaded Delvin. "I just wanted to know if he was dead."

"Well, you should be worried about the penalty," said the chief elder severely. "The penalty is death."

The sudden realisation stunned Delvin into silence. His mind could not take it all in.

The chief elder turned to Berman and asked him to give his account.

Delvin listened in disbelief as Berman recounted running up to the room after hearing shouting, and finding Delvin, the black robed stranger and the body of Borlock.

The man in black then told how he had heard crashing and entered the room to see Delvin stabbing Borlock. He had at once called for the landlord.

Delvin's mind suddenly seemed to lose its lethargy. If he had stabbed Borlock, why had he had a chair leg in his hand and not a knife? If the man in black had just entered the room, why had he been standing by the window and not the door?

"Sir," began Delvin. "What he says can't be true." Delvin was aware of the man in black's eyes upon him. "If I had stabbed Borlock I couldn't have..." Delvin suddenly couldn't seem to remember what he was about to say.

"Yes?" enquired the chief elder.

"I'm sorry sir. I seem to have forgotten what I was going to say."

"Your forgetfulness seems rather convenient today. You cannot accuse people of lying if you cannot back it up."

"I am sorry sir."

"We have heard the evidence. It only remains for us to decide upon it." He glanced at the other two elders seated next to him who both nodded their heads grimly.

"Delvin Farmhand, we have found you guilty of the murder of Borlock the magician. You will be taken to the village green and hanged by the neck until you are dead. Take him to the green."

If the elders had expected an orderly procession to the green, they were wrong. As hands grabbed Delvin's arms, the whole crowd began to push towards the door. The chief elder tried shouting to let him through, but the crowd ignored him, everyone intent on getting the best position to see the execution.

Delvin and the people holding his arms were swept along. Most of the crowd ignored him and avoided his gaze, but occasional kicks and sly punches landed on his legs and body.

The Ploughman's Inn faced the green, and once through the door the crowd was able to spread out. An ancient tree stood about twenty paces from the inn. The branches seemed bare and threatening against the sky.

The crowd had begun to form a circle around the tree's trunk as the chief elder emerged from the inn

"Get a cart and some rope," he demanded. "Find one in the Ploughman's stables...come on we haven't got all night."

Delvin was dragged towards the tree. Someone had produced a short length of rope, and his hands were tied roughly together behind his back. He winced as the knot was yanked tight.

Heads turned towards the Ploughman's Inn, and a lump came to Delvin's throat as he saw that the horse and cart being led from the stables were Borlock's. The cart was still piled with the boxes that Delvin knew contained the tricks that Borlock had used in his shows, plus all sorts of other bits and pieces that he had collected over the years.

The cart was brought under the tree. Several hands bundled Delvin onto the back of the cart, scraping his leg on the edge as they did so. Rough hands hauled Delvin to his feet amid the boxes.

"Where's the rope," called one of the men.

"Didn't you get it when you got the cart from the stables?" said the chief elder testily. "Greg, go and get some rope."

Greg reluctantly went off and returned with a length of thick rope.

"Tie a noose in it," said the chief elder.

"I've never tied a noose before," said Greg looking at the rope unhappily.

"I'll tell you how to do it," said Delvin, suddenly having an idea.

"All right," said Greg reluctantly.

Under Delvin's instructions, the rope soon had a noose at the end.

Greg gave Delvin an embrace, which Delvin was not able to return with his hands tied, but he was able to whisper a goodbye in Greg's ear. A quizzical look crossed Greg's face as he jumped off the back of the cart.

One of the men put the noose around Delvin's neck. The other end was thrown over a branch and secured to the tree trunk. The man who had been on the cart jumped down leaving Delvin standing alone in the failing light, looking down at all those whom he had thought to be his friends. He saw his parents on the edge of the crowd, his mother crying and his father looking anguished and trying to comfort her. He saw the stranger in black leading his horse out of the Ploughman's Inn's stables, mounting it and heading away down the Havelock road.

"Right. It is time. Drive the cart away," ordered the chief elder.

Delvin felt the cart move and moved his feet along the back until the cart ended and there was nothing beneath them. The noose tightened around his neck as he swung out into the air. Then the noose unravelled, and Delvin landed in a heap on the grass.

A titter of laughter went up from the crowd.

The chief elder was not amused. "Is this another of your jokes?" he said angrily.

"I didn't tie it," said Delvin. "Isn't it the law that if someone survives an execution, he is set free?"

"You told Greg how to tie the noose," spluttered the chief elder, who was then was momentarily lost for words.

"I told you he would play another of his tricks," came a voice from the crowd. "Last month he put sheep paint outside my door. I stepped in it and had blue footprints all across my path."

"Aye," said another voice, "He hid behind a wall and made a loud clicking nose as I drove my cart past. I thought the axle was going. I only realised it was him when I heard him laugh."

An argument was starting up in the crowd. Some voices spoke up for Delvin saying he should be released, others saying the original sentence should be carried out.

Then an upstairs window of the inn was flung open, and Meril, Berman's wife's head appeared.

"Stop! Borlock's come round! Delvin didn't do it. Borlock says it was a magician from the Guild of Magicians."

There was a moment's silence in the crowd. Everyone's attention was on Meril. Then they turned back to Delvin who was still sitting on the grass with the remains of the noose around his neck.

"A magician? Who was he," demanded the chief elder.

"I don't know," replied Meril.

"What was his name?" someone asked.

"Did he give his name?"

"Where is he?"

"He's gone down towards Havelock, he left a few minutes ago," said another man.

"Follow him," called a voice.

"What on? Our horses couldn't keep up with his."

"And he's a magician," came another voice.

"We must tell the watch at Havelock," pronounced the chief elder.

"We had better release Delvin," said one of the other elders.

"He was perverting the course of justice with his tricks," said the chief elder severely. "That's a very serious offence."

"Just a moment," interrupted one of the other elders. "He's innocent."

"Innocent? He didn't know that at the time. He was perverting the course of justice."

There were murmurs from the crowd and the chief elder looked around and saw hostile looks directed towards him. The other two elders were looking at him expectantly.

"I think perhaps a pardon?" said one.

The chief elder looked around again, then cleared his throat importantly.

"Delvin Farmhand, it appears you did not murder Borlock. You are free to go. But keep out of trouble in the future."

"Yes sir," gasped Delvin amid cheers from the crowd.

The chief elder turned away, and Delvin was suddenly smothered by the embrace of his mother and pats on the back from men who had been trying to hang him only moments before. Over his mother's shoulder he could see his father and Greg both grinning in relief. He got up and walked over to Greg.

"I was worried you wouldn't follow my directions on tying the noose," he said quietly with a grin. "Borlock taught me that knot."

"I knew you were up to something," said Greg grinning back.

A hand touched Delvin's shoulder. It was Berman the landlord.

"Borlock is asking for you. You had better come quickly. I don't think he has long."

The relief at his escape was instantly replaced by sorrow for the injury to his friend. He gasped, "I'm coming."

"Will you be all right?" his father asked concerned.

"I'll be fine," replied Delvin, releasing himself from his mother's embrace and turning to follow Berman back into the inn.

As he walked past the villagers, some wouldn't meet his eye, others muttered "Well done," and, "I knew you hadn't done it." He ignored them, his mind on his old friend Borlock, hoping with all his heart that he would recover.

He followed Berman through the door into the inn, up the stairs and along the passage to the room, where, only a short time before he had been accused of murder.

The room had been straightened, the broken furniture removed and Borlock's chest placed neatly by the wall. Meril and one of the kitchen maids stood by the bed where Borlock lay. His long hair and beard that had always made him look a caricature of a magician, were spread out around him on the pillow. His face looked grey and drawn and Delvin could see a large bandage around his chest with a slowly growing red stain on its centre.

As Delvin slowly approached the bed, Borlock's eyes opened, and he moved as if he was trying to rise to meet his friend. But the effort was too great, and Meril put her hand on his head, telling him to lie still, that all would be all right.

Delvin looked down at his old friend and took his hand in his.

Borlock smiled up at him. "Thank you for trying to save me Delvin." Borlock's voice was weak and hardly more than a whisper. "Because of you he didn't find it." Borlock coughed and his face twisted in pain. "He got a copy I once had made. He'll realise it's only a copy eventually and come for the real one. I want you to have it. You are a good boy, and you may be able to do some good with it, but you must be careful. Don't let anybody know you have it. That's important. Nobody, absolutely nobody must know you have it. I want you to have all my things as well. I have no family… Berman," Borlock turned his head to the innkeeper. "You are my witness. I leave everything to Delvin."

"I'll see to it," replied Berman gently.

"What is this thing?" asked Delvin puzzled.

But it was too late, Borlock had died.

Berman quietly led Delvin downstairs. Greg was waiting at the bottom of the stairs, and when he saw Delvin's face, he didn't need to ask what had happened, but simply said to Berman, "I'll take him home,"

Greg guided Delvin back down the track to the cottage he shared with his parents. Neither spoke, Greg realising Delvin needed time to grieve and that Delvin was wrapped up in memories of his friend. When Greg opened the door, Delvin's parents were waiting for him and rushed to comfort their son.

Greg quickly signalled to them that he thought Delvin wanted to be alone. The three stood in silence as they watched Delvin climb the ladder to the loft where he slept. When he was out of their sight, Delvin threw himself down on his bed and sobbed himself to sleep.

CHAPTER 3

Delvin was up at dawn as usual, determined the events of the day before would not affect his work. Tynan, the farmer Delvin worked for, had heard what had happened, and after Delvin had finished his morning's tasks, told him to take a break and go to the inn to see if anything needed doing. Delvin thanked him and trudged sadly down to the Ploughman's where he found Berman had everything under control. Berman told him to leave it all to him, and he sat Delvin down at a table with a tankard of ale. Delvin just sat there, looking into his drink, asking himself why, why had it all happened.

The funeral was that afternoon, and Delvin stood sadly by as the rough wooden coffin was lowered into the grave.

He returned to the farm to do the milking. Supper that night was a quiet affair with neither of his parents wanting to intrude on his private grief. After they had finished, his father offered to go down to the Ploughman's with him to check through Borlock's effects.

When they got there, they found Berman had laid out Borlock's personal belongings in the room where he had died. Meril had washed the blood out of the clothes he had been wearing, and had even sewed up the tear made by the murderer's knife.

"There's his purse and the other things he had on him," said Berman embarrassed. "Then there's his cart in the stables and the things there, and his horse."

"Has anybody fed his rabbit?" asked Delvin.

"I'll see to it," replied Berman, glad of an excuse to leave the room.

Delvin looked through the bits on the bed. The purse contained eleven gold royals, six silver carls and eleven copper bits. There was a bag of charms he used to sell, including, Delvin saw with a lump in his throat, the one he had given him the day before containing the piece of glass. There were the little paper packets containing love potions that Delvin knew were really powdered chalk. Delvin remembered helping him crush some blocks of chalk with a pestle and mortar only three months ago. There was his tinderbox and the small knife he carried on his belt. There was the piece of crystal that he looked into when telling fortunes. Delvin picked it up and looked at it, it was clear with several facets forming a point. On impulse Delvin put it in his pocket. Four brightly coloured handkerchiefs, washed, and carefully folded by Meril, lay on the bed beside the clothes.

Together with his father Delvin collected the bits and made his way downstairs. He found Berman in the bar and thanked him for his kindness and help. He then asked how much the funeral had cost and what else was owed. Berman apologetically said the one royal four carls would cover it, and Delvin paid him the money and asked if he would look after the horse and cart until he had decided what to do with them. Berman nodded his agreement, and Delvin and his father trudged back home.

As Delvin lay on his bed that night, he wondered what he should do with all Borlock's props. Suddenly a thought came to him, why shouldn't he become a magician? Borlock had said he might take him on as an assistant. Borlock had been teaching him tricks for almost four years. He knew enough to convince people at a fortune telling, and he could make charms and love potions. At only twenty he was rather young for a magician, and with his slim build and average height, he was not the imposing figure a magician should be. Maybe he should put on weight and grow a beard, that would make him look older. No, he decided, he didn't want to be fat, and with his blond hair, if he grew a beard, it would hardly show up. His mind began to race at the thought of what he might do and where he might go. He thought of all the tricks in Borlock's cart. There were some small illusions and a device that Borlock called a magic lantern. The previous year Borlock had got the villagers to hang up a sheet, and he had used the magic lantern to project pictures onto the sheet. He had even made some of the pictures seem to move which had amazed the villagers who were watching.

It was a long time before he finally got to sleep, but before doing so, he resolved to talk to Greg about it the next day.

In the morning Delvin was feeling better. He had got over the initial shock of Borlock's death, and as he worked, he found himself thinking more and more of how he might live as a travelling magician, and how it would get him away from Byford.

He met Greg in the Ploughman's after they had both finished work and as they sat down, he put it to him.

"I'm thinking of leaving Byford and becoming a magician."

Greg looked at him.

"This is not one of your jokes, is it?"

"No, I'm serious," he replied. "I've never wanted to stay here all my life, and after what happened…I won't get another chance like this again. I've got the props, some money, the horse and cart. Borlock has been teaching me magic. Things aren't the same here anymore. All those people I thought were friends turning against me. I just want to get away."

"I could do with getting away from here," replied Greg wistfully. "This place can't afford another groom, so I'm stuck as a stable boy until Eddie retires or dies, and that's going to be years."

"You could come too," said Delvin.

"Don't be silly, you won't need a groom as a travelling magician. Anyway, you'll probably have enough trouble earning enough to keep yourself, never mind me as well."

"How about if we go to Hengel?" suggested Delvin. "I could set up somewhere in the city, and you could find an inn that needed a groom. There's sure to be one in a place as big as Hengel."

"Aren't there already magicians in Hengel?" asked Greg.

"Probably, but there should be enough work for more than

one."

"Do you really mean it?"

Delvin nodded and Greg grinned back. Delvin went to get another ale for them both, and they spent the rest of the evening planning what they would do.

Delvin woke with a thick head in the morning. He had spent longer discussing and planning with Greg than he intended. He climbed down the ladder from the loft and went out into the yard, blinking in the early morning sun. He put his head under the pump, and the shock of the cold water brought him awake. His mother looked up as he came in, and the thought suddenly struck him, what would his mother and father think about him leaving the village. He was about to tell his mother of his plans when he thought better of it. He wanted a clear head when he told them, so he grabbed a slice of bread, waved goodbye to his mother and went off to work.

Tynan noticed he was distracted that day and twice had to tell him to pay more attention. Delvin kept going over in his mind different ways he could break the news to his parents.

At supper that evening, Delvin at last outlined his plans to his parents. They listened to him carefully. Then to Delvin's surprise, rather than trying to dissuade him as he thought they would, they discussed it with him carefully, his father making several good suggestions as to how he could find business in Hengel.

When Delvin met Greg again in the Ploughman's that night, he found that he too had been discussing it with his mother, and she had also agreed that it was a good idea. So, over several drinks they resolved that they would actually do it, and that the following day they would give notice to their employers.

Tynan smiled when Delvin told him what he wanted to do, and said there would always be a job for him at the farm if he needed it.

When they met again at the Ploughman's that night, Greg told him that when he had told Berman he was leaving, Berman had also been helpful and had given him suggestions as to which inns in Hengel would be the best ones to try for a job.

So, three days later, Delvin and Greg found themselves seated on Borlock's cart heading out of Byford on the road to Havelock on the way to Hengel. Half the village had turned out to see them off. Delvin could see his mother trying to hide a sob, and as he gave her a wave a sudden pang of sadness filled him too. Greg's mother was also looking tearful as she gave them a last farewell. The other villagers all waved, seeming to have forgotten that only a few days before they had been crowding out of the inn to see Delvin's execution.

As the last house in the village went out of sight, Delvin suddenly felt homesick, and he wondered with sadness mixed with excitement what lay ahead.

CHAPTER 4

They reached the walls of Hengel in the late afternoon. Neither of them had been to the city before, and as they waited their turn to pass through the massive gates, they both wondered if they had made the right decision to leave Byford.

Their first priority when they got into the city was to find somewhere to stay. Delvin's father had suggested they try the East Quarter; that was an area where there were small general shops and traders and also a lot of residential buildings. He had said that if they looked in the windows of general food shops, some of them put up small advertisements, and they might find lodgings advertised there.

The soldier on the gate waved them through, and they went under the huge arch. Inside the gate they found themselves on the North South Road. It was a mass of people, carriages and carts as it drove its way across the city to the North Gate on the other side. The road was lined with inns and large shops with many-paned windows displaying their wares. In contrast to the North South Road, the streets leading off were narrow with overhanging buildings housing all manner of businesses, many with their goods displayed outside, or hanging from their first or second floor windows.

Delvin and Greg paused and took in the new sights, sounds and smells of the city. Delvin felt apprehensive as he looked about him. The city seemed so big. Would he really be able to make it as a magician here? They turned down one of the alleys to the right of the main road into the maze of back-streets that were the East Quarter. The first two food shops they stopped at didn't have any advertisements, but the third one did. People were trying to sell horses, dresses and a sword, and offering all manner of services, some of which Delvin could only guess at, but no one had rooms to let. It was three shops later that they found one that seemed to specialise in lodgings. They noted the details of the three that looked the best.

The first on their list had already been taken, and the second was owned by an unshaven narrow-faced man. Greg stayed with the horse while Delvin went up to look at the room. There were damp stains on the walls and rat droppings on the floor. Delvin told the man he would need to discuss it with his friend. He went back downstairs feeling depressed and wondering if that would be the best he could find.

The door of the third, in a little lane by a chandler's, was opened by a large lady of indeterminate years. She had brown hair cut in the style of a younger woman, and she eyed Delvin speculatively as he stood on the doorstep.

"What can I do for you, young masters?"

"Do you have a room to let, mistress?" Asked Delvin.

"A room is it? Yes, I do, but you can't keep that horse and cart here. I don't have space for those."

"We were going to sell those, mistress."

"You are, are you. In that case come in and I'll show you the room. I am Mistress Wilshaw. Is it both you young gentlemen? You don't have girlfriends living with you, do you? I don't allow girlfriends in my gentlemen's rooms."

"It's both of us and we've just arrived in Hengel, so we don't have girlfriends," replied Delvin.

"Well, you won't have girlfriends in here either. It's up these stairs. It's a lovely room. It was decorated by my late husband before he died, rest his soul. I will charge seven carls a week each for the two of you, but that does include breakfast and a lovely meal in the evening. And no cooking in the room, that encourages mice."

As Mistress Wilshaw talked, she was climbing the stairs. At the top she opened a door to a room on the left. It was a pleasant room, though the decorations were starting to look a bit old and chipped, and Delvin wondered how long ago it was that Mistress Wilshaw's husband had done the decorating. A window looked out on an alley behind the house, and two other walls were taken up by narrow beds. A washstand stood by the window, and next to the door was a table with a mirror over it and two chairs.

"Well young master, what do you think of it?"

"I think it is very nice Mistress Wilshaw," replied Delvin as he inspected the beds. "I will need to talk to my friend first though," he added.

"What do you and your friend do, and why have you come to Hengel?"

"We've come to find work, he's a groom." Delvin took a deep breath. "And I am a magician." It was the first time Delvin had actually called himself a magician, and it somehow sounded presumptuous to him, but not to Mistress Wilshaw.

"Ooo, a magician! Can you tell fortunes?"

"Yes mistress," replied Delvin, knowing he had never done it before, but hoping he could follow the basic principles of drawing information out of people that Borlock had taught him.

"Ohh! You'll have to tell my fortune. What's your name?" She gave an excited giggle.

"Delvin," he replied.

Mistress Wilshaw looked disappointed, as if he should have been called Delvin the Magnificent, or the Great Delvin, but she quickly recovered.

"You go and talk to your friend. I'll wait for you here."

Delvin went back down the stairs and let himself out. Greg looked at him expectantly.

"It looks all right," began Delvin. "She looks a bit much though."

Greg grinned back.

"I'm sure you can handle her. How much is it?"

"Seven carls a week each including breakfast and an evening meal."

"Sounds all right, let's go for it!"

Delvin went back in and called up the stairs.

"We would like to take it, Mistress Wilshaw. May we leave our horse and cart in your yard tonight, since it is rather late to get to the horse dealers?"

"Well just this one night, Master Delvin. And mind you clean up after it goes. I don't want to go out and tread in anything. I have cooked a nice stew for dinner, there should be enough for you as well. Get your things in and the horse out of the way, then come down when you have washed…"

Delvin was already signalling Greg to bring the horse through to the yard.

CHAPTER 5

First thing the following day, Greg and Delvin took the horse and cart to the dealers and sold them. Greg then went to look for the inns that Berman had told him about, to see if they needed any grooms. Delvin meanwhile made his way back to Mistress Wilshaw's house. He had been thinking about how he could get himself business as a magician, and eventually decided to try putting small advertisements in food shop windows, like the ones he had seen when looking for lodgings.

On getting back to the room he sat down at the table and began to write. His first few attempts he screwed up and threw away, but eventually he came up with one he thought might work. It read:

DELVIN THE MAGICIAN
Children's shows, fortune-telling, mind reading, divination and good luck. All your wishes and desires come true.
Leave a message or call at 3 Chandler's Lane, East Quarter.

He sat back and read it through again. Delvin the magician he thought. Would he be able to make people believe in him as a magician? He took a deep breath and looked at the advertisement again. He couldn't think of any way to improve it, so he carefully copied it out five times and set off to find five shops that would take it.

Delvin soon found that different shops specialised in advertisements for different things, so that it was almost an hour before he had found five suitable ones. Most of the shops charged one copper bit a week, but one large establishment, on the other side of the North South Road near the Temple and the

Market Square charged him two. He decided that if that one did not quickly produce results, he would remove it.

When the last advertisement was up, he made his way back to Mistress Wilshaw's, buying himself a meat pie from a street vendor on the way. As he walked down the road munching his pie, he wondered how long it would be before he got his first reply.

When he got back to Mistress Wilshaw's he went up to his room and sat down, but he couldn't sit still. Every time he heard someone go past the front door, he was on his feet hoping they would stop and knock.

After an hour of getting up and down, pacing the room and looking out of the window, he decided he must do something to keep himself occupied. He thought he would look through Borlock's tricks, so he got out one of Borlock's boxes. It contained Borlock's magic lantern and several hand painted slides mounted in wooden frames. Borlock hadn't shown him how it worked, so he spent some time experimenting. The lantern was made of very thin metal, painted black and was quite light to carry. There was a lamp and a flask of oil that obviously fuelled it. He put some oil in the lamp and lit it and then tried projecting some of the slides onto his bedroom wall. After viewing a few slides, he decided that he should add magic lantern shows to his shop window advertisements.

He then started looking through the other boxes. Over the years Borlock had amassed the most amazing collection of bits and pieces, tassels and ribbons, springs and hinges, bits of soft pliable material and wax, fragments of cloth of almost every colour and pattern imaginable, and a large array of other odds and ends.

Delvin pulled out of the box a very strange contraption. He had looked at it before and still had no idea what it was. There was a curled spring that could be tightened that was connected to a complicated arrangement of gears, that in turn was connected to a rod on the end of arms that only allowed it to go up and down. He was deep in thought about what it was used for when he was startled by a knock at the front door. Could this be a customer?

Delvin dropped the contraption back in the box and dashed down the stairs. He reached the door just before Mistress Wilshaw, who was coming out from the kitchen.

"I'll get it," Delvin gasped.

He opened the door and a stout lady stood there.

"Is Delvin the magician in?"

"I am he, mistress," said Delvin bowing.

"I want a love potion. How much?"

"Five copper bits, mistress," replied Delvin.

"Right, I'll have two," said the lady, her stomach rumbling as she spoke.

"If you would care to come in off the street, I will get them for you," said Delvin ushering her into the house.

He sedately climbed the stairs and got two of the little packets of powdered chalk that Borlock had sold as love potions. Even if they don't bring her love, they might cure her indigestion he thought, grinning to himself.

He went back down the stairs and handed the love potions to the lady and she paid him one silver carl. Delvin bowed and thanked her and then ushered her back out into the street.

"I hope this works, young man!"

"There can never be any cast iron guarantees in matters of love, but that potion will pave the way."

He closed the door and let out a deep breath. He had done it. He had sold his first magical service. He was a magician! His thoughts were interrupted by Mistress Wilshaw, who had come back out of the kitchen.

"Will you be needing to entertain clients Master Delvin?"

"I thought I could do it in my room," said Delvin in some trepidation.

"That won't look very good with the clients. You may use the parlour, but I'll charge you five copper bits per person."

"Thank you, mistress," said Delvin relieved.

"Right," said Mistress Wilshaw, putting a hand on his arm.

"And there is no need to break your neck coming down the stairs like that. I can open the door."

"Yes mistress, thank you," said Delvin smiling. Mistress Wilshaw patted his arm and turned back to the kitchen.

The afternoon was drawing on before there was another knock on the door. Mistress Wilshaw opened it, and this time a nervous looking man asked if Delvin the magician could read his fortune. Mistress Wilshaw ushered him into the parlour and summoned Delvin, who was hovering at the top of the stairs.

Delvin came down with Borlock's crystal ball, and thanking Mistress Wilshaw, entered the room. The man turned as Delvin entered, and by the slight change in expression, Delvin could see he was disappointed in his appearance. Maybe he should dress in Borlock's gown and cloak he thought, that would make him look more impressive.

Delvin pulled out a chair by the table and asked the man to sit down, taking the chair opposite himself. He put the crystal ball on the table between them and took the small crystal out of his pocket as he had seen Borlock do. Then he began the series of questions he had heard Borlock use, making general comments and listing groups of words that if he saw a glimmer of recognition, would allow him to start making more definite statements and tell the man about himself. Borlock had taught him that most people would not realise that they were feeding the magician with information that he could then use to make his predictions and divinations. The main thing, Borlock had said, was to find out what people wanted to hear, and then tell it to them. That was the way to get happy customers and the best fees.

Delvin soon found out that the man was embarking on a business venture and was wanting reassurance that it would be successful.

"I can see a great enterprise ahead," said Delvin looking deep into the crystal. "All the signs are good."

He decided he had better give himself an excuse in case the venture was to fail.

"I can see luck has shown both her faces to you in the past." The man nodded sadly. "This will happen again, but at the moment she is smiling on you. Now is the time to move forward before luck changes her face again." The man looked relieved and pleased.

Delvin passed his hand over the crystal ball again, touching it with his crystal as though that would somehow activate it and enable him to see visions in its depths. He then told the man about his family and background, managing to change the information he had got from his initial questions and comments to make it sound different and new.

Suddenly a thought flashed into Delvin's mind of someone pushing a barrel and many barrels falling, crushing people beneath them.

"Keep away from falling barrels," he blurted out before he realised what he was saying.

"What was that," said the man.

"Oh nothing," said Delvin. "I'm sorry, I lost concentration."

"Falling barrels, where would I be in the way of falling barrels."

"It's nothing, now let me tell you about your father."

Delvin continued to tell the man about his family, and the man appeared to forget his comment about the barrels. Delvin soon brought the session to a close.

"And that magister is your fortune, and may luck walk with you. The fee for my service is one silver carl."

"One carl is it? I hope you are right in what you say." He took a carl from his purse and handed it to Delvin who showed him out through the door.

As the door closed behind him, Delvin shut his eyes, leant back and let out a deep sigh. The short interview had exhausted him, but he had actually done it. He had managed to convince the man that he could tell fortunes. His mind flashed back to the thought of falling barrels that had come to him. Whatever had that been, he wondered.

"Dinner!" called Mistress Wilshaw through the door, startling

Delvin from his thoughts. He tucked the crystal into his pocket and went through into the kitchen.

Greg was already sitting at the table. He must have come in while Delvin was doing his fortune telling.

"I've had two clients," grinned Delvin.

"Fantastic! I've got a job," responded Greg.

Delvin sat down and Mistress Wilshaw brought a bowl of stew for him and Greg

"Now you eat that up before it goes cold. You'll have plenty of time later to tell each other what you have done."

Delvin and Greg thanked her and started to eat while Mistress Wilshaw fetched her bowl and joined them at the table, her chair creaking under her weight. Delvin hadn't realised how hungry he was, and it was only a few minutes before he had finished his bowl.

"I sold two love potions to one lady and told a man's fortune."

"I tried the inns Berman mentioned. They were all on the big North South Road or on the Great East Road. They were really big places, one of them had an amazing clock tower over the gate to its yard, but none of them were looking for a groom or a stableboy. So I started trying the smaller inns in the side streets and I've got a job as a stable boy at The White Bear. It's just off the Great East Road. It's about three times the size of the Ploughman's in Byford, and they say they will make me a groom if I do well."

"Would you like some more stew?" broke in Mistress Wilshaw.

"Yes please," they replied, and it was again several minutes before they could resume telling each other what they had been doing.

CHAPTER 6

On the following day Delvin waited all morning for a knock on the door but no one came. He had gone down and looked out of the door several times, and even checked that the number on the front door was visible and that people couldn't miss it. By midday he was wondering if there would be any calls and sat down on his bed feeling depressed.

In mid afternoon a girl of about sixteen came nervously to the door, looking over her shoulder to see if anyone was watching her, and bought a love potion.

I am going to have to go out and get the business thought Delvin. He got up off the bed and went downstairs to the kitchen where Mistress Wilshaw was preparing supper.

"Do you know when market day is Mistress Wilshaw?"

"It's tomorrow Master Delvin."

"Do you know if any magicians perform there?"

"I don't remember seeing any."

"Do you think mothers would pay me to entertain their children while they went round the stalls?"

Mistress Wilshaw cocked her head while she thought about it.

"They might, Master Delvin, though I'm not sure if they would want to leave their children alone."

"I'll try it anyway," said Delvin determinedly.

Just then there was a knock ay the door. Mistress Wilshaw brushed the flour from her hands and went to answer it while Delvin waited, hardly able to keep still.

The door opened to reveal a man dressed in servant's clothes. Delvin's heart sank. That didn't look like a customer.

"What may I do for you?" asked Mistress Wilshaw.

"My mistress has asked if the magician Delvin could come and read her fortune?"

Another client and a rich one thought Delvin excitedly.

"I will see if he is available, wait here," said Mistress Wilshaw shutting the door. She walked back to the kitchen smiling.

"A lady wants you to read her fortune. You go along and do it. I'll keep your supper warm if you are late. And if anyone else comes to see you I'll make appointments for them."

"Thank you, Mistress Wilshaw," said Delvin grinning.

He dashed up to his room to get his things, then came down and followed the servant to his mistress's house. She turned out to be a haulier's wife. The reading seemed to go well, and when Delvin charged her two silver carls, she paid it without comment.

That night he worked hard putting together a show for market day. He had decided he would do something short and simple. Something that would amuse the children, but wouldn't take so long that the parents would get bored. He thought that a puppet made out of a sock with two eyes painted on it would do the trick. By the time he got to bed he had a short routine worked out.

Delvin was up early the next day and set himself up at the corner of the Market Square. The show seemed to go down well, and as the day wore on Delvin improved it as he learned which bits the children liked best.

After each show he checked his hat. There were only a few copper bits in it, but after a while he began to do better. Just before the market began to pack up, a well-dressed lady with a kindly round face came up to him.

"Do you do children's parties?"

"I do mistress," replied Delvin, rapidly trying to think what tricks he could do at a children's party.

"How much do you charge?"

"Four carls mistress,"

"Are you free the second day next week?"

"I am mistress."

"Splendid. I am Mistress Audley. My daughter Wenda's birthday is the second day next week. Her party starts two hours after midday. It's at our house next to Audley's Merchants, Rider Street in the Merchant's Quarter. Can you remember that?"

"I can mistress. I'll be there."

"Thank you and good day."

Mistress Audley turned and left Delvin grinning in excitement. He had got his first booking for a children's party.

During the next few days Delvin worked hard putting the children's show together. He patched up some more of Borlock's props and made some other bits and pieces himself. The room he shared with Greg became full of half stuck paper flowers, cards with magic symbols drawn on them and all manner of other bits and pieces, including a box Delvin had designed himself that would disappear small objects with a flick of the wrist. At last he felt he was ready and packed the props carefully together to carry to the merchant's house.

When the day of the children's party arrived, Delvin carefully packed up his props and got ready to go. Greg had offered to come with him. He had the afternoon off, and although he had arranged to meet Polly his new girlfriend later, he thought he would just have time to walk along with Delvin, help him set up and watch the show before he would have to dash off. Delvin was glad of the help and readily agreed.

They found Mistress Audley's house without too much difficulty and Delvin and Greg began to set up for the show. Mistress Audley kept popping in to see how they were doing, breaking the thread of Delvin's thoughts as he concentrated on the tricks he was planning to perform.

Soon they were ready, and Delvin put his head through the door to tell Mistress Audley. The children streamed through laughing and giggling as they came. Delvin raised his hands to call for quiet and the children looked up expectantly. Taking a deep breath, he began the show.

He started the same way Borlock had done, producing a red handkerchief out of an empty box, then making it disappear again only to be found on his back.

The children laughed and clapped, their smiles and cheers fuelling his confidence. He performed the trick with the cups and balls that had been the first magic he had learned, and one where an egg seemed to disappear and reappear from a small black bag to gales of laughter from the children.

The show was going well. Mistress Audley at the back was looking pleased, and her daughter Wenda, a pretty blond girl, was jumping up and down with glee.

His final trick was the same as Borlock's final trick. He built up the story of the wicked genie, and asked the children to help him overcome the genie's magic. The children held out their hands and started to wiggle their fingers just as Delvin directed.

"Has your magic overcome the genie?" He asked dramatically, gripping the box decorated as the genie's palace.

Then panic gripped him. He had forgotten to load the rabbit under the palace, it was still in its travelling box. He had been distracted by the merchant's wife when he had been setting up. What could he do, the whole show would fall flat.

"Lift the palace," screamed the children.

Delvin desperately wished the rabbit was under it, but it wasn't. He would just have to pretend the rabbit had disappeared and that he didn't realise it.

"Lift the palace," screamed the children again.

He looked into the children's expectant faces, took a deep breath and lifted the palace, waiting for the sudden quiet of disappointment. It didn't come. The children cheered and clapped. Delvin looked down and didn't have to act his astonishment. The rabbit was there, large as life, looking at the children.

Delvin overcame his surprise, picked up the rabbit, bowed to the children and their parents at the back, and walked off to the side with the applause ringing in his ears. How did the rabbit get there? Had his memory gone? Was he going mad? He didn't understand it.

In a daze he walked up to Mistress Audley who thanked him

smiling and pressed his fee of four silver carls into his hand. He knew four silver carls was probably a much lower fee than the Guild of Magicians would have charged, but as he got better, he could charge more.

He was still slightly dazed by the appearance of the rabbit, and as he packed up his props, he surreptitiously looked in the travelling box. He half expected to see another rabbit there. But no, it was empty. He folded the props down, packed them together with a strap and put his rabbit in its travelling box. He then said goodbye to Wenda, bowed and thanked Mistress Audley, and left.

As he trudged back through the grey drizzle of early evening, avoiding the puddles building up on the cobbled streets, he kept thinking…how did the rabbit get under the palace.

He hardly noticed the cold and rain that had kept most of the citizens of Hengel in their homes. He turned into the vegetable market, quiet now that most of the traders had left, leaving the smell of cabbage and rotten vegetables, and a litter of leaves squashed into the grey mud underfoot. Only a few people hurriedly walked across the market square, hunched against the weather which had now started to rain in earnest. Delvin was still puzzling over how the rabbit had appeared as he turned into a road past a candlemakers and a pharmacy, and then into Chandler's Lane and back to Mistress Wilshaw's.

CHAPTER 7

"Come in here out of the rain Master Delvin, you'll catch your death of cold. Look, your clothes are all wet. Now take them off and I'll dry them for you." Delvin stepped through the door out of the rain.

"Thank you, Mistress Wilshaw, I'm quite alright thank you," said Delvin trying to sidle past her and get to his room. Mistress Wilshaw followed him up the stairs, her generous size brushing the walls on either side.

"Now I'll have no arguments, if you catch a cold, you'll be expecting me to wait on you hand and foot. Take them off. I've seen it all before."

As Delvin reached the top of the stairs, he shrugged off his jacket and handed it to Mistress Wilshaw.

"Come on, let's have the rest," She demanded. Delvin reluctantly removed his breeches and shirt and handed them over.

"Are your drawers wet?" Mistress Wilshaw placed a hand on the front of his drawers. Delvin stepped back quickly.

"They are dry enough thank you, Mistress Wilshaw."

Delvin retreated quickly into his room, thanking Mistress Wilshaw again and shutting the door behind him. In his rush to escape he had left his rabbit outside the room. He wondered if his memory was slipping. Thinking of the incident with the rabbit, had he just forgotten he had put the rabbit in the palace?

Delvin opened the door a crack and checked that Mistress Wilshaw had gone. When he was sure, he tip-toed out and brought in the rabbit and his bundle of props.

Delvin sat down at the small table and looked in the mirror.

He must start getting ready since he had a visitor coming after dinner. A message had been pushed through the door saying simply, 'I shall visit an hour after sundown.' Probably a lovesick girl wanting a love potion. Still, it was all good business. He looked at his reflection critically. He still looked too young.

He shrugged, and his mind turned again to the rabbit. How had it got under the palace? And then there was that sudden thought of falling barrels he had had when he had done his first fortune telling. What had that been?

"Dinner!" called Mistress Wilshaw. Her voice snapping Delvin out of his dream. Maybe it would be chicken pie. Chicken pie was his favourite, and he had been hoping it would be that for dinner. He quickly put on his spare breeches and hurried downstairs.

"It's just the two of us tonight with Master Greg working late," said Mistress Wilshaw as she placed the tray on the table.

"Chicken pie, I know it is your favourite. Let me give you a nice big helping." Mistress Wilshaw heaped a large helping of chicken pie onto one of the plates with some cabbage from the other bowl. "There, that should feed you up."

She put another much smaller helping on to the other plate and set it before herself.

"I mustn't spoil my figure now, must I." She sat down on the chair next to Delvin, her bulk slightly spreading over the edges.

"Mistress Wilshaw," began Delvin.

"Yes," she replied.

"May I use the parlour this evening? A visitor has asked to see me."

"What time will that be."

"An hour after dusk."

"Oh good. Yes certainly. That will give you time to tell my fortune after they've gone. You've been saying you will. Now eat up your pie. I don't want you fading away." Mistress Wilshaw gave a little wriggle of anticipation.

Delvin had prepared the parlour carefully for his visitor. The only light came from two candles on the table. He had spread out the cloth so he could sweep his hand across the table, making either a packet of chalk powder or a charm seem to appear by magic. His crystal ball was to one side together with the small crystal. He was wearing Borlock's deep red gown. In the dim light it could have been velvet and looked much richer than the shabby garment it actually was.

There was a knock at the door. Delvin could hear Mistress Wilshaw open it and ask the visitor in. The door to the parlour opened, and a dark cloaked figure walked in, their head covered with a hood and a scarf pulled across their face, so all Delvin could see was a sparkle from the light of the candle reflected in the two eyes that met his.

"Come in, sit down," said Delvin.

The figure came in and sat in the chair opposite Delvin then looked back towards the door. Mistress Wilshaw, who had been standing staring after the visitor, quickly moved back shutting the door, leaving Delvin and the figure alone.

"How can I be of help?" began Delvin.

"Are you a magician?" asked a determined female voice.

"I am."

"What can you do? What powers do you have?"

"What would you wish me to do?"

"Do you know about enchantments and how to remove them?"

"I perform magic," said Delvin wondering what he was getting into.

"Can you send people to sleep?" asked the voice.

"I can make things appear and disappear," said Delvin trying to get onto firmer ground, and he swept his hand across the table making the charm appear.

"Oh no, you are like all the rest, a fraud!" cried the figure, sweeping up and heading towards the door before Delvin could move.

"Wait!" cried Delvin. The figure hesitated. "I may be a fraud, but I do sincerely wish that what you want will come about." He briefly pictured people going to sleep in his mind's eye.

"Fraud!" snarled the figure disgustedly, as she opened the door and was gone.

Delvin sat back. Whatever was that all about, he thought.

The door opened again before he had time to think further on the subject, and Mistress Wilshaw entered.

"You did that nice and quickly. That leaves us plenty of time for you to read my fortune."

Delvin gestured towards the chair which had been recently occupied by the cloaked figure.

"This table is in the way," said Mistress Wilshaw, moving the table to one side. "That's better, now we can get closer." She pulled her chair next to Delvin's and sat down with her knee brushing his.

"What are you going to do, read my palm?" Mistress Wilshaw held her large hand towards Delvin.

Delvin took the hand between his and looked at it placing his crystal between her hand and his. What would Mistress Wilshaw like to hear? He thought.

"I can see a tall figure," he began. "He has a beard and is broad across the shoulder."

"Ooo…" said Mistress Wilshaw.

"I don't think he is very nice," he had better not raise her hopes too high.

"Ohh…" said Mistress Wilshaw sadly.

"But he is well respected and looked up to by everyone who knows him."

"Ahh…" responded Mistress Wilshaw.

"I can see him coming here," said Delvin, wondering what to say next. "I can see him knocking at the door, and you are opening it for him."

"Ooo…" The hand gave a squeeze.

"I can see him coming in. You are embracing. I think he is your husband."

"Ahh…" gasped Mistress Wilshaw. The hand squeezed again, and she wriggled excitedly.

"You are happy with him," Delvin desperately tried to think

what he could say next. Mistress Wilshaw seemed to be getting too carried away. He'd get himself into trouble if he went any further.

"What else are we doing, are we going upstairs?" breathed Mistress Wilshaw.

"You are looking into his eyes," what could he say?

"Ooo…" she wriggled again.

"He has a smile on his face," Delvin wished he hadn't started on this tack. He couldn't think how to get out of it without either disappointing Mistress Wilshaw or being drawn into embarrassing details. He wished he wasn't there or that Mistress Wilshaw would faint or something.

A gurgle came from Mistress Wilshaw. Delvin looked up and saw that her face had gone red and then suddenly pale. She started to slump in her chair. Delvin started up and caught her as she slipped to the floor, her weight pulling him down too.

Was she still breathing, he wondered? She seemed to have just fainted. Her eyes opened.

"Oh dear, I came over all faint!" she gasped. "I got so excited by what you were telling me." She started to get up. "I think I had better go and lie down. Oh dear, I don't know what came over me."

Mistress Wilshaw got up and went out, leaving Delvin looking after her in amazement. What was happening? First the rabbit appearing, then Mistress Wilshaw suddenly fainting just when he wished it, and even chicken pie for dinner after he had wished for that. No that must have been a coincidence. His thoughts suddenly turned to his mysterious visitor. What had he wished for there? No, he pulled himself up. Magic did not exist. It was all trickery, he knew that. What was he thinking of, he was fooling himself with his own tricks. He walked back up to his room.

Delvin was feeding his rabbit scraps left over from the cabbage when the door opened, and Greg walked in grinning from ear to ear.

"How was your show?" asked Greg.

"Fine thanks, I think it went down well."

"How did the rabbit trick go?"

Delvin looked up. "It went fine, why are you asking?"

Greg's grin became even broader. "Oh, no reason. I was wondering how the appearance of the rabbit under the palace went."

"Was that you?" gasped Delvin.

Greg burst out laughing. "You should have seen your face. It was a picture. Oh dear, that'll teach you for putting nettles in my breeches."

"What did you do?" laughed Delvin.

"I saw that you had forgotten to put the rabbit under the palace when that merchant's wife interrupted you, so I did it for you. I was going to tell you. Then I remembered those stinging nettles, and I thought I would get you back by not telling you. You should have seen your face when you lifted the palace. It was great!"

Delvin was laughing too, and they continued to joke and laugh as they climbed into their beds. As Delvin lay back in the dark thinking of the day's happenings, he smiled to himself. Fancy thinking magic was real, how could he have thought that? Probably Mistress Wilshaw had just got too hot. He quietly grinned. How could he get back again at Greg? He'd think of something.

CHAPTER 8

The following afternoon Delvin had his first booking for a magic lantern show. It was for a group of butcher's wives who met together every month.

As he walked downstairs carrying the magic lantern, he saw Mistress Wilshaw.

"Mistress Wilshaw?"

"Yes?" she replied.

"You know that tin bath you have hanging in the kitchen?"

"Yes."

"Greg was wondering if he could have a bath before the festival this evening. You know he always smells of horses from working in the stables. He thinks it is putting off the girls."

"I'll see to it," she replied. "As soon as he comes in, I'll have him in that bath…I'll see to it myself."

Delvin grinned as he thanked Mistress Wilshaw and went through the door. That would get Greg for giving him such a shock with the rabbit.

There were not many people in the streets as Delvin made his way to the butcher's house where he was to perform his show. Maybe people were getting ready for the festival, thought Delvin, or maybe it was the general depression with the high taxes and the war with the neighbouring country of Argent that seemed to be dragging on. Argent was claiming Duke Poldor had kidnapped Princess Fionella. In his proclamation, Duke Poldor claimed he was protecting her from her scheming father. That was a laugh, the idea that Duke Poldor would protect anyone other than himself. Delvin had never met the duke, but just the mention of his name sent shivers down people's backs. Whatever the rights and wrongs of the case, Argent's army had been held for almost three weeks at the bridge over the River Septim that separated the two countries, with neither side able to get across the river.

Delvin came out of his dream as he turned into the Butcher's Quarter. On both sides of the road were shops with sides of meat hanging in the window. At least there was no shortage of food in the city, if you could afford it. The prices seemed to be going up and up. Delvin looked for number 17 where the show was to take place. He soon found it. It was a smart, fastidiously clean shop, with fresh yellow sawdust on the floor and an assistant with a red and white striped apron behind the counter.

"May I help you?" asked the assistant.

"I've come to give a magic lantern show," replied Delvin.

He was shown through to a house at the back where the merchant's wives were waiting for him. The show took half an hour, and Delvin earned two more silver carls. He hoped the ladies would tell their friends and he would get more magic lantern bookings.

He walked back through the city feeling content and happy. He felt he was starting to get established as a magician, and the magic lantern shows now gave him another string to his bow. Soon he would be able to charge more than just two carls.

He got back to Mistress Wilshaw's, and as he opened the door to go in and get ready for the festival, he could hear voices and splashes coming from the kitchen.

"I am quite all right, Mistress Wilshaw."

"Now you just let me wash that dirt from your hair, Master Greg."

"No, please Mistress Wilshaw, please!"

"That's right, we'll soon have you clean all over."

Delvin grinned as he climbed the stairs.

CHAPTER 9

The sock with two eyes painted on 'looked' towards the children, then 'looked' towards Delvin. The children roared it on. The sock on the end of Delvin's hand seemed to attack Delvin. He grabbed it with his other hand and wrestled against it. Eventually he got it next to a box, put it inside and shut the lid, in the same instant taking the sock off his hand. The sock monster was apparently shut safely in the box. Delvin bowed, the children clapped and cheered. Smiling, Delvin walked round the children and their parents with his hat, though some had already moved away before he got to them. He reached Greg and the two girls who had been watching from the back. One of the girls was bright and blond with a low-cut dress showing off her trim figure. The other was darker with curling brown hair and dancing eyes.

"That's the last one for tonight, I think most of the children have gone home now or gone to the square. I'll get this lot packed up, and we can have some fun."

"Was that really your hand in that sock?" giggled the blond girl Polly, Greg's girlfriend.

"I'd wriggle like that if he had his hand in mine," joined in Meg, the other girl.

"Shall I try?" grinned Delvin.

"Come on, let's head towards the Square," said Greg. "The pageant will be starting soon."

Delvin quickly packed, and the four friends headed down the street towards the Square in front of the Castle. The street was lined with stalls selling everything from hot pies to hats and toys. Some of the stalls had games of skill or chance. Meg stopped by a hoopla stall.

"Oh look Delvin, hoopla! I've always wanted to try that. Will you show me how to do it?" Delvin handed a copper bit to the attendant and received three hoops.

"The problem is to get the hoops over the blocks at the bottom," said Delvin.

"Ooo! I do like the bracelet, I'm going to go for that," said Meg, launching the first hoop which sailed over the bracelet and landed at the back of the table.

"Try spinning it a bit," suggested Delvin. The second hoop went over the bracelet, but failed to go over the block. The attendant cleared it away.

"You guide my arm," said Meg.

Delvin took Meg's arm just above the wrist, and Meg gave a little wriggle. Then he flipped her wrist, concentrating on the bracelet and willing the hoop to go over it. The hoop left Meg's hand, sailed over the bracelet, but again got stuck on the block.

"Ooh, almost!" cried Meg. "Ooo, that was really good." She turned to Delvin and planted a big kiss on his lips, and the four moved down towards the Square.

The Square was the centre of Hengel. it was surrounded on two sides by the colonnaded fronts of the Guildhall and municipal buildings. The third side was faced by the ancient buildings of the oldest part of Hengel, which was now the Metalworker's Quarter, and the fourth side was taken up by the grim walls of the Castle, its great barbican facing the Square.

By the time they reached it, the Square was almost full. A large low stand had been erected to one side with several tiers of seats at the front. Someone had put two rows of barrels at the back with another row on top, so the people standing there could climb on them and see over the heads of those in front. In the centre of the Square, in front of the Castle, was a raised platform with a pavilion behind. That was where the pageant was to take place.

Delvin manoeuvred himself and his friends closer to the stage, since he didn't want to miss anything. A hush descended on the crowd as guards moved round in front of the platform, and a group of people climbed the platform's steps at the back. The figure in front arrested Delvin's attention. Tall, and dressed completely in black, his hair had been set to form a series of huge black spikes pointing straight up from his head. His black beard was also cut as a spike, giving the impression that one of the spikes from his head had somehow escaped and become stuck on his chin. Around his neck was a great black ruff cut into a ring of black spikes, each one with a red jewelled pendant at its tip, like drops of blood, swaying as he moved. The overall impression was of a deadly black and poisoned flower with dark eyes and a hooked nose at its heart.

"Is that the duke?" gasped Delvin.

"Yes," whispered Meg. "The others are his son Gustov and his daughters. The dark one is Princess Jarla, the blond one Stella".

"Does he always look like that?"

"I think so. Someone told me he does it to scare people into paying their taxes and doing what he wants."

Delvin shivered as he remembered he hadn't registered himself for tax yet.

The duke lifted his arms. There was momentary silence.

"People," boomed the deep hard voice. "Today is the festival to celebrate the founding of our state. Yet even now the warmongers of Argent are trying to destroy us. Your brave husbands and sons cannot be with us today as they are defending our border. We shall have to strive even harder to defeat them and ensure they will never threaten us again. Enjoy the festival. Let the pageant begin!" A low sporadic ripple of applause went round the Square.

"Sound like he's going to raise taxes again," groaned Greg.

The duke and his party left the stage and moved to sit in the seats at the front of the stand. A huge dragon came onto the stage, worked by ten men under great hoops that formed its back and tail. The dragon was covered with cloth scales that were coloured green and blue. Its head was on a long thin neck that swung from side to side. Hengel, the city's legendary founder, after whom the country was named, stepped forward with his great sword and shield. The crowd gasped as the head swung towards him, the great tail thrashing. Hengel gave a huge sweep of his sword cutting the head from the dragon. The crowd surged up cheering.

The cheer was suddenly drowned by a crash. One of the barrels from the top tier of the stand had slipped and was falling down towards the front bringing the others with it. The cheers turned to screams as the spectators on the top were pitched forward onto those in front, and a wave of slipping, grasping, falling bodies and barrels came crashing down the stand. The duke and his party would have been swept from their seats had they not managed to leap up and get out of the way.

Delvin could see guards running towards the back of the stand, but the surging crowd then blocked his view.

"I think we had better get out of here," said Greg. Many of the others in the crowd had had the same idea, and the four friends joined the mass of people leaving the Square and going back towards the taverns and stalls in the surrounding streets.

"Let's get a drink," suggested Greg.

The four friends went into The Red Phoenix on the Great East Road and were soon settled with their drinks.

"Do you think Greg smells better today?" Delvin asked Polly grinning.

"I think he smells nice all the time," replied Polly giving Greg a hug.

"Was it you that set up that bath?" laughed Greg. "What a rotten thing to do! I never thought I would get away from her."

Greg and Delvin explained to the girls what had happened, embroidering the details as they went.

Some more people started to move into the tavern, and Delvin saw that Prince Gustov, and Princesses Jarla and Stella were moving through the stalls with a group of guards close by. People were moving away as they saw them coming, only returning after they had passed.

Delvin had not really looked at the prince and princesses on the platform, the duke's extraordinary appearance having held his attention. He could now see that Prince Gustov was short and broad with a course featured face, and hair cut very short so that it stuck up straight. His nose was slightly flattened as though it had been broken, and he walked with the swagger of a bully. Princess Jarla was tall and thin with straight jet-black hair contrasting with her pale white skin. She was wearing a crimson dress slit to her navel, with a necklace consisting of a single large red gemstone resting between her breasts. Her most striking feature was her hands, since she had grown the nails on her two forefingers so they extended into two long claw-like curves. Princess Stella was also tall, but she was blond, with a pale blue dress trimmed with fur. She had a penetrating look in her eye, and Delvin looked away as she looked towards him.

They stopped by the hoopla stall, and Gustov held out a peremptory hand. The attendant gave him three hoops which he handed to Jarla. She tossed them towards the stall, the second going over the bracelet that Meg had wanted, but again failing to go over the block. Gustov held out his hand, and the attendant started to explain. Gustov looked at him, and the attendant quickly gave the bracelet to Princess Jarla.

They moved to the archery stall next door, where if you could hit a bull's eye you won a soft bear. Gustov picked up a bow and took an arrow. He drew the bow, changing aim at the last minute and shooting one of the bears between the eyes.

"Bull's eye!" said Gustov. He laughed, and the three moved on out of sight, the crowds moving out of the taverns and returning to the stalls as they left.

"There's no one at the stables tonight," said Greg. "Everyone is at the festival. There's a nice quiet hayloft there."

"Oh, you are terrible!" giggled Polly.

"Only a little kiss now," said Meg.

It was some time later, after seeing Meg home, that Delvin entered the lane where he lived. As he was about to open the door, he was startled by a clocked figure emerging from the shadows.

"Did you think you were trying to help?" hissed a voice. "Your meddling has now made things worse."

Delvin realised with a start that it was the same figure that had visited him the evening before. Again, the face was covered with a scarf.

"What did I do?" gasped Delvin.

"You know what you did. You cast a spell to send the guard to sleep. But I didn't know it was going to happen, so I couldn't use it. The guard has now been doubled. Whatever did you think you were doing? You will not get away with this." With that the figure turned and was gone before Delvin could pull his wits together again.

All he had done was wish what the mysterious figure wanted would happen. Had some of it really happened, or was it just coincidence? And what about the falling barrels? In his first fortune telling he had suddenly had the thought of falling barrels, and in the Square that evening the barrels had fallen from the stand. What was happening? How could that be a coincidence? He was sure 'real magic' didn't exist. Magic was just tricks.

Delvin had trouble getting to sleep that night. As he tossed and turned, he kept wondering, had he really made something happen?

CHAPTER 10

Delvin was determined to find out if other people had experienced these odd coincidences. As he lay awake, he decided what he would do. He had no shows or appointments booked the next day, so he would visit Magister Meldrum. Magister Meldrum was a member of the Guild of Magicians. He performed for the nobles. If anyone else had experienced odd coincidences when doing magic, it would be him.

Delvin set off soon after breakfast and made his way to the Professional Quarter of Hengel where Magister Meldrum lived. Delvin had rarely been to this part of the city before, since so far, his customers were mainly the shopkeepers and their children. The houses in this district were tall and built of stone with large impressive double doors. The ground floor windows had ornate carved lintels, and some had iron bars across them. It took Delvin some time to find Magister Meldrum's house, between a doctor on one side and a banker on the other. The door knocker had been made in the shape of a curious magic symbol. And other magic symbols had been painted in gold paint across the top of the door.

Almost the second Delvin struck the knocker, the door was opened startling him. Inside he saw a tall man with a completely expressionless face, wearing a long red robe which reached down to the floor.

"Yes?" enquired the man.

"I've come to see Magister Meldrum," gulped Delvin.

"Is he expecting you?"

"No, it is a professional matter."

"Yes…"

"I'm a magician and I was wanting to ask his advice."

"A magician..." The tall man's eyes looked Delvin up and down.

"I was hoping he could spare me a few minutes."

"I will ask him if he will see you."

The door was shut leaving Delvin on the street. It was opened a minute later by the tall man beckoning him in.

"Magister Meldrum will consent to see you."

Delvin was led through a hall lined with glass cabinets containing curious pieces of apparatus that Delvin had never seen before. They stopped outside a dark carved wooden door, and the man turned to Delvin.

"Your name?"

"Delvin."

The man knocked on the door.

"Enter."

He opened the door and announced, "Delvin the magician, magister."

Delvin entered the room. Two walls were covered with bookshelves filled with ancient looking volumes. The other two consisted of cabinets, one side containing more of the strange apparatus, and the other lined with bottles and containers. The room had no windows, the light coming from candles in sconces extending at regular intervals from the bookshelves and cabinets. There were three armchairs and a couch upholstered in deep red velvet. Behind a huge desk covered with books and papers, sat a small man wearing a round pill box hat with a gold tassel. His hair was grey and shoulder length and he peered at Delvin through a pair of gold rimmed spectacles.

"Sit down."

Delvin pulled up a chair. It must have been slightly lower than Magister Meldrum's chair, since Delvin found himself looking up at him.

"You asked to see me about a professional matter?"

"Yes," began Delvin. "Things have started to happen when I perform magic. It may just be coincidences, but it is as if it is really happening. I was wanting to ask if you have found the same thing. When you want something to happen, does it happen. Can you perform magic?"

Magister Meldrum seemed to expand like a bullfrog. "You are asking me if I can perform magic," he roared. "You come to this town. You have no connection with the Guild of Magicians. You take business from me, and now do you hope I'll say I don't perform real magic so you can tell all my customers. Then I presume you will claim that you can. You are a fraud! Only Guild members can perform magic. Get out!" he roared.

The door opened and the tall man was there. "I believe you are leaving."

Delvin was too startled to make any reply, and before he had got his wits together again, he was out on the street, and the door had shut behind him. He made his way back towards his lodgings, trying to work out whether Magister Meldrum's reaction was because he did perform real magic, or because he didn't.

As Delvin entered the small lane where he lived, he noticed three guards waiting outside the door of Mistress Wilshaw's house. As he opened the door a fourth guard was inside.

"Are you the magician Delvin?" asked the guard coming out through the door.

"Yes," replied Delvin shaken.

"You are under arrest. Surrender any weapons."

"I don't have any weapons, only a belt knife."

"I'll take that," said the guard deftly removing the knife. "Come with us."

Delvin was spun round by a guard at each elbow, and the next moment found himself being marched towards the Castle with one guard in front, another behind and the two others each holding an arm.

Why didn't I register for tax? thought Delvin.

CHAPTER 11

As Delvin was marched through the streets by the four guards, people stopped and stared. He tried to look straight ahead hoping no one would recognise him and wondering how this would affect his bookings.

As they came to the Castle's great barbican, Delvin looked up and saw the heads of Hengel's enemies stuck on spikes above the gate. He shivered as he was marched under the gate's arch, the gatekeeper and other Castle visitors standing back to let them through.

They came into the main courtyard which was surrounded by the Castle's walls and towers. Delvin had never been in the Castle before and was surprised at the bustle going on all around. The doors to the stables on his left were open and he could see the rows of horses inside. The great hall built against the Castle wall to his right, reared up in complex pattern of pinnacles and buttresses that despite his fear made him gasp in awe. He had no time to stop and admire, as he was being marched inexorably towards the main Castle building that was built around the ancient square keep that had been built by Hengel himself.

The guards marched him up the steps to the huge iron-studded doors set in the square tower that had once been the inner bailey's gatehouse. The doors were open to let in light and air, and they hardly paused as they went inside.

It took Delvin's eyes a moment to adjust to the sudden gloom. They passed through a long stone arch with doors at the side, and then came out into a huge hall with a grand staircase leading up on the left, and doors on the right open to what appeared to be a courtroom.

The guards appeared to be heading towards the courtroom, but to Delvin's surprise they marched past the courtroom to a narrow passage in the corner of the hall.

The passage was dark having no windows. As they passed a slight bend Delvin could see that it was lit by a single torch held in a bracket at the far end. Fear gripped him and he tried to drag back, but the guards holding his arms took a firmer grip. He gasped as the guard on the left hit him hard in the back and he was half dragged down the passage.

As they reached the torch, the guard in front took it down from the bracket and they turned left through a stone archway that led tunnel-like through a massive wall that Delvin took to mean they were entering the ancient keep itself.

Inside the keep a spiral stair led downwards into the dark. The guards half marched, half dragged him down the stairs. He had to be careful since the stairs were wet and slimy and he did not want to fall into the dark unknown.

As they reached the bottom of the stairs, in the flickering light of the torch Delvin could see an arch leading into a chamber that contained strange devices and things hanging from the ceiling. His heart seemed to stop as he realised where he was, but the guards turned right down a passage lined with heavy doors. As they passed one, an inhuman sounding wail came from within that chilled him to the bone.

They turned left, and the passage continued with more doors. As they reached the end of the passage, the guard in front stopped at the last door on the right and pulled it open. Delvin started struggling, but with two more punches in the back and a shove he was propelled through the door. He hit the wall at the far side and crashed to the floor as the door was slammed shut behind him, blocking out even the flickering light of the torch. The bolts screeched as they were slammed home, and as Delvin crept to his knees, the faint sound of the guards retreating feet faded away into the distance.

He was in total dark. He felt towards the walls and found them only a single pace in each direction. The walls were damp and slimy, and the cell had a sharp sour musty smell that made his stomach turn. There was the sound of dripping water, and Delvin felt a drop fall on his neck. The floor sounded and felt as though it was covered with rotten straw, and when he stood still, he could hear a scurrying and scraping as some animal or insect moved about.

He didn't feel like sitting or lying so he leant against a wall and tried to think. Whyever was he here? What had he done? And the thing that really terrified him, what was going to happen to him?

Delvin rapidly lost all sense of time, and it seemed to him that he had been in the cell for hours when he once again heard the sound of feet.

There was a screech as the bolt was drawn back and Delvin was momentarily blinded by the brightness of the torch. Two guards grabbed him by the shoulders and pulled him out, frogmarching him down the passage and up the stairs.

At the top of the stairs, rather than head back through the thickness of the keep wall, they went through an arch into the lower chamber of the keep. As Delvin was dragged along, he could see rack upon rack of weapons and armour, the light of the torch glinting dully off the blades and iron helmets. At the left-hand corner of the armoury another stone arch led to a spiral stair. Delvin was half dragged up, one guard in front, one behind. The spiral stair opened into a huge guard room that seemed to occupy the next level of the keep, but the guards headed through an arch, again leading through the massive thickness of the keep walls into a service passage beyond. A maid was in the passage, but when she saw Delvin and the guards she quickly ducked through a doorway.

At the far end of the passage the guards turned left, then opened a door and Delvin found himself on the landing at the top of the grand staircase. He was marched along the landing towards a pair of huge double doors guarded by two magnificently dressed sentries. Several people sitting on seats and benches around the walls gave him curious, pitying or annoyed looks. Delvin wondered if they were waiting to see someone, but before he could speculate any further, the sentries had flung open the two doors and Delvin was marched straight through into the room beyond.

The room was long with a high hammerbeam ceiling. The bosses of the hammerbeams had been carved into grotesque faces and the beams and the roof between were decorated in rich colours. The lower walls were covered in tapestries with narrow windows above through which the sun sent shafts of light down the length of the hall.

The bottom of the hall where Delvin had entered was empty, but as his eyes drunk in the splendour, he saw a group of people standing on a dais at the far end. In their midst was a figure seated in a huge chair. Delvin immediately recognised the seated figure as Duke Poldor. He was once again dressed completely in black, but this time each of the black spikes of his hair and beard had a piece of black ribbon tied to their tips so they waved every time he moved his head. Delvin also recognised Prince Gustov and Princesses Jarla and Stella.

The guards marched Delvin up the hall and stopped in front of the duke.

"The traitor Delvin, Your Grace."

At the word 'traitor' Delvin's heart seemed to stop and he suddenly felt faint. Traitor? He had never been a traitor! He had thought he had been arrested for not paying his tax.

The duke looked up and his dark eyes stared at Delvin for several seconds, his face completely expressionless.

"Why were you trying to kill me?" snarled the duke.

"I was not trying to kill you," gasped Delvin.

"Really, do you expect me to believe that," snapped the duke. "I have a witness who heard you say that barrels were going to fall, days before they actually did. If you knew they were going to fall it must have been deliberate, and you must have been part of it. Now why?" Duke Poldor suddenly slashed Delvin across the face with a riding crop he was holding and Delvin reeled back and cried out in pain.

In shock Delvin gasped, "I don't know what happened, the thought of the falling barrels suddenly came into my head."

Duke Poldor sat up, his hooked nose approaching Delvin's. "You don't know? Is that the best you can come up with? Are you going to tell me you saw it in your crystal ball?"

Delvin's cheek stung furiously from the duke's blow.

"No, Your Grace, I've never seen anything in a crystal ball."

"Well that at least is clear. So, who told you? Who are you working with?"

"I'm not working with anyone Your Grace. The thought of the falling barrels just came to me."

"Do you expect me to believe you can see visions of the future? What do you take me for? Just look at you, you don't even look like a magician," the duke sneered. "You didn't even predict your own arrest."

"It is the truth," muttered Delvin, wishing that Duke Poldor would go bald, whatever would he look like if one of the big spikes fell out.

"Father!" a sharp feminine voice broke in, and Princess Jarla stepped forward. She had replaced her crimson dress with a dark green one with a crossover bodice that left her midriff bare apart from a large emerald set in her navel. "Let me find the answers." She poked her right hand towards Delvin, and he saw that the long-curved fingernail had been filed to a sharp point. She placed the point under his chin and moved it slowly up. Delvin tried to move his head back as he felt the fingernail cut into his skin. As the fingernail moved inexorably up, Delvin forced his head back as far as it would go. The fingernail started to cut deeper. He could just see the duke looking towards his daughter.

"All right my dear, if you like."

"I do like," she replied, her tongue flicking her lips. "I shall do some... probing... to find out everything he knows."

"I want the answers tonight...without fail," hissed the duke.

Jarla gave a sudden quick twist of her nail, cutting a thin circle under Delvin's chin. She then pulled back her hand and examined the drop of blood on the tip of the nail.

"Take him back to the dungeon. I will be with him in due course."

Delvin's knees and legs felt weak with shock, and as the guards spun him round and marched him off, he could hardly make his legs obey him.

CHAPTER 12

As the dungeon door slammed shut behind him once again and the bolt crashed home, Delvin wondered fearfully what Princess Jarla would do to him. Her talk of probing to find answers filled him with dread. What or where would she probe? He shivered. He had told all that he knew. How could he convince her that he had told her everything. He thought back over what had happened. Was that image that had come into his mind like the magic that seemed to keep happening? What else could he tell her?

In desperation he wondered if there was any way he could get out. He put his hand in his pocket and felt what he had in there. There were a few coins, Borlock's piece of crystal and a cloth. Nothing he could use to prise back the lock.

Delvin grew more and more restless as he waited with increasing dread the sound of feet in the passage.

There was a sudden screech as the bolt went back and the door swung open. Delvin hadn't heard any footsteps, had the magic happened again?

"Stop standing there like an idiot and get a move on!" demanded a female voice.

Delvin pulled himself together and started to move out of the cell to be brought up short by the sight of Princess Jarla. She was standing outside the cell holding a torch, wearing an old leather riding jacket and leather trousers, and with her hair tied back behind her head.

"Snap out of it, we haven't much time," demanded Jarla. "Up the stairs, fast!"

In a half daze, Delvin moved out of the cell, staggered down the passage and climbed the stairs.

"Quicker, get a move on!"

As they came to the ground floor Delvin hesitated.

"Turn right, move it!"

Delvin turned right and went through the arch he had been through earlier into the armoury. But this time Jarla directed him diagonally across the chamber moving between the racks of equipment the torch throwing strange shadows across the room. They reached the corner and Jarla nodded at an arched doorway.

"Through there and up."

There was another spiral stair through the doorway and Delvin climbed upwards. As Jarla was behind him with the torch he could see little ahead but the dark. He seemed to be climbing for a long time before a crack of light appeared around a door to the side.

"Stop!" Jarla commanded.

Delvin stopped and Jarla carefully opened the door and peered through. When she was sure there was nobody there, she signalled for him to follow. They were in a narrow service passage that seemed to run through the thickness of the keep wall and then bend to the left. As they moved round the bend Delvin could see it was lit by a single torch ahead.

As they approached the torch Jarla stopped again. She carefully opened a door opposite the torch and peered out. Again, silently signalling Delvin to follow, she stepped through the door.

They were in a richly decorated passage with tapestries on the walls and candles at regular intervals giving a steady light. Some way down two guards lay asleep outside a carved door. Jarla advanced down the passage with Delvin following. The other doors opening on the right were also richly carved, but before Delvin could wonder what lay behind them, they had reached the door with the sleeping guards and Jarla was opening it, being careful not to disturb the guards as she did so. Delvin followed behind her and found himself in a beautifully furnished bed chamber. Pictures in ornate frames hung on the walls and a massive canopied bed stood against the wall to the left. It was a moment before Delvin saw a female figure slumped on the floor where she must have fallen from a chair in front of a dressing table. She had long blond hair covering her face and was wearing a beautifully embroidered long yellow dress.

"Pick her up, quick, we haven't much time," whispered Jarla.

"Who is she?" asked Delvin, desperately wondering what was going on.

"Fionella of course, now move fast."

Too stunned to object, Delvin picked up the prostrate figure and followed Jarla back out of the room.

Jarla turned right and then almost immediately right again into a narrow unlit passage. She was still holding the torch and in its flickering light Delvin could see a door in an arch ahead. Jarla opened the door and went through into a bare square chamber with an arrow slit opening in the far wall.

We must be in one of the Castle towers thought Delvin as Jarla turned left to an opening in the corner of the room that led to a spiral stair.

She moved quickly down the stairs, Delvin trying to keep up under the burden of Princess Fionella, not wanting to fall behind since Jarla's torch was the only light. On the floor below Jarla moved out into the tower chamber and opened a door similar to the one they had passed through above. They were in another short service passage, this one blocked off by a door at the end. Jarla carefully opened it and looked through. She turned back to Delvin.

"Run to the next door."

As Delvin was still taking in what she had said, she was through the door and had set off down the passage to the right. Delvin followed as quickly as he could and as he got to the door, he could just see her disappearing to the right. He ran after her as fast as he was able, panting under the weight of Fionella. The passage curved round a central wall and then opened on the right into a wide hallway with pillars down the centre. It was well lit and he could see doors to either side. Jarla was well ahead of him and he only just saw her disappear through a door on the far side. Delvin was now panting hard, and his arms ached by the time he reached the door. He pushed it and it swung open. He staggered through, past another spiral stair into another tower chamber. Jarla was standing there with her torch.

"Did anyone see you?"

"I don't think so," panted Delvin.

"Good," said Jarla heading for the stair.

"Can I have a rest?" gasped Delvin, putting Fionella down and stretching his arms.

Jarla glared at him. "Don't be so pathetic, come on."

Delvin picked Fionella up again, this time putting her over his left shoulder and followed Jarla up the spiral stair. They went up one floor, and then Jarla put the torch down on the stairs and opened a door.

Fresh air hit Delvin as he followed Jarla through the door. They were on the Castle wall walk. The tower they had just come up was on the corner of the Castle. They were level with the roof of a large building filling the inner bailey of the original castle.

Jarla had already reached the next tower and was signalling furiously to Delvin. He set out after her. As he passed the roof and chimneys of the building, he could see down into the courtyard which was lit by a series of torches fixed to the walls. It seemed full of activity, with guards checking people and carts entering and leaving the Castle. He reached the next tower and Jarla pulled him through the door shutting it behind them. Without a torch it was completely dark. Jarla's voice came out of the darkness.

"This way."

He followed the sound feeling carefully with his feet.

"Down here."

Delvin's foot felt open space and he realised there was a step down. It must be another spiral stair he thought. He felt out with his free hand and felt the stone wall, and by keeping his fingers on it was able to guide himself down the stairs.

They seemed to be going down a long time when he heard

Jarla's voice ahead hiss, "Stop!"

Delvin stopped and he heard a scratching and a rattle, then light flooded in as Jarla opened a door. He followed her into a chamber that was obviously a guardroom since six guards lay slumped over a table in the centre of the room. They had been drinking and playing dice and their goblets and winnings were spread across the table. Delvin reached for one of the goblets, he had had nothing to eat or drink for hours.

"Leave it you idiot!" snapped Jarla.

Delvin looked towards her angrily.

"I drugged it you fool. You don't think they fell asleep on their own do you? Now this way quickly."

Jarla led the way down a narrow stair at the back of the tower to a small door. She removed a key from her pocket, unlocked the door and a moment later they were out of the Castle and standing opposite the entrance to a narrow lane on the edge of the Metalworkers Quarter.

"This way," said Jarla. "I've three horses stabled down here. You can ride, can't you?"

"A bit," replied Delvin.

"Oh no, a bit! That means you will be bumping along like a sack of potatoes."

"Is it far?" asked Delvin. "Fionella's getting heavy."

"Keep quiet, or you'll join the heads on the gate."

After only a few yards down the lane Jarla turned into an alley beside a disused house. At the back of the house past a small yard was a stable. Jarla opened the stable door gesturing Delvin in. It was pitch black in the stable and Delvin could see nothing until Jarla struck a tinderbox and lit a lantern. The stable was small with three horse boxes each occupied by a horse. There was a pile of bundles in one corner and a heap of straw to the side. A door appeared to lead through to a coach house.

"Put her on the straw over there and help me get the horses ready."

"What are we doing?" asked Delvin." Why are you doing this?"

"To save Hengel and my father of course," replied Jarla in an exasperated voice. "My father is under an enchantment. It must have been done by a magician. And you're a magician, you sent the guards to sleep and predicted the barrels falling. That's why you're coming. You're going to help me find out what's going on. I do know it is something to do with Fionella. That's why we are taking her back to Argent, to stop this war"

"I thought the duke was protecting her from the Duke of Argent," said Delvin stunned.

"Protecting her? You must be joking. You didn't believe all that rubbish did you" sneered Jarla. "Fionella came here on a short visit. We thought it was to meet Gustov. My father falls under some sort of spell and becomes infatuated with her. She refuses to go home. My father refuses to let her go and the Duke of Argent claims she has been kidnapped. A nice simple straightforward excuse for Argent to go to war with us."

"You mean it was all just an excuse for Argent to declare war?"

"Of course it was. Why else put a spell on my father to become infatuated with her. Marrying her off to my dear brother Gustov would have been the logical thing to do if they wanted peace."

"But if she is refusing to go home, why was there a guard on her door?"

"My father thinks Argent will send people, agents, soldiers, to take her back. They won't. Argent wants her to stay here as an excuse for the war. But my father doesn't believe that. He thinks Argent will try to get her back. So, if Argent won't send people to get her back, we must do it ourselves instead. We are going to take her back and so get this war stopped. Once she is back in Argent, they can't claim she has been kidnapped."

They had been saddling the horses and now Jarla led the first one forward.

"Put her in the saddle. We'll have to tie her on until she wakes up."

Delvin was about to hoist Fionella into the saddle when they heard an urgent trumpeting and shouting from the Castle.

"Sheffs!" exclaimed Jarla. "They must have found the guards. We will just have to lie low until we can work out how to get out of the city."

"Won't they search the city?" asked Delvin.

"Yes," replied Jarla.

"Won't they find us?"

"They might."

"You don't seem worried. Kidnapping princesses is probably treason."

"It is, but I have evidence that you did the kidnapping. I am just another of your victims." Jarla gave a quick evil smile.

"You…a victim!" choked Delvin. "We have to get out of here. We are almost next to the Castle. We must get out of the town."

"And how do you propose to do that? The guards at the gate will have our descriptions."

Delvin thought fast. In his magic if he didn't want people to see something, he would make it look like something ordinary that they would expect to see.

"We need to change out appearances."

"What, a long beard and false moustache?"

"No. They will be looking for a man and two women. We need to change that to two men and one woman."

Jarla looked up as Delvin continued.

"That will do once we are out of the gate, but we need something better to get through it."

Delvin looked around he stable. In the coach house beyond he saw an old cart that must once have been used to bring produce into the city. It was now covered in dust but it looked sound enough.

"We could use that cart," said Delvin. "You driving and Fionella and me covered by sacks in the back. They won't be looking for a woman on her own."

"It will take forever getting to Argent in that…and how do you propose to turn Fionella into a man?"

"Cut her hair and put her in men's clothing."

"What men's clothing? Do you happen to have a spare set hidden somewhere?"

"I'll have to get to my lodgings and get some of mine. You

could be cutting her hair while I do it."

Jarla looked at him for a moment. "Your lodgings are one of the first places they will look."

"I'll be quick."

"You had better be…get on with it. I'll sort her out, and remember," Jarla looked him in the eye. "If you run off you will be hunted down as a traitor. My father has some particularly inventive, and messy ways of dealing with traitors… Your only chance is if I tell them that you were helping me."

Delvin turned and was out of the stables and running towards his lodgings as fast as he could go. His mind was racing with what Jarla had told him. How had he got mixed up in all this?

As he approached the lane where Mistress Wilshaw's house stood, he slowed down. He must be careful he thought, the guards may be waiting for him. There was a back entrance to the house and Delvin made it there without being seen. He couldn't see any guards, but he knew they wouldn't be long.

"Oh Master Delvin, I wondered if we would ever see you again when those guards came to take you away," exclaimed Mistress Wilshaw as she came out of her kitchen to see who had come in.

"I don't think you will see me again Mistress Wilshaw. I've come to get my things. I think the guards are after me."

"Whatever have you done?"

"I haven't done anything, but they think I've kidnapped Princess Fionella."

"You, kidnapping a princess. Well of all the silly ideas. You get along quickly and get your things. If anybody comes, I'll hold them up… go on, get on now."

Delvin quickly ran upstairs and bundled up his props and clothes as fast as he could. He didn't have time to decide what to take or leave, so apart from a few large magic props and the magic lantern he just grabbed everything. Suddenly he heard a loud banging from downstairs and shouts outside.

"Now you wait a minute while I get to the door, what a noise you're making," came the voice of Mistress Wilshaw.

Delvin looked around the room. He had got just about

everything. He looked at his rabbit, and on a sudden impulse quickly put it in its travelling box and headed for the stairs with his bundles and his rabbit. As he reached the back door, he heard a stern voice from the front door.

"Have you seen the magician Delvin?"

"I saw him this morning when you came to take him. He hasn't escaped, has he? Oh, my goodness, he must be a real magician then. He said I would meet a tall dark man with a moustache. You are dark, and you've a moustache, and you are tall…"

Delvin grinned as he crept quickly out of the back door. Mistress Wilshaw seemed to have the matter well in hand.

He avoided the main streets where possible, and when he crossed the North South Road, he tried to keep to the shadows for he could hear running feet and shouts to his right. The West Road was quieter though he could still hear noises coming from the Castle Square. He slipped across the road without being seen, and dodged into the alleys of the Metalworkers Quarter and was able to get back to the stable without being challenged.

As he entered the stable Delvin saw that Jarla had been busy. Fionella seemed to be just coming round from the drugs but her appearance had dramatically changed. Jarla had cut her hair off short in a man's style so that her face now looked like that of an adolescent boy rather than a beautiful princess. She had also removed Fionella's long and sumptuous dress so that now she was wearing just her undergarments. The dress had been bundled up, and was with a pile of other bundles that had obviously been left at the stables by Jarla for their escape from the city.

"Have you got the clothes?" said Jarla turning towards Delvin. She saw the rabbit in the carrying box. "Good, at least you have thought to bring dinner."

"That's my rabbit," said Delvin protectively. "Yes. I do have the clothes."

"Well, we have nothing else to eat. I'll kill it for you if you are too squeamish." Jarla reached towards the rabbit's box flexing her fingers.

"You are not going to eat my rabbit!" Delvin thought fast. "We need it for misdirection. If the rabbit is on the seat of the cart when we drive it out of the city, the guards will tend to look at the rabbit and not at you or the cart. It is how magicians stop you seeing what they are doing."

Jarla looked at him. "They'll probably be thinking who is stupid enough to have a rabbit on the front seat."

"That's exactly my point. They won't be looking at you."

"All right. We'll try it. But if it gets in the way it goes. You might have changed your mind by morning since we've no food and we won't be leaving until tomorrow when the guards will have relaxed a bit. Right, give the clothes to Fionella... Fionella put them on."

As Delvin fumbled in his bundle to get out his spare clothes Fionella stood up from where she had been sitting in the straw. The drug had now almost worn off though she still looked a bit wobbly, but her eyes sparked dangerously.

"What the sheffs are you doing?" spat Fionella. "What have you done to my hair? You will take me back immediately. Immediately I say!" She stamped her foot and almost fell over as her balance was not yet quite right.

"We are taking you back," sneered Jarla. "To Argent."

"You will take me back to the duke. He'll have your head for this."

"But your dear father has gone to war to rescue you. Don't you think it will warm his heart to have you back?"

"Duke Poldor is protecting me, and we love each other."

"How convenient. When you are back in Argent, if you still love my father, it can all be arranged properly and you can have a state wedding. Now you are going back."

"I am going nowhere," snapped Fionella. "I am going straight back to the Castle." With that she began to stride to the door. Jarla reached her with one pace and grabbed her by both her arms. Delvin could see that where Jarla was gripping, stains of blood were slowly spreading from where her fingernails had dug into Fionella's flesh.

"You are staying here and leaving with us," said Jarla very quietly and deliberately. "You are going to do exactly what I tell you."

Fionella was now squirming in pain as the fingernails bit deeper. Jarla nodded to Delvin.

"Hold her arms."

Delvin, slightly shocked, moved behind Fionella and held her arms. Jarla released her grip and moved her face to within half a handspan of Fionella's nose.

"Let me tell you what we will do," purred Jarla. "At night you will be tied up so you can't escape, and if…" Jarla moved closer and raised her right fingernail towards Fionella's eye, "you try to escape," Jarla's fingernail moved closer towards the eye, "I shall get great pleasure in pricking your eyeballs." Despite Fionella's head now being as far back as it would go, the sharp pointed tip of Jarla's fingernail was now only a hair's breadth from Fionella's eyeball. "Do you understand?"

"Yes," gasped Fionella.

Jarla moved back and Fionella slumped forward.

"Good, we understand each other," said Jarla. "Now get into those clothes."

Delvin released Fionella, and she did as she was told with Jarla standing over her to make sure.

"Get me the rope from the bag."

Delvin had ben trying to move away, but was brought up by Jarla's command. He found the rope and handed it to Jarla, who proceeded to tie one of Fionella's ankles and one of her wrists to a ring in the wall, probably intended for tying horses to.

"There's a pump outside, get some water," commanded Jarla. Delvin looked around and found a bucket. He went out to the small yard beside the stable where he found the pump next to the building. He washed out the bucket and filled it with water.

"When you've watered the horses, get some for us." As Delvin trudged back out again, he was tempted to tell Jarla to get her own water but thought better of it, and brought water for all three of them.

"Right," said Jarla. "We will sleep on the straw in here, you go in there." She pointed to the coach house. "We start at first light."

"Wouldn't it be better to wait till the afternoon when the farmers are leaving the city with their empty carts? suggested Delvin.

"You may be right, but we'll be good and hungry by then."

With that Jarla blew out her lantern and Delvin was left in the dark to try and find his way to the coach house. He banged his ankles twice before he got there, and then could not see to find a place to sleep. In the end he found a pile of sacks and lay down on them.

Delvin's mind kept turning over what had happened, there were so many things he still did not understand.

"Was that you who came to see me the day before yesterday?" asked Delvin into the dark. It now seemed much longer than just two days.

"Of course it was," came Jarla's voice from the stables.

"What did you want?"

"I told you. I wanted to get the enchantment taken off my father and get Fionella away. But it didn't work, I wasn't ready for it so couldn't organise things. Anyway, this is much better, everyone will think you have abducted us both, so will blame the magicians."

"Why do you want to blame the magicians?"

"They are getting much too rich and powerful. No one knows how they are doing it. But here in Hengel and also in South Bridge there's one very rich influential magician. I believe it's the same in Argent. They need their wings clipping."

"You might not know how they are doing it," muttered Fionella.

"What was that?" Demanded Jarla.

"Nothing, I'm just here for the ride," sneered Fionella.

It was some time before Delvin finally got to sleep.

CHAPTER 13

Delvin was woken by a kick in the ribs. Jarla was standing over him.

"Get up and get us some water," she demanded.

For a moment Delvin wondered where he was, and then it all came back to him. He rubbed the sleep out of his eyes and got stiffly to his feet. His stomach felt empty and his cheek throbbed where Duke Poldor had hit him the day before. He looked around the stable and coach house. Daylight was coming in from the shuttered windows. Fionella was sitting on the floor, glaring furiously at Jarla who was checking her bundles.

Delvin went out to the pump and washed his face in the cold water having a deep drink as he did so. He then brought a bucket-full back to Jarla and returned to the pump to shave. Jarla had decided to wait until the afternoon before leaving, and as there was no food, and as neither Jarla nor Delvin wanted to risk being seen in the city, they were unable to have breakfast. They sat on the straw, watered the horses and occasionally got up and walked around, waiting for the time to leave.

Eventually, about two hours after midday, Jarla stood up.

"Time to get ready."

They hitched one of the horses to the cart and loaded their bundles in the back. Jarla ordered Fionella into the back where she tied her hands and feet and then gagged her. Jarla then tied another rope around Fionella's neck into which she inserted a stick to act as a lever.

"If Fionella makes any movement or noise," Jarla told Delvin. "Turn this stick. It will throttle her, which will shut her up and stop her wanting to do it again. I'll show you." She gave a sudden jerk on the stick and Fionella's eyes popped wide open and her face quickly reddened. She released it again and Fionella slumped forward.

"You will lie in the back with Fionella. Keep hold of the stick. We will have to leave two horses here, leading two horses behind the cart would look too suspicious. Right, lie down."

Delvin lay down in the back of the cart next to Fionella and Jarla heaped sacks on top of them. It was musty, dark and hot under the sacks, but through the smell of dust and age, Delvin could smell Fionella's perfume. He heard Jarla put the rabbit box on the seat beside her and then the cart was off. Delvin suddenly gave a start.

"Which gate are you heading for?"

"Quiet and stop moving," snapped Jarla.

"Which gate?"

"The North Gate, we are heading for Argent. Now will you keep quiet or am I going to have to shut you up too?" Jarla stopped the cart and turned towards the pile of sacks.

"They'll be looking for us at the North Gate, we should go through the South Gate."

"That's the wrong way, we are not going to Pandoland."

"No, we turn off at Havelock and head towards the Grandents. There'll be side roads that lead along the edge of the mountains towards Argent."

"There are only two ways into Argent if you don't want to swim, South Bridge and Cragley. I don't fancy Cragley, too many narrow mountain roads with the castle at the border.

"I saw a map that Borlock had. There's a road that goes through Gaverton. You can get to South Bridge from there. I don't know the roads in detail, but I'm sure side roads are better than main ones."

"All right, we will use the South Gate. It will take us longer and if you are wrong about it not being guarded you will pay for it!"

Jarla flicked the whip and the cart moved off again. Delvin kept track where they were for the first few minutes, but then the stops and turns lost him and he just concentrated on staying as still and as quiet as he could. He gripped the crystal that was in his pocket and hoped that the guard at the gate would not want to examine the sacks in the back of the cart. After what seemed a long time, he heard a gruff voice.

"What have you got young lady?"

He hardly recognised the voice that replied as being Jarla's.

"I dropped off our turnips, now I'm off home."

"And where is that?"

"Endelson's farm near Havelock."

"What's that you've got there?"

"Ahh, that rabbit. Got that for my sister. If she don't like it, I'll have it for supper."

Delvin heard a harsh laugh. "Right on you go. Next!"

The cart started again, and Delvin relaxed slightly as he felt the cart move off the smooth stones under the gate, and onto the rougher surface of the road beyond.

CHAPTER 14

It seemed an age later when Jarla stopped the cart and pulled the sacks off Delvin and Fionella. Delvin's legs were cramped from not being able to move and he blinked in the sudden light. Fionella was breathing raggedly, the gag making it difficult for her to breathe through her mouth, and dust having got up her nose. She gasped as the gag was removed and sucked long gulps of air into her lungs. Jarla untied her and removed the rope from around her neck.

"Your idea of putting the rabbit on the front seat seemed to work," said Jarla with a brief smile.

They had stopped by a small wood that partially screened them from the road. Ahead the road wound gently between low walls, bounding fields containing the early growth of summer grain. There was no sign of other travellers, though Delvin knew it would not be long before some came past.

"Just a minute," said Delvin reaching for the rabbit box.

"What are you doing?" demanded Jarla, as Delvin took the rabbit's travelling box to the side of the road and opened it.

"I'm letting her go. She's done me good service and helped us get out of Hengel, she deserves her freedom."

The rabbit looked around and lolloped a few steps away from Delvin. She then sniffed the air, turned round and came back.

"Go on," said Delvin flapping his arms. "Freedom, go on!"
The rabbit ignored him, sniffed the air once again and jumped back into the box.

"It looks like we have a meal organised after all," said Jarla. "Get back in, we have a long way to go before dark."

"You are not eating Freda," muttered Delvin as he climbed

back in the cart with the rabbit box.

The cart swayed as they set off again with Delvin clutching the rabbit box protectively. They were travelling through gently rolling countryside. The fields were planted with either grain or root crops. Narrow tracks led to farmsteads, often surrounded by a few worker's cottages and shaded by large trees. There were frequent small woods, and other trees bordered the road. They occasionally saw merchants travelling towards Hengel, their carts piled high with their merchandise. There were other travellers too, some looking like farmers others like gentlemen. There was even a carriage of giggling girls, probably being taken to a party.

Apart from stopping once to let the horse drink they continued on throughout the afternoon. As the light began to fade the rolling fields began to give way to low hills. Some of these still had fields of crops but others were dotted with sheep.

Eventually, to Delvin's relief, as they rounded a bend in the road, they could see the lights of a large village ahead.

"Is that Havelock?" asked Fionella.

"It had better be or we've taken the wrong road," replied Jarla.

"I'm so hungry I could eat a horse," said Fionella.

"Don't let Delvin hear that, he's already protecting that rabbit."

Jarla drove the cart into Havelock. They passed a row of cottages that led to a village green with a small duck pond. Facing each other across the duck pond were two inns, The Troubadour, a large inn which looked like it catered for the merchants and gentlefolk, and a smaller inn, The Green Duck. Delvin could also make out in the gloom two or three shops now boarded up for the night, and beyond them a crossroads.

Jarla drove the cart into the yard behind The Green Duck where a stable lad ran out and took the horse's head,

"How much to stable the horse?" asked Jarla.

"Three copper bits ma'am, one more if you want oats."

"Give him oats," said Jarla climbing stiffly down from the cart and reaching into the back for her bundles.

"Can you give her some as well?" added Delvin handing the rabbit box to the boy.

"I suppose so sir," said the boy turning back towards the stable door.

"I'm famished" said Jarla. She suddenly turned towards the stable boy and fixed him with a look. "Brush him and look after him properly, understand!"

"Yes ma'am," replied the boy looking frightened.

Jarla was about to walk into the inn when Delvin stopped her.

"Don't you think it will look odd with you ordering things?"

"What do you mean, odd?"

"Women don't usually do it. Men do."

A flash of anger crossed her eyes and then went again as quickly as it had come. "You are right. You do it. Two rooms and some food." Jarla turned back towards the door.

"I'll need some money." Delvin didn't want to spend his small savings on Jarla and Fionella.

Jarla glared at him and reached into her belt and removed one gold royal and two silver carls from her pouch. "This is not for you to get drunk."

They entered the inn and a large lady with red cheeks and a white apron came up to them.

"What can I do for you lady and gentlemen?"

"Have you got two rooms for the night?"

"Ooo no sir, I don't have. I've only the one room. But if you two gentlemen wouldn't mind sleeping in the barn, the lady can have that."

Delvin looked desperately at Jarla who scowled back at him.

"If the room is big enough the men can sleep on the floor," said Jarla.

"Ohh, I think it is," said the landlady. "That's three carls, payment in advance please."

Delvin handed over the royal and the landlady fished the change out of her apron pocket.

"Top of the stairs, last door on the left. Have you a horse in the stables?"

"Yes," replied Delvin.

"Right, I'll take for that too," said the landlady.

Delvin settled up for the stabling and oats and followed Jarla and Fionella up the stairs.

The room was under the eves and contained one large bed that sagged in the middle, a washstand with jug and bowl, and a few threadbare rugs on the floor. It had one small window that looked out onto the stable yard.

"If we had travelled direct by horse, we would have been there by now, and not stuck in this sheffs awful hole," muttered Jarla. "Right... Out while we get washed."

Delvin was left standing outside the room while Jarla and Fionella got washed.

When they eventually emerged, Delvin whispered to Jarla. "It's going to look very odd, you and a lad disappearing into a room every time we stop. What do you think people will start thinking?"

Jarla gave him a cold look and brushed past him towards the stairs. They entered the inn's common room which had a fireplace at one end and tables set about the walls. The room was filling up, with labourers coming in after their day's work.

Jarla led the way to a table by the wall and a young girl came up to them. She was not much older than fourteen, slightly breathless and flushed.

"If you want to eat, we have sheep stew, sausages or fresh bread and cheese."

Jarla gave a grimace and looked at Fionella who was scowling. "Stew?"

Fionella nodded.

"Three stews."

"What will you have to drink?"

"Wine," said Jarla.

"And two ales," said Delvin before Fionella could say anything.

The serving girl dashed away to get their order and Fionella turned to Delvin. "Why did you order me ale? I wanted wine."

"Young lads don't drink wine, they drink ale. You'd have given us away."

"I can't stand ale. It smells horrible."

"Have you ever drunk it?"

"Of course not."

"Well, you are going to."

"Quiet!" said Jarla. "Do you want everyone to hear with all this bickering."

The food and drink soon arrived. The young girl concentrating hard as she carried the three drinks. The stew was thick and meaty with vegetables and potatoes. Fionella looked with disgust at the chipped bowl and spoons.

"Are we meant to eat with these?"

"Either that or your fingers," replied Jarla.

Delvin tucked in, he was famished and the stew tasted delicious. He watched out of the corner of his eye as Fionella took a sip of the ale and grinned when he saw her grimace at the taste.

"Something is puzzling me," began Delvin. "I know we left by the South Gate, but I would have thought there would have been guards down this road looking for us by now."

"Of course not," replied Jarla between mouthfuls. "Do you think my father wants to be made to look a fool? He will be keeping things quiet. It will be bad enough for you to have escaped, but to have kidnapped two princesses as well?"

"What will he do then? He won't just leave us, will he?" asked Delvin hopefully.

"Of course not. He will send Grimbolt after us."

"Grimbolt?"

"Yes, Grimbolt. His real name is Grybald, but he was nicknamed Grimbolt after he put a crossbow bolt through a protester outside the Castle. The name stuck."

"What does Grimbolt do?"

"All the dirty work. If my father wants someone silenced, Grimbolt sees to it. He's very good."

"Very good?"

"Yes, I haven't known him fail."

"What will he do?"

"Whatever my father has told him to do. Either kill you or bring you back. That was why I wanted to get to Argent quickly. To keep ahead of him. We will just have to hope he concentrates on the road between Hengel and South Bridge."

"I hope he puts a crossbow bolt through both of you," said Fionella scowling.

"Hardly my dear," said Jarla sweetly.

They finished their meal in silence and retired to the room where Delvin tried to make himself comfortable on the hard floor. As he was about to get to sleep, he heard a sharp yelp as Jarla stopped Fionella rolling onto her in the sagging bed.

CHAPTER 15

They woke early, and Delvin was dispatched with six carls to buy provisions while Jarla and Fionella got up.

He walked round the pond in the early morning sunshine, and was able to buy two loaves of fresh bread, cheese, carrots and apples. He also bought three cups since they had nothing to drink from. He had visited the stables before he left, and taken out one gold royal from the secret pouch where he kept his money in the bundle of his magic tricks. He had been worried about leaving his money with his bundles in the stable, but it would have looked odd to have taken his magic tricks to bed with him. With the royal he was able to buy a new belt knife to replace the one that had been taken when he was arrested.

Delvin was in a happier frame of mind when he returned to the inn and joined Jarla and Fionella at breakfast in the common room.

Jarla's dark hair was tied back behind her head. The contrast of her dark hair and pale face made her look severe. Fionella's blond hair was tousled after the rough cut it had received, and together with her sullen look, it made her look like a sulking lad annoyed by his elders.

"Come on, eat up quick, we want to make good time to Shappley," said Jarla rising from the table.

"I haven't had anything yet," complained Delvin, breaking off a piece of bread with one hand and pouring a cup of hot leaf with the other.

"You can always walk," said Fionella following Jarla from the common room.

Delvin took a quick sip of his hot leaf, spooned some jam on his bread, grabbed the rest of the loaf and followed them out to the stable.

The stable lad had already hitched the horse up to the cart, so by the time Delvin emerged they were ready to go.

Delvin climbed into the back and saw that his rabbit box was there as well.

"I gave him some grain like you asked, and some cabbage leaves," said the stable boy.

"Thanks," said Delvin smiling at him. The stable boy returned the smile as the cart moved out into the road.

They turned left at the crossroads and were soon out of the village. The low hills continued with the fields bounded by dry stone walls. In the distance Delvin could see the crags of the Grandent mountains stretching across the horizon. They formed an almost impenetrable barrier across the continent from the far north to the deep south, the only road through being the Sheepstone Pass. Much of Hengel's wealth came from controlling that pass and the trade that came through it. The pass was guarded by Sheepstone Castle and a toll was charged on all travellers passing through.

The day was fine with a light breeze blowing a few clouds across the blue sky. After a few miles they saw a man sitting on the wall ahead with his horse grazing nearby. As they drew level with him, he looked up and Delvin could see his unshaven scarred face and hard cruel eyes.

"Stop! There's an arrow aimed at your throat," said the man.

A second man with a bow and arrow aimed at Jarla stood up from behind the wall. His hair was long and lank and his features narrow and sunken.

Jarla reined in the horse scowling. Fionella looked frightened.

"Do you know who we are?" began Fionella.

"Quiet," snapped Jarla, not taking her eyes off the two men.

"Oh, we are someone are we?" said the first man. "That means you should have plenty to help poor working men like us. Hand me your purses. Now!"

Jarla undid her purse from her belt and threw it down to the man.

"And yours," said the man to Fionella and Delvin.

Delvin undid the purse containing the change from buying his knife and threw it down as well.

"I'm carrying his money," said Jarla indicating Fionella.

"I wonder what else you have?" said the man. "Get down... Cover the other two," he told his companion with the bow.

Jarla slowly climbed off the cart, her eyes never leaving the two men. The first man stepped quickly over to her and expertly ran her hands over her and through her pockets.

"Not much here," said the man disappointedly. "But maybe there's something here." He leered putting a hand on her breast. "Come and see what a real man is made of." He started to undo the buttons of her leather riding jacket.

Jarla looked into his eyes. "I like strong men," she said huskily. "That idiot of a man over there hasn't enough to satisfy a milksop." She put her arms around his neck and drew him towards her.

"I like a woman with spirit," he replied putting his hands around her waist.

"Kiss me," she breathed.

The man grinned, and Jarla kissed him passionately, wrapping her arms right around his neck. Then her body, arms and two forefingers tensed and jerked, as she suddenly dug her sharpened nails into the jugular veins on either side of the man's neck. The man jerked and tried to draw back from her kiss, but his neck was pinned from either side and his movement just helped dig the nails in deeper.

The other robber who had been covering Delvin and Fionella with his bow, was transfixed by the sight of his companion jerking in Jarla's grip. Delvin used the distraction to grab the knife from his belt and throw it at the man. The knife bounced harmlessly off his arm, but the blow made him release the arrow which flew away over their heads.

Delvin leapt off the cart towards him. The man gave one glance at his companion who was now covered in blood, leaped up, grabbed the two purses, jumped into the saddle of his horse which was tethered by the road, and galloped off as fast as he could.

Jarla released her grip on the first robber who fell at her feet.

"Disgusting man, I'm covered in blood. Is there a stream nearby?"

Delvin, still slightly in shock from the encounter, pointed over the wall. "I think there is one just ahead."

"I'm getting cleaned up... Sort her out." Jarla pointed a bloody hand at Fionella who was as white as a sheet and shaking uncontrollably.

Delvin retrieved his knife and returned to Fionella.

"It's all right, they've gone now," he began.

"A lot of good you were," snapped Fionella forgetting her shock. "Left to you we'd have been raped and cut to pieces. A schoolgirl would have been better than you with that knife."

Delvin tried to explain that he had never been trained to fight.

"Sheffs! You let him get my purse." Delvin turned to see Jarla, who had now returned from the stream, and was standing over the dead robber, staring at him.

"I couldn't reach him in time."

"We are in the middle of nowhere with no money," wailed Fionella.

"Keep quiet," snapped Jarla. "Let's see if he has any money on him."

She quickly went through the robber's pockets and brought out his purse.

"Two carls and four copper bits. That's not enough for the inn tonight." Jarla looked around thinking. "Have you anything we can sell?"

"We could sell that smelly rabbit," said Fionella.

"My stuff is only magic tricks. People wouldn't buy those. Haven't you got anything Fionella? How about selling Fionella's dress. It must have cost a fortune."

"You are not selling my dress. I will not be stuck forever in these smelly old clothes. You will not sell it."

"No, we can't sell that. A dress like that would attract far too much attention." Jarla turned to Delvin. "You are going to have to earn the money. You've got your magic tricks. You're going to have to perform when we reach Shappley."

Delvin thought quickly. "It won't look right if I'm doing magic and you are sitting in the cart doing nothing."

"I thought you were meant to be a magician," said Fionella.

"I am, but travelling magicians don't have hangers on that do nothing."

"I see, pretending you don't have a stone, and magic is just tricks."

"What on earth do you mean?" said Delvin.

"Nothing. Forget it. We'll do it your way. I'm sure Jarla will act as a helper."

"You'll help as well," said Jarla.

"You know magicians don't earn very much," said Delvin.

"Oh, I believe you," said Fionella.

Jarla kicked the dead robber. "We'll just have to earn what we can... Right... Delvin, take his sword. You don't seem to know how to use it, but if you waggle it around you might impress somebody."

Delvin undid the belt holding the robber's sword in its scabbard and put it in the back of the cart.

"Should we do something with the body?"

"Why? He's a robber. It will be a deterrent to other robbers."

Jarla mounted the cart and flicked the reins. Delvin had to run to climb into the back.

CHAPTER 16

As they drove on towards Shappley, Delvin wondered what Fionella had meant when she said he was pretending that magic was just tricks. Did Fionella know if some magicians could perform real magic? If so, how did they do it? Had he inadvertently performed real magic back in Hengel? But any attempts to get her to say more were met with dismissive comments that she had meant nothing. Soon he had to think of more pressing matters. What sort of show was he going to perform in Shappley? What tricks was he going to do and how would he use his two assistants?

They stopped for lunch by a small stream where they ate some of the bread and cheese that Delvin had bought that morning. The new cups came in useful, and as Delvin went back to the stream to refill his, he collected a number of snails and put them into a bag, grinning to himself as he did so.

"Right," said Jarla. "We will be in Shappley soon. Tell us what you want us to do."

"Fionella must announce the show. Go round shouting 'The Great Delvin is about to perform.'"

"What!" shouted Fionella.

"That's about right," said Delvin. "Then organise the audience and take round the hat."

"I will not beg," muttered Fionella.

"It's not begging, it's getting paid," said Delvin.

"And you will do it," commanded Jarla. "And you had better be the great something else if you don't want half of Hengel after us."

"How about The Great Dollop," suggested Fionella.

Delvin looked up thinking, "I shall be The Great Casper," he announced. "And you will act as my assistant in the show," he said turning to Jarla. "But we will need to make you more glamorous, leather riding gear isn't quite right. Have you got something a bit glitzy."

"You want me to show myself off to country bumkins," said Jarla very deliberately, glaring at Delvin.

"As you said, we must help," said Fionella starting to grin.

Jarla looked angrily at the two of them.

"I have one dress, but it is not the sort of thing that a travelling magician's assistant would have, or afford."

"let's take a look," said Delvin supressing his grin.

Jarla removed the dress from one of her bundles. It was full length black silk.

"No, that's not quite right," said Delvin. "How about your underwear?"

"I am not performing in my underwear."

"We could trim it so that it becomes a costume."

"We must do this properly," said Fionella.

Glaring furiously, Jarla took her underwear from her bundle. Delvin held it up. It was a short black camisole reaching to just below the buttocks with a deep cleavage. The halves of the top held together with a black lace bow.

"That looks better," said Delvin. "But it is a bit too short at the moment and..." He thought a moment. "It needs a few tassels and beads. I would need to see it on to know just what was wanted.... We could make it a bit longer with a silk scarf. I should have a few tassels and things in my bundles. I'll get them while you change."

"The one I am wearing is the same," said Jarla dangerously as she undid her jacket and took off her outer clothes.

Delvin and Fionella, keeping very straight faces whenever they faced Jarla, tried positioning Delvin's tassels, silk scarves and beads in various places until they felt they were right. They then pinned them in place. They also undid Jarla's hair so that it hung down over her shoulders. When they had finished, they stood back and surveyed their handiwork.

Strings of beads had been pinned around the bottom of the camisole covering a brightly coloured silk scarf that now made the camisole longer. Tassels hung from each shoulder and Fionella had adjusted the bow at the top of the cleavage to give maximum effect.

"Well, I don't think anyone will recognise you," said Fionella.

"There had better not be anyone who will recognise me," snapped Jarla. "I feel like some concubine from the east."

"Oh no, they have veils over their faces," replied Delvin stifling another grin. He stood back looking at her critically. "I think you'll do. Right, you need to learn some poses. When I perform a trick, you raise one arm in the air and point the other at me like this..." Delvin posed in the way he described. "You try it."

Jarla still glaring, posed half heartedly like Delvin had done.

"No, your arm should be straighter, big smile, chest out."

Delvin tried to rearrange her and Jarla slapped his hand away furiously.

"Get your hands off me!"

"Right, try the walk."

Delvin demonstrated the walk with a sway of the hips. This time Jarla did it with more conviction, her eyes blazing.

"Sway the hips more...big smile." Jarla smiled through gritted teeth. "Ok, the applause position at the end." Delvin again demonstrated.

Jarla followed what he had done.

"Let's go through those again." Delvin ran Jarla through them again. "Right, I think we are ready to give it a try."

"Hitch the horse up and get in the back," ordered Jarla as she put her riding clothes back on.

"Fionella must go in the back. I am The Great Casper. I need to ride in the front."

"In the back Fionella."

Delvin hitched up the horse and they set off again. After about half an hour they came to the outskirts of Shappley. As their cart rolled past the first cottages Delvin told Fionella to shout:

'Casper the great magician will perform in two hours time.' Her first attempts were rather feeble but after Jarla had turned round and glared at her, she improved.

Soon small boys and girls were following the cart, shouting and asking to see a trick. Delvin smiled loftily to the left and right and told them to come to the show. Doors and windows opened as people came out to see what all the noise was about. Soon there was quite a crowd following the cart. In the centre of the village was a small square, and to the side of it the village green.

"Just the place," said Delvin and directed Jarla to pull the cart a little way onto the green close to the square. Delvin stood up on the cart and said to Fionella out of the corner of his mouth, "announce me."

"The Great Casper," shouted Fionella.

Delvin spread his hands and a hush came over the crowd. "Tonight, I shall be performing stunning feats of magic and prestidigitation the like of which you have never seen before. Come to the show and be amazed, bewildered, astonished and entertained. Bring your family, your friends, your neighbours to see a show you will remember for all your days. Come and see The Great Casper and his beautiful assistant Carolina." He turned and produced a bunch of flowers apparently out of thin air, which he handed to the astonished Jarla. "In the meantime, I shall repair to the inn. If any of you would like me to read your fortunes, or your minds, divine the future or provide any other magical service, come and see me there. Boy!" He turned to Fionella, "See to the horse, leave the cart on the green then bring the bags."

Delvin climbed down from the cart and strode purposefully towards the Shappley Arms Inn at the side of the square. Entering the inn, he called for the landlord and requested two rooms.

"That will be four carls." Said the landlord standing foursquare in the centre of the passage blocking their way.

"Splendid," said Delvin. "But before checking if the rooms are suitable, I must see to my public. May I use the common room?"

"All right," said the landlord eyeing him carefully. He followed Delvin into the common room and moved behind the bar to take any orders.

Delvin selected a table in the corner. He then requested the rest of the crowd to wait by the bar so he could not be overheard. He spread his special cloth in front of him and asked who was first.

It took an hour and a half, and several charms and packets of chalk love potions before the last customer had left. He had made five carls and three bits. While he was working, he had frequently leant forward to whisper in people's ears, giving him plenty of cover to secretly place three of the carls in a hidden pocket in his jacket. He reasoned that as he was supplying the charms and love potions, he should get some payment. He stood up, smiled round the room and swept up the remaining two carls and three bits and handed them to Jarla.

"A little more for our coffers. Let us examine the rooms. Landlord!" he looked towards the landlord who came from behind the bar. "If you would kindly lead the way so we can examine our rooms."

The landlord led the way to two small rooms at the back of the inn. One contained a double bed, the other two singles. Each had a washstand and two chairs, and they both looked out onto the stable yard behind.

"These should do very well. Carolina, will you settle with the gentleman please."

Jarla took four carls from the robber's purse which she now carried, and handed them to the landlord. When the landlord had closed the door behind him, she turned furiously to Delvin.

"Carolina! Who do you think you are?"

"The Great Casper who has just earned the extra money we needed for the rooms. We start in twenty minutes. Time to get changed." With that he turned on his heel, picked up his bundles and left for the next-door room.

There was a good crowd waiting to see the show. Delvin,

wearing Borlock's red robe, had positioned the cart so he could either stand on it to use as a stage, or could climb down to move into the audience. Jarla and Fionella stood by him looking apprehensive.

"Right, Fionella. After announcing me, I want you to take the hat round and try to get everyone to put something in while the show is going on. If you leave it till after the show, half of them will go without paying anything. At the end, stand at the back with the hat, you may get a bit more. I think we are ready. Announce me."

"Ladies and gentlemen. The Great Casper," Fionella smiled, "and Carolina."

The audience clapped and Delvin began his show with the first trick he had learnt from Borlock, the cups and balls. This time though he used their new drinking cups and the snails he had collected that afternoon.

Fionella saw what he was doing and whispered furiously, "get that disgusting snail out of my cup." Delvin lifted the cup and the snail had gone, only to reappear a moment later.

"Get it out of my cup!" hissed Fionella.

The crowd by now had realised what was going on and roared with laughter each time the snail returned to the cup. Fionella was torn between her embarrassment at the crowd's laughs and her anger at Delvin, which made the crowd laugh even more. She gave Delvin a furious look and started to take the hat round the crowd. Each time she looked back towards Delvin she scowled at him. The audience, thinking it was part of the act, egged her on and roared with laughter at her reactions.

Delvin moved on from the cups and snails, to making a lucky charm belonging to a member of the audience disappear, to be found again in the middle of a cabbage. He cut a rope in half with his belt knife and then mysteriously joined it together again. He made ball after ball appear apparently from nowhere that he held up between his fingers. He ended with the rabbit trick, making the rabbit appear from under the 'palace' to a round of thunderous applause.

Delvin bowed, and presented Jarla who was also applauded, and Fionella whose scowl brought both applause and laughter.

The crowd drifted away apart from a few curious youngsters who wanted Delvin to tell them how the tricks were done.

"With magic, practice and great skill." Delvin told them loftily, making sure his props were securely put away so that the boys couldn't try to examine them.

Fionella came up with the hat and they tipped it out onto the cart so they could see how they had done. The coins were all copper, but there was a good pile of them.

"There should be plenty for supper here," said Delvin.

"And some towards tomorrow's inn," said Jarla. "I'd prefer not to go through that again."

"Nor me," said Fionella. "I've never been so humiliated in all my life. You will wash those cups out Delvin, or I assure you, you will regret it!"

"I'll wash the cups," said Delvin. "Let's see what we have got." They counted the coins and found they had six carls and three bits all in coppers.

Jarla looked up with a slight smile, "That's the first money I have ever actually earned."

"I'll get the landlord to change them into silver carls," said Delvin as they packed up their things and headed towards the inn. "Get the stable lad to help you get the cart into the inn's yard," he told Fionella. "Meet us in the inn."

Fionella looking furious, did as she was asked, and Jarla and Delvin entered the inn.

When they had changed, and Delvin had checked that his rabbit had some food and water, they went down to the common room. Jarla had resumed her leather jacket and trousers, but she had left her long hair hanging free which softened the expression on her pale face. Fionella had washed her face which made her look pink faced and younger but she still wore a sullen look. The room was beginning to fill and several people made comments to them about the show, one telling the landlord to make sure there were no snails in his cups, which brought a laugh from his companions and a blush from Fionella.

They selected a table by the wall and a waitress came up to take their order. She was about sixteen with brown wavy hair, a plump figure and a shy look in her eye.

"Good evening magister, ma'am," she began in obvious awe of Delvin. "We have skirtles, cold meat or roast chicken."

"Whatever are skirtles?" asked Delvin.

"Oh, haven't you heard of skirtles," she said in a rush. "They are a speciality of the Grandent area. They are like a sausage made from sheep, with mutton, onion, parsnips and spices. My mum makes the best skirtles anywhere." She blushed at this admission. "They are roasted and served with chopped cabbage."

"Does your mum cook here?" asked Delvin kindly.

"Yes magister," she blushed again.

"Well, I shall have skirtles," said Delvin, and he turned to Jarla. "What would you like?"

"I shall have skirtles," said Jarla.

"Cold meat," said Fionella.

"What would you like to drink?"

"One wine and two ales please," replied Delvin seeing Fionella scowl out of the corner of his eye.

The girl rushed off and returned shortly with the drinks and the food. The skirtles were delicious with a strong spicy taste. Delvin sat back in his chair feeling calmer than he had since his arrest. He had no idea what was going to happen to him, but he had shown he could do a show as a travelling magician, just like Borlock had done.

The girl rushed back.

"That will be seven bits each for the meals, two bits each for the drinks. Two carls seven bits please magister," she gasped.

Delvin nodded to Jarla who counted out the money and the girl rushed off.

"We won't have enough money for both an inn and food tomorrow night," said Jarla grimly.

"He should be a proper magician," said Fionella sullenly.

"What do you mean by that?" said Jarla sharply. "You said

something similar earlier then tried to dismiss it. You are not going to dismiss it this time. You said something about a stone earlier. What did you mean?" Jarla had turned towards Fionella who was starting to look frightened.

"I didn't mean anything."

Delvin saw Jarla make a move towards Fionella who had gone almost as pale as Jarla.

"Tell me what you meant."

"Get your fingernail off my leg," cried Fionella.

Delvin saw that Jarla's hand was around Fionella's thigh and that the tip of the fingernail was already starting to bite through the fabric of the trousers.

"Don't make a scene," said Delvin urgently. "We have already attracted enough attention with the show."

"Smile please Fionella," said Jarla.

Fionella gave a watery smile.

"Now, what did you mean?" Delvin saw Fionella tense and wince as the fingernail began to bite into her.

"Get off me. I'll scream. You don't want to attract attention," sobbed Fionella."

"There's a large artery in the thigh. I wonder if I can reach it first go," mused Jarla. "Now tell me. What did you mean?" Jarla's voice had an edge of steel.

"It's a secret. No one is meant to know. I can't tell you. If they even thought I knew they would kill me."

"Who would kill you?"

"The magicians of course. And he says he's one. I don't know anything," she said desperately, looking at Delvin and suddenly realising she was admitting in front of a magician that she knew their secret.

"What is the magician's secret?" Jarla asked Delvin.

"I haven't any idea," replied Delvin.

"You are just saying that," sobbed Fionella.

"Are you going to kill her for knowing this secret?" Jarla asked Delvin.

"Of course not. I don't even know what it is," replied Delvin.

"Right, Delvin is not going to kill you. What is this secret? I am going to find out."

Delvin saw Fionella wince as Jarla again tightened her grip.

"Stop it, stop it!" gasped Fionella. "I'll tell you, but you mustn't tell anyone. You must promise me that you won't tell anyone you heard it from me."

"Get on with it," said Jarla coldly.

"I don't know much. But I overheard the Duke of Argent, my father, talking to Drandor. He's a magician in Argent. They were talking about taking Hengel. It involved using a stone."

"A stone?"

"I think they meant a magician's stone."

"How could they take Hengel with a magician's stone?"

"I don't really know, but the duke told Drandor to use his stone to put a thought into somebody's mind."

"Into their mind?" asked Jarla frowning.

"I don't know the details. Just that these stones can put thoughts into people's minds, and if you put thoughts into peoples minds you can influence them, and make them do what you want. They said nobody would be able to stop them."

"So that's what they did," said Jarla grimly. "They used a stone to make my father infatuated with you. Were you in on it?"

"No, No! They must have used a stone on me as well," said Fionella frightened.

"In a battle you could put fear into the other side's men," said Jarla reflectively. "I wonder if you could make them look the wrong way, or give them an idea to do the wrong thing… I bet that is how the magicians have made their fortunes," she mused. "Imagine, at a race meeting, giving a jockey the suggestion of losing, or giving two the idea to move over, both at once, so they collide… I wonder if an idea could be put into a horse's head as well… We must do something about this and quickly. If Argent is putting suggestions into our soldier's heads, there could be problems at South Bridge… They could even take the town… We need get there and get this war stopped as quickly as we can… Do you know anything else about these stones or where they come from?"

"No, that's all I know. I wasn't even meant to know that. I just overheard it. You won't tell anyone that I know will you. The magicians would kill me."

"I won't tell anyone." said Jarla. "But something needs to be done about the magicians." She turned sharply to Delvin. "Did you know about this?"

"It's all news to me," said Delvin quickly. "The magicians with these stones must be members of the Guild of Magicians. I'm not a member. I just do tricks."

Jarla continued looking at him.

Delvin gulped. "Look. If I had one of those stones, do you think I would have let myself get into this mess?"

Jarla grunted, then lapsed into silence thinking over what Fionella had said, while Fionella sagged in her chair looking frightened.

Delvin's mind was racing. Was that what Borlock had been referring to when he said that his murderer hadn't found it, and had only got a copy? He had also said, not to let anybody know he had got it and that the murderer would come after it. He shivered and put his hand in his pocket and felt Borlock's crystal. Was that Borlock's stone? Was that what had caused things to happen that he had thought was real magic? He remembered he had been holding the crystal when he had got the message about the falling barrels. He needed to try it out and see if it worked. He looked across the bar for someone to try it out on. He selected a tall thin man in a green jerkin, and sent him a thought to take a sip of his drink. The man did so. Was it a coincidence? He saw the waitress who had served them, and projected a thought of them kissing and making love. She looked up towards him and blushed furiously. Delvin felt guilty and looked away. There was a dog sitting with its master by the fire. Was it possible to influence animals as well? Delvin tried to send a thought to the dog that one of the logs stacked by the fire was a bone, but the dog made no movement. Oh well thought Delvin, it doesn't look like it works with animals. Then he got another idea and projected a feeling of excitement to the dog. The dog jumped up barking, the owner tried to restrain him but the dog was too excited. Ah! Thought Delvin, you can project feelings but not messages to animals. That must have been useful at the races.

He looked towards Jarla and Fionella. They had both finished their meals. Fionella sat slumped in her chair looking unhappy and frightened and Jarla was leaning back obviously thinking hard. Delvin wondered if the stone could set off involuntary actions in people. He smiled to himself as he projected the thought of a hiccup to Jarla. She suddenly lurched and her eyes snapped back from their faraway look with a look of surprise on her face. That seemed to work thought Delvin with a grin.

The hiccup had brought Jarla back to earth.

"We haven't enough money for any more drinks so we can't sit here all night. Time for bed."

"And we were having such a good chat," quipped Delvin and got a stony stare from both Jarla and Fionella.

The three got up from the table and made their way through the bar into the passage beyond. The front door of the inn had been left open so they could see out into the road beyond.

Jarla suddenly pushed them both back into a doorway.

"Flat against the wall, keep of sight," she whispered urgently.

"What is it?" breathed Fionella frightenedly.

"Grimbolt. He's just ridden past. Right, he's past now. Up the stairs quick."

The sudden shock that Delvin felt at Grimbolt's name was still with him as he followed the others running up the stairs. They reached their rooms panting. Their candles had gone out in the rush and they relit them from the one lighting the passage.

"We leave as soon as there is enough light," said Jarla. "How did he get here this quickly? We will have to hope he doesn't find out we are in Shappley until after we have left tomorrow. With luck he won't know which road we have taken."

"Can't we leave tonight?" asked Fionella.

"It's too dark. We'd be in the ditch before we had gone half a league. Right, we will be up early. Bed." With that Jarla ushered

Fionella into their room and left Delvin to go to his.

Delvin entered his room quickly. The elation of finding he had a magician's stone had gone. He wondered what Grimbolt would do if he caught up with them. If the Duke had given him orders to kill him, the first thing he would know about it, would be a crossbow bolt through the heart. Well, thought Delvin, I'd better prepare as best I can. He placed his candle on the washstand, went over to his bundle and took out the sword he had taken from the robber. He hadn't actually looked at it until then.

The sword looked very old. The leather scabbard was stained and blotched with white bits by the seams that looked like salt or mildew. The brass fittings at the top and bottom were almost black from corrosion and dirt. The guard was plain and made from iron pitted with rust. The hilt had been wound round with wire. This was now starting to come off showing a black surface underneath. The pommel too was iron and pitted with age. Not a very prepossessing weapon thought Delvin as he pulled the blade from the scabbard.

The blade slid out smoothly and the sword felt light and balanced in Delvin's hand. The blade was in far better condition than the rest of the sword. It was straight with a cutting edge along its length. There were nicks on the edge, and dark marks where some previous owner had neglected to clean blood off the blade before it had time to corrode the metal, but it looked serviceable and deadly.

Delvin tried it giving a few practice swings. He felt awkward and clumsy. He had never needed to learn swordplay when he worked on the farm, and he was sure he would be no match for an experienced soldier like Grimbolt. Delvin's thoughts were interrupted by a knocking at his door. He quickly returned the sword to its scabbard and dropped it on the bed. He was halfway to the door when he thought, what if it was Grimbolt? He quickly stepped back to his bed and retrieved the sword, his heart beating faster and breath coming quickly. He managed to calm himself enough to ask. "Who is that?"

"Anita, the waitress," came the soft reply.

He let out a long breath, put down the sword and went to the door. At the door was the young waitress who had served them. She had carefully arranged her wavy hair and Delvin could smell her perfume. She looked nervous and not quite sure what to do with her hands.

"I saw you come up magister," she said breathlessly. "I wondered if there was anything more you might like before going to bed."

Delvin looked down into the wide eyes, that momentarily looked away, and then back into his.

"Oh magister," she breathed, then looked away again and said in a rush. "I shouldn't have come. It was Adam the stable lad. He said I was no good, just because I turned him down. He said I couldn't attract anyone decent, and I saw you magister, and ohhh." She burst into tears. Delvin put his hands on her shoulders and guided her gently into his room.

Delvin mentally kicked himself. He must be more careful in using his stone on innocent and inexperienced young girls.

"Anita, you are one of the loveliest and most attractive girls I have ever seen," he began. "But you must save yourself for your true love. There are great advantages and great curses in being a magician. The curses are that the future I see is often not what I might wish, and your future I see with a handsome husband you love, and the husband is not me. The other curse, and the one that haunts me all the time, is that if I was to make love, I would lose my powers. That is why I sleep alone. Let me give you a token of my regard for you." He took one of the charms from his pocket and pressed it into her hand. "Look after it well, it will bring you good fortune. Now one kiss, that is all I dare ask."

Delvin bent down and kissed her on the lips. He could feel her body trembling as he released her.

"Oh magister, I will treasure it always," she whispered.

"Go now Anita and sleep well. I will always remember this moment."

Anita opened the door and slipped into the passage and away into the darkness.

Delvin shut the door and sat down on the bed with a sigh. He knew he had done the right thing, but part of him still wished he hadn't. He put his hand on his crystal and projected a thought to Anita of self confidence in her attractiveness, and the thought that she had been able to attract and tempt a magician... And she had too he thought wryly.

Delvin had difficulty getting to sleep, tossing and turning. Fionella had said the stones only put ideas into people's minds. He needed to know more about what they could do.

Just before going to sleep, he touched the crystal and tried to project to himself the thought of waking an hour before dawn. As he finally drifted off, he wondered if the crystal would work on him too.

CHAPTER 17

When Delvin awoke it was still dark. He stretched, got out of bed and looked out of the window. The stable yard was quiet with the still of predawn. He lit a candle and quickly shaved, dressed, fitted his sword's scabbard to his belt and packed his bundle. The unfamiliar sword almost tripped him as he moved to the door. The passage was dark, and he had to feel his way to Jarla and Fionella's door. He gave it a light tap that was met by grunts.

"I'm going down to the stables to get the horse ready," he whispered.

He moved on down the passage until he saw the vague outline of the head of the stairs. He carefully made his way down making sure his sword didn't bump on the stairs as he went. The inn continued sleeping as he pulled back the bolts of the rear door and went into the stable yard.

The air was cool and fresh after the stuffy, stale beer smelling air of the inn. He took two deep breaths and walked over to the stables. As he entered, the sleepy face of the stable boy showed itself from the loft.

"We have to make an early start," explained Delvin.

"Do you need a hand magister?"

"No thanks, I can manage," replied Delvin.

By the time he had the horse hitched up to the cart, he could see the first hints of light in the sky through the stable door.

Jarla and Fionella came out through the inn's rear door still looking half asleep. Jarla's black hair was brushed severely back and the early dawn light made her pale face look almost white. Fionella was yawning, and there was a smudge of dirt across her cheek that made her look even more the young lad.

They threw their bundles into the cart and climbed aboard. Delvin bade goodbye to the stable lad and they moved out into the square.

As they left the village, the first lights were starting to appear at some windows and the sky began to brighten as the new day dawned.

"Do you know where you are going?" asked Fionella glumly.

"To Gaverton," replied Jarla briskly. There's a road from there that leads down towards South Bridge.

"How far is Gaverton?"

"Quite a way. It will probably be fairly late by the time we get there."

"What happens if Grimbolt catches up with us?"

"Hopefully he won't. If he doesn't find out till this morning that we were in Shappley, we will have a few hours start on him. He will then need to check out the road to Endby. By the time he has done that we will be past the Great East Road and he will need to check if we turned down there to the Sheepstone Pass. With luck we will keep ahead of him."

"Well, I hope he catches us. You deserve a crossbow bolt in the back."

"The most likely person to get a crossbow bolt in the back is you." said Jarla sweetly. "He won't shoot me because I am a princess."

"I'm a princess too," said Fionella hotly.

"Let me finish. He may or may not shoot Delvin depending on whether he has been told to bring him back to my father for questioning. But as for you, all he will see is a young lad, possibly acting as a bodyguard, certainly an accomplice. If he shoots anyone, you'll be the target."

Fionella had turned white. "Let me put my dress back on."

"Don't be an idiot, all we have to do is keep ahead of him."

"You've got to let him know it's me," said Fionella desperately looking this way and that.

"Keep still," snapped Jarla, "or I'll make you keep still." Jarla paused. "You don't actually think I want him to kill you, do you? I need you so I can stop the war between Hengel and Argent."

"But what if he sees me and shoots me before you can tell him who I am. You've got to do something."

"I can't put up a big sign saying 'Princess'. You'll have to take your chances."

"I'll hide. I'll go under the sacks again."

"All day?" said Jarla surprised.

"If I have to," replied Fionella stoutly.

"All right. If you must."

Fionella climbed into the back of the cart and piled the sacks over herself, muttering to herself as she did so.

They were now travelling parallel to the mountains, and Delvin could see the great snow-capped peaks on his right as the road ran through the low foothills. It was still sheep farming country with small fields bounded by dry stone walls. The few farms they passed were also made of stone, with small windows and thick stone walls able to withstand the winter snow and storms caused by their proximity to the mountains.

They stopped briefly in midmorning by a stream to let the horse drink and to stretch their legs. But no one wanted to delay long and they were soon on the road again, frequently looking back over their shoulders to see if anyone was following them.

Just past noon they crossed the Great East Road that went from Hengel to the Sheepstone Pass. The Great East Road was a far better road than the side road they had been travelling on. Delvin could see several trader's caravans and other travellers making their way in both directions. The war with Argent did not seem to have stopped trade.

There was an inn at the crossroads and Delvin would have liked to have stopped, but he did not want to admit he had any money, and there was the ever-present threat of Grimbolt following them. The country past the crossroads began to change. The small fields gave way to woods, and soon they were travelling on a winding road cutting through the hills and thick forest. Being past the crossroads and enclosed by the trees they began to feel safer.

After an hour they stopped in a small clearing with a stream and ate what remained of the food that Delvin had bought the day before. The bread was a bit stale, but having missed breakfast they were hungry and quickly finished it.

They set out again, and a little while later came to a larger clearing. A horse was tethered at one side of the road. Its rider was seated behind a rock so they could only see his feet sticking out. As they drew near, the rider suddenly got up and turned towards them bringing a crossbow up as he did so. Delvin felt himself sucking in his breath in fright.

"Good afternoon Grimbolt," said Jarla.

"Captain Grybald if you please, Princess Jarla."

"Oh, you've been promoted Grimbolt. Congratulations."

"Grybald, Captain Grybald."

"Absolutely," replied Jarla.

Delvin's hands were shaking and his breath was coming unevenly. He glanced left and right to see if there was any way out, but Grimbolt's gaze caught him and he felt a shiver down his back as Grimbolt pointed the crossbow directly at him.

Grimbolt moved from behind the rock and Delvin could see him more clearly. His appearance was not what Delvin had expected. He was short and wiry and slightly bowlegged. His head was round and fleshy and bald on top. More the head of a baker than a soldier he thought.

Grimbolt waved his crossbow at Delvin indicating he should get down from the cart.

"How did you manage to get ahead of us?" asked Jarla.

"After your performance yesterday, it was not difficult to find you had been in Shappley. The road to Endby is a dead end. If you had gone that way you would have had to come back to Shappley, so I took the other road. If I hadn't found you, I would have returned to Shappley to wait for you. Please could you also get down from the cart Princess Jarla and stand by that rock so that I can see you."

"Don't you trust me Grimbolt?"

"Captain Grybald. I know your tricks Princess Jarla, and I would rather you didn't play any on me."

Jarla climbed down from the cart and stood by the rock Grimbolt had indicated.

"You haven't told us how you got ahead of us."

"I came up behind you shortly before the crossroads. There were too many people around for our sort of business, so I cut across the fields to get ahead. I waited down this road as you reached the crossroads, then watched to make sure you came this way and didn't take the Great East Road. Then I went ahead to check there were no other travellers in front and found a good vantage point to check there were none behind. And then I waited. Now Magister Delvin, undo your belt and let it fall very, very slowly."

"How did you find us in the first place?" asked Jarla.

"I heard a report of a man being killed by a vampire. Just two small holes in his neck. And I thought, that sounds like Princess Jarla," He smiled thinly. His smile was slightly lopsided, which somehow made it particularly threatening. "Right Magister Delvin, if you have any more weapons tell me now. I would prefer not to have to put a crossbow bolt through your leg or arm, so I'm looking for a bit of co-operation in return." He smiled lopsidedly again.

"I've no more weapons," replied Delvin swallowing hard.

"Excellent, now we can get onto the interesting bit. What have you done with Princess Fionella?"

"I'm here," said Fionella standing up in the cart.

Grimbolt spun towards the cart. Delvin put his hand in his pocket and touched the crystal projecting the thought of a sneeze. As the sneeze hit Grimbolt, he doubled over triggering the crossbow, the bolt flashing narrowly over Fionella's head. Before he could recover Jarla calmly picked up a stone, took one step towards him and struck him over the head. Grimbolt slumped to the ground as Fionella screamed.

"He shot at me, he shot at me. You've killed him." She started trembling violently and slumped back into the cart.

"I sincerely hope not," said Jarla. "He was following my father's orders and I wouldn't want to kill him for that. Right. Delvin, over here. I need your help. Get his clothes off."

"His clothes?" asked Delvin dully.

"Yes, his clothes," said Jarla annoyed. "We need to slow him up. And finding a new set of clothes will take even Grimbolt a few hours out here. Anyway, Fionella could do with a change. Also put his weapons in the cart and give me his purse."

While Delvin did as he was asked, Jarla untied Grimbolt's horse and hitched it to the back of the cart. She found a rope in one of his saddlebags and returned to Delvin who had just finished removing Grimbolt's trousers.

"Right, roll him over and help me tie him up," said Jarla.

"Will he be all right?" asked Delvin.

"Of course he will. He has a head like steel. He will get himself untied in a couple of hours. Make sure you take his boots. We don't want him walking to Gaverton. With no boots or trousers, he will need to find a forester's or charcoal burner's cottage. It will be almost dark by then. He won't get to Gaverton till nearly noon tomorrow, by which time we will be almost at South Bridge."

"That was a bit of luck running into Grimbolt," said Jarla with satisfaction. "Now we have enough money for supper. Climb up, we're off."

"Aren't you going to check he's alright?" asked Delvin.

"Of course he's alright. I told you, he has a head like steel. Now climb up."

"I'm going to check anyway," said Delvin.

"Suit yourself," said Jarla giving the horse a flick and setting the cart in motion.

There was a big bump on the back of Grimbolt's head. Delvin rolled him onto his side. He seemed to be breathing evenly and Delvin felt relieved.

Suddenly Grimbolt's eyes snapped open. "Come to finish me off, eh?"

Delvin leapt back. "No, no," he said quickly. "I was checking you were all right."

"Checking I was all right? And what were you going to do if I wasn't? Put me out of my misery?"

"We could have taken you somewhere to be looked after."

"Oh, a comedian. Is comedy going to be your new act? If you are going to kill me, get on and do it, and stop being so lily livered. Remember when I catch up with people, I do to them what they've done to me, but I do it double."

"Come on, hurry up," said Jarla coming up behind Delvin. "You've checked him, now come on."

"You've found a right one there Princess Jarla," said Grimbolt. "He hasn't even the guts to finish me off."

Jarla who had already turned back towards the cart, turned again in surprise. "Finish you off, he was checking you were all right." She grabbed Delvin by the shoulder. "Come on, I told you he was fine. On the cart, move it."

Delvin, slightly dazed, climbed onto the cart as it began to move off. They spoke little as they continued down the forest road. Delvin was thinking about how Grimbolt might get himself free and Fionella still seemed shaken by the crossbow bolt that had narrowly missed her.

They saw no other travellers. The only signs of life being an occasional path leading off the road, and twice as they got closer to Gaverton, they saw charcoal burner's clearings with their cone shaped heaps, and the huts from which Delvin could feel the eyes of the charcoal burners watching them as they passed.

The sun was low in the sky as they reached the outskirts of Gaverton. Most of the buildings were wooden with a raised boardwalk bordering the street. Behind, Delvin could see large sheds with chimneys, some of which belched smoke. A stream ran down from the mountain and rushed under a bridge turning waterwheels as it passed the sheds. The door of one of the sheds was open. In the failing light the inside glowed red from a furnace, a great bellows powered by a waterwheel, pumping rhythmically.

"What do they make here?" asked Delvin.

Jarla looked up. "Iron. There used to be just a few loggers here, but they found iron ore a few years ago."

They had reached the centre of the village. There was only one inn. It was a two-story building with the downstairs double doors standing open to the boardwalk. Delvin could see through the door that it led straight into the bar and he could hear singing and the sound of music.

"Check that they have rooms then we'll stable the horses," said Jarla eying the inn dubiously.

"I'll need some coin."

Jarla gave Delvin two royals and five carls from Grimbolt's purse and he climbed down from the cart and entered the inn.

The bar was large but was already half full of miners and ironworkers. There were few women, and those there were, seemed to Delvin to be wearing too bright clothes and too much make up. A musician played in one corner with a group of miners singing a popular song. He walked to the bar.

"What will it be?" asked the barman.

"I'm looking for two rooms for the night."

"Magister Jael! Gentleman looking for two rooms."

A smartly dressed man that Delvin took to be Magister Jael walked over. "You need two rooms?"

"Yes."

"One gold royal each, payment in advance."

"That seems a lot."

"That's the price."

"All right," said Delvin and handed over the coins.

"Are the rest of you outside?"

"Yes."

"Ladies with you?"

"Yes."

"Stable the horses and come in the back way if you want. It'll be half an hour before the rooms are free." With that he turned and walked away.

Delvin went back out to Jarla and Fionella, and explained the position.

"Half an hour," exclaimed Jarla. "What are they doing?"

Delvin blushed and Jarla looked at him. "Oh sheffs. That's all we need. Right. Get the horses stabled."

Delvin led the horses to the stables behind the inn where they unhitched the cart, paid for the stabling and made sure the two horses were brushed and fed. Delvin dropped some fresh grass he had picked up into his rabbit Freda's box and gave her a quick stroke before re-joining Jarla and Fionella. He nodded towards the rear door of the inn that faced the stableyard.

"The innkeeper said we could use the rear door."

"I'm not accustomed to being shown the tradesman's entrance," said Jarla, determinedly walking round the building to the front. Delvin tried to catch up with her.

"That may not be a good idea."

"I do not go sneaking into places."

They had reached the double doors, and without pausing Jarla strode in with Delvin and Fionella at her heels. The noise at the bar died as she entered, heads turning towards her.

"Come over here darling," shouted a voice that was instantly quelled by a look that would have shivered steel. There were a few laughs and another voice called, "You're too young to be in here lad, or does she have you for afters." There was more laughter and Fionella went red.

Jarla stopped and spun. Glancing at where the comment had come from, she located the person by his grin and advanced upon him. She stopped in front of him, looked him slowly up and down, and calmly picked up a knife the man had stuck in the table in front of him. She examined the sharp point of the knife, and looking the man directly in the eye, dropped the knife in front of him. The man yelled in pain as the knife speared through his shoe and into his toe. Jarla turned on her heel and walked calmly back to the others.

The man's friends guffawed with laughter as Delvin tried to project a thought to the man, that he had better not do anything since she might be even more dangerous than she looked. And she was too thought Delvin.

Magister Jael came up to them. "Mistress, magisters, have a seat while your room is prepared. Can I get you a drink?"

"A wine and two ales please magister," said Delvin holding a chair out for Jarla.

Magister Jael flicked his fingers at a waitress who ran off to get the order. "Welcome to our inn. We get very few travellers here and even fewer ladies. Most of the men here have come to work in the mines for a season or two before moving on elsewhere. They can get a bit rowdy. Please excuse their manners."

"No offense taken," said Jarla loftily. Magister Jael bowed and walked off.

"As you see, no problem," said Jarla sitting back.

The waitress arrived with their drinks and set them down. "One carl two coppers please." Delvin paid for the drinks and the waitress went off, expertly avoiding the clutches of various men as she returned to the bar.

A short while later Magister Jael returned to say their rooms were ready and escorted them through a rear door that Delvin had seen several people come and go through, and then up the stairs behind. The rooms were at the end of a passage, and Delvin could hear grunts and moans coming from the other rooms as they passed. Each of their rooms contained a large bed with frilled bedcovers, a chair, a washstand with two candles, frilled curtains at the windows and smelled strongly of perfume.

They thanked Magister Jael and retired to their rooms to wash the dirt of the day from their faces and get ready for dinner.

About a quarter of an hour later Delvin heard a knock on his door. "Dinner," called Jarla. Delvin joined Jarla and Fionella and they made their way back to the bar where they sat down again at the table they had left earlier.

The waitress hurried up to them. "Stew, skirtles or bread and cheese?"

"Skirtles for me," said Delvin remembering the ones at Shappley. He looked at the others who nodded. "Three skirtles please."

Delvin looked around the inn. More people had now arrived.

In one corner a man was playing the three-shell game. The game was simple. There were three walnut shells, the man placed a pea under one, moved the shells around quickly and asked people to bet which shell it was under. Borlock had explained the principle of it to Delvin. It was an age-old scam for getting money from unsuspecting people. The man placing the pea under the shells could cheat and control which shell it ended under. So if he was skilful, he would always win, or lose, just as he wanted. Borlock had said there was usually an accomplice. His job was to encourage people to bet. When the accomplice placed bets he won, so making people think that winning was easy and persuading them to continue betting their money. Delvin watched idly and soon identified the accomplice. He wondered if he could influence the game with his crystal and put his hand in his pocket feeling the crystal's smooth faces under his fingers. The accomplice was playing and about to decide which shell to select. Delvin tried projecting the thought of him selecting the middle shell. The accomplice selected it. Delvin then tried projecting the thought to the man placing the peas under the shells that it would end up under the left-hand shell. When the shells were picked up, the pea was under the left-hand shell. This might be fun thought Delvin.

The skirtles arrived, but they were nothing like as good as the ones at Shappley. As Delvin ate, he continued to observe the three-shell game. He tried to influence it without actually touching the crystal, just having it in his pocket. After a few tries he discovered that the closer he was to the crystal, the stronger the influence. So if he was touching it, he could influence where the pea was every time. If there was just the material of his pocket between his leg and the crystal, he was only right about half the time. But if the distance was greater than that, the crystal didn't seem to have any noticeable effect at all.

One miner who had lost most of his money was about to leave the game. Delvin sent him the thought that he should have one last go. He then projected the thought to the man with the shells that the pea would end up under the right-hand shell, and sent the miner the thought to select that one. The miner won and the man with the shells looked annoyed. Delvin grinned to himself. He was starting to enjoy this. In the next half-hour he carefully controlled the game. Not letting the miners win too often, but just enough to recover some of their losses. He could see the sheen of perspiration and the look of worry on the faces of the man and his accomplice, as they realised that they were losing but didn't understand why.

"Time to get to bed, we're starting early in the morning."

Delvin jumped, and turned to see Jarla and Fionella rising from the table. He glanced back at the game.

"You are not going to spend my money on the dubious pleasures of this place, come on."

Delvin reluctantly followed them out of the bar and back towards their rooms. He was briefly tempted to go back down later with some of his own money, but quickly dismissed the idea when he thought of Jarla's reaction if she found out.

When he got back to his room, he washed some of his clothes and laid them out to dry. Before going to bed he took his breeches and eased open the threads on the seam of his pocket. If he pushed the crystal into the hole he had made, he found he could control whether the crystal rested against his leg or not. He had decided that he did not want the crystal to be always touching him, since he was not yet sure just how many of his thoughts might get transmitted. After the previous day's incident with Anita, he wanted to control what he transmitted and what he did not. When he had got the seam just as he wanted, he put the breeches back with his other clothes, climbed into bed, touched the crystal, willed himself to wake before dawn and blew out the candle.

CHAPTER 18

Delvin woke just before dawn and quickly got himself dressed. He lit a candle to shave by, and when he had finished, checked the clothes he had laid out to dry. They were still slightly damp and he shrugged as he repacked them in his bundle. As he left his room, he banged on Jarla and Fionella's door before going down to the stables to get the horses ready.

There was a faint drizzle as he went out into the yard and the air was chilly. The inn still slept but he could hear a dull thudding from the ironworks like a huge hammer rhythmically beading.

He roused the stable boy to help him with the horses and gave him a copper for some grain, some of which he gave to his rabbit Freda. They had the horses and cart out in the yard by the time Jarla and Fionella emerged yawning in the growing light. They threw their bundles in the back, climbed aboard and set off on the last stage of their journey to South Bridge.

The road from Gaverton towards South Bridge was much better than the one from Shappley. This was the road down which the finished iron was brought to Hengel, to the port at Cavid or through South Bridge into Argent. As they left Gaverton, the road wound through a series of sharp bends as they came down from the foothills of the Grandents. At some points the road had been cut into the side of the hill, at others there was a sheer drop on one side. The forest was still thick and the trees dripped with the early morning dew and the thin drizzle.

After a while the bends gave way to smoother curves as they began to leave the mountains behind. The trees also began to thin out, and soon they were travelling through open country with fields dotted with sheep interspersed with an occasional field of grain.

They stopped at a farm near the road, and Delvin was able to purchase some bread, cheese and ham from the farmer's wife. They drew up by the next stream and ate a late but welcome breakfast. They were soon on their way again, as they all wanted to make sure there was no way that Grimbolt could catch up with them again.

The drizzle gave way to pale sunshine and the day became warmer. There were few other travellers. And those they saw, were intent on getting to their destination and not stopping to talk.

As the sun got higher, the land flattened out. Most of the fields were now given over to grain, but in a few, cattle grazed. The small farms with their brightly painted doors and windows looked peaceful enough, but the farmers they passed gave them suspicious looks, as if they thought that any travellers might be foraging for provisions or looking for fresh mounts for the army.

There were wisps of smoke rising in the distance. As they grew closer Jarla's face grew grim. "Something's burning at South Bridge."

"Are we nearly there?" asked Fionella.

"Not far now."

"What are we going to do when we get there?"

"Go up to General Gortley and tell him my father has sent me as a special envoy to the Duke of Argent."

"What if the duke is there leading the army?" asked Delvin.

"He won't be. You presumably haven't seen the bridge at South Bridge. The River Septim is quite wide. You can't get across if the drawbridges are raised. Whenever there is a war between Hengel and Argent, they raise the drawbridges. The dukes come down and make speeches and there is a big show of strength. But with the drawbridges up, no one can get across so there is no actual fighting. After a day or two the dukes go off leaving it to the generals. Usually after a week or two, common sense prevails, peace is made and the drawbridges are lowered. This war is going on too long. Something needs to be done to sort it out and get it over. That's why we are here."

"What are you going to ask General Gortly to do?"

"Tell him to escort us to the bridge. Demand to see the Duke of Argent or his general. Take Fionella across and hand her over. That should sort it out."

"Just like that?" said Delvin incredulously.

"I shall use a flag of truce."

"Won't General Gortly have orders to send you back to Hengel?"

"Possibly, but they will be a few days old. It would take him half a day to get a messenger to Hengel and back to check if they are still in force. Delaying a special envoy from the duke for half a day is not healthy."

"Fionella was looking pale and scared. "You can't do that."

"Of course I can. Just watch me."

"I can't go back looking like this."

"You can get changed when we get to South Bridge."

"You can't do it," muttered Fionella looking even more frightened.

"Right, we need to get ready," said Jarla. "Delvin, you will drive the cart." Delvin nodded as Jarla pulled the cart to a stop. "I'll take Grimbolt's horse. I'll look more like an envoy that way." Jarla swung down from the cart and unhitched Grimbolt's horse while Delvin moved over to where Jarla had been sitting. They set off again.

Fionella tugged at Delvin's arm. "You can't let her do it. You've got to let me go." Delvin ignored her and Fionella lapsed into silence.

They could now see the first encampments of the army, and were twice stopped by guards on the road asking where they were going. As soon as they saw who Jarla was, they snapped to attention and waved them through.

The walls of South Bridge came in sight with smoke rising from somewhere in the town. Across the river they could see

North Bridge, with the long multi-spanned bridge joining the two. The bridge was impressive. There were two towers and a drawbridge at the end, then three arches before two more towers supported Hengel's side of a central double drawbridge, wide enough to let large ships pass through. Argent's side was similar, with two towers supporting their side of the central drawbridge, three more arches, and a further drawbridge and two towers leading into North Bridge.

Jarla suddenly stiffened. "Sheffs, the drawbridges are down!"

They looked, and sure enough the drawbridges at each end and in the middle were all down. As they looked more closely, they could also see that the silver and red flag of Argent was flying on all the towers.

"They've taken the bridge," said Jarla grimly. She pulled over to an encampment near the road. "Get me your officer!" she demanded.

An officer shortly appeared looking annoyed at having been disturbed, but when he saw who it was, he stiffened and saluted.

"What's going on. How did Argent take the bridge?"

"Your Highness, they took the end towers last night. The first anybody knew the drawbridge was half down. Some of Argent's soldiers had got into the tower. A detachment from the town saw it and raised the alarm. They stopped them getting through the tower until more troops had arrived. The town detachment managed to jam the drawbridge so it wouldn't go fully down. Then suddenly they broke and ran. My friend, he's in that detachment. I spoke to him this morning. He said he doesn't know what it was. They were holding them. Then suddenly he felt scared and had to run. They say it's haunted."

"Haunted?"

"Yes, Your Highness. Everyone suddenly getting scared like that, and what's been happening on guard duty."

"What has been happening?" asked Jarla grimly.

"It's hard to explain Your Highness. Sentries dropping to sleep or suddenly looking the wrong way, and always when Argent are about to attack. That's probably how they got into the tower last night."

"How do you know this?"

"I was on sentry duty two nights ago. I came to do my rounds. Two sentries were asleep and another was looking towards the town. And there were soldiers from Argent creeping along the bridge. I got them awake and we beat them off. But those were good men. They wouldn't have gone to sleep. Not normally Your Highness."

"Did you report this?"

The officer looked guilty. "No. Your Highness." I thought it was the haunting. Others have had the same thing happen. We decided, that is us officers decided, that we had better do regular rounds every ten minutes in case it kept happening. Freeman, he was the officer last night, he must have forgotten to do it."

"And the centre towers?"

"That was the same Your Highness. They were just suddenly there."

"When did that happen?"

"There had been attempts like I explained, for some time. They actually took it four nights ago."

"And what is the position now?"

"The streets leading to the bridge are barricaded. The customs post was burned down to stop them using it to get closer. We are bringing up more materials to try to build walls across the ends of the streets."

"They haven't got further than the tower?"

"Not yet Your Highness. The drawbridge being jammed stopped them getting too many men across."

"We must make sure they don't get any further. You may go." Jarla turned to Delvin and Fionella. "They are using a magician's stone. We've only just got here in time… Fionella, we have to get you back to Argent and get this lot stopped as quickly as we can. Right, let's get going."

Delvin flicked the reins and they set off again.

Fionella pulled on his sleeve. "You've got to stop. Please you must stop." Delvin ignored her. "You must stop, you don't understand, please, please. I'm not Fionella."

"What?" said Delvin turning to her.

"I'm not Fionella. I look like her, and the Duke of Argent told me to take her place and come to Hengel."

"Jarla you'd better hear this," said Delvin grimly. Jarla pulled up her horse and glared down.

"This had better be good, we haven't much time."

"You had better hear it."

"Right, what is all this?"

"I'm not really Fionella," she began in a frightened voice. "I'm Maegar, I worked as a maid at the palace. I've always looked rather like Fionella. About six weeks ago the duke told me I was to take Fionella's place on a trip to Hengel. He said I must try to make the Duke of Hengel fall for me, and then I must refuse to come back to Argent. He said if I told anybody I wasn't Fionella I'd be killed." She burst into tears.

"What happened to the real Fionella?" asked Jarla.

"I don't know. It's been nine or ten weeks since I last saw her. It was a few weeks after that, that I was asked to take her place."

"So, this was all a put-up job," said Jarla pensively. "I presume a magician's stone was used to make sure my father fell for you."

"I don't know," whispered Maegar.

"Well, Maegar, we can still take you back. Everyone thinks you are Fionella, so that should do."

"You can't. He'll kill me," wailed Maegar.

"It wouldn't work Jarla," said Delvin. "The Duke of Agent would say she was an imposter. And to prove it, he would have her publicly executed. He wouldn't do that to his daughter. We'd be in even more of a mess then."

"You may be right," mused Jarla. "Right. We have a lot of work to do. We must sort out the situation here in South Bridge, and then we must find the real Fionella."

"What about me," sobbed Maegar.

"You're coming too, come on."

CHAPTER 19

They found General Gortly supervising the building of barricades across the streets. Stones and mortar had been brought in, and already a thick wall blocked off the end of the road. The windows of the houses were filled with archers in case Argent attacked again. Teams of men, horses and waggons were bringing still more materials to the men building the new defences.

General Gortly turned as Jarla walked up to him. He was a short stocky man, with short grey hair sticking straight up from his weather-beaten head. He wore a plain brown leather jerkin and trousers, and if there had not been an air of strength and power around him, he could have been mistaken for a common workman.

"Not now Priness Jarla, I'm busy."

"This is important General Gortly. I need a detachment of soldiers."

"And I need another army. Anyway, I'm meant to send you back to Hengel."

"I think I know how to beat Argent. I need just one company for an hour."

"Are you up to your tricks again Princess Jarla?"

"I am trying to get us out of this mess," flashed Jarla.

General Gortly put his hands on his hips and stared at Jarla. "You are, are you. I've been a soldier all my life. I've worked my way up from being a trooper, and you think you know how to beat Argent. Do you realise what we are up against here? The men are deserting. We've lost the bridge. It'll be a miracle if we can hold South Bridge. The duke is trying to get another army together to meet them on the road to Hengel in case they get through here. And now you are wasting my time and getting in my way...princess."

"I'm not wasting your time," hissed Jarla.

Delvin touched the crystal in his pocket and projected the thought to General Gortly that Jarla might know something, and one company for an hour would not make much difference. Jarla and General Gortly stared at each other angrily, neither wanting to back down.

General Gortly turned away in exasperation. "Just one hour, and you'd better know what you are doing, because if this is some worthless escapade, I'll tan the hide off you myself... Berman!"

"Yes Sir."

"Take Mendip's company. You are under the command of Princess Jarla. Report back to me here in one hour without fail... and with Princess Jarla."

"Yes Sir." Berman turned and nodded towards Jarla. "This way Your Highness."

"Thank you general," said Jarla. "You won't regret it."

General Gortly had already turned back to the work companies and was shouting orders to the men on the wall.

Jarla and the others followed Berman back through the town. He stopped outside a large building with a guard outside the door and turned to Jarla. "Mendip's company were in the thick of it last night. They've been given two hours rest before they go on duty again." He turned to the guard. "I am Captain Berman, please let Captain Mendip know we are here."

The guard showed them down a passage and into a hall and went off to find Captain Mendip. A few moments later a tousled and very tired looking officer appeared. "Berman, what's up. They aren't attacking again, are they?"

"Not yet. Your company's been placed under the orders of Princess Jarla for the next hour. We are then to report to General Gortly."

Captain Mendip looked at Jarla for the first time and snapped to attention. "Your Highness."

"Captain," acknowledged Jarla. "Please assemble your men, fully armed. Are any of you from South Bridge?"

"Sergeant Haston is from South Bridge Your Highness. Excuse me." Captain Mendip turned to face the doors leading off the hall and roared, "Company assemble. On the double."

Jarla watched as the men of Mendip's company poured from the rooms hastily buttoning their jerkins and pulling on their boots. Most of them looked tired and several supported bandages. She turned to Captain Mendip.

"Is Sergeant Haston here?"

"Yes Your Highness."

"Tell him to come over here."

"Sergeant Haston. Approach Her Highness," roared Mendip.

A huge soldier fell out from the ranks, marched up to Jarla and saluted. "Sergeant Haston at your service Your Highness."

"Sergeant Haston," began Jarla. "I believe you are from South Bridge?"

"Yes Highness."

"Does South Bridge have a magician who is a member of the Guild of Magicians?"

"I don't know about Guilds Highness, but Magister Perball is the magician here."

"Where does he live?"

"Silver Street Highness. He has a big house there."

"That's where we are going," said Jarla. "Captain Mendip, your men will guard all entrances to the house, and I will need six men to accompany us inside."

Captain Mendip gave the orders, and the company moved off guided by Sergeant Haston towards Silver Street.

Silver Street was in an obviously wealthy area of town. The houses were made of stone with ornate iron railings at the front. They had short flights of steps leading up to the large front doors that were flanked by stone pillars holding up carved stone porches.

"Second house on the left Highness," said Sergeant Haston.

Captain Mendip rapidly deployed his force. One troop going into the street behind the house to check the rear entrance. Others covering the front of the building on either side. When they were all in place, he was left with five troupers and Captain Berman.

"Ready Your Highness. I will accompany you with these men here."

Jarla turned to Delvin and Maegar. "Maegar stay out here, you'd get in the way. Delvin you're coming with us. Right, come on."

With that, she strode up the steps and banged on the door. The door was opened by a large burley man. He wore black trousers and a black shirt that looked too small for him with his muscles bulging beneath it.

"We have come to see Magister Perball. Show us to him."

"I will see if he is in," said the man, making to close the door. Jarla nodded to Captain Mendip, and his men stepped forward and pushed the door fully open.

"Show us to him," demanded Jarla. The man looked at Jarla and Delvin, and seemed for a moment to be about to bodily push them out, but as the soldiers stepped up, he thought better of it.

"Who shall I say is calling?"

"Princess Jarla, now get on with it."

The man led them down a corridor lined with pictures of magicians, to a room at the back of the house. He stopped in front of a black wooden door with a curious gold symbol on it and rapped once. There was a short wait.

"Come," said a petulant voice from inside.

The man opened the door and announced, "The Princess Jarla to see you magister."

As Jarla and Delvin stepped into the room, Jarla glanced back towards Captain Mendip. "Have two men stay out there with him. The rest follow me."

The room was lit by four huge candelabra standing in the corners of the room. Like Magister Meldrum's study, there were no windows, the walls being covered with ancient tapestries.

There was a large desk to one side, and in the centre of the room there was a couch and a circle of easy chairs. In one of the chairs sat a plump florid figure wearing a long red gown that in the flickering candlelight made his fleshy face seem almost purple. His sparse hair was worn shoulder length and Delvin could see makeup on his lips. On the couch sat a lady of about thirty. She looked annoyed and flustered. She was trying to straighten her hair, and Delvin noticed that her lipstick was smudged and the buttons of her bodice had been done up in the wrong holes. The man rose from his chair.

"You do me a great honour Princess Jarla. As you can see, I have a client. I have almost finished her consultation. If you could wait a moment."

"Get out, now" snapped Jarla at the lady. The lady looked furiously at Jarla, and was about to say something when she saw Jarla nod to Captain Mendip and two troopers started towards her. She rose with as much dignity as she could muster, and made for the door glaring angrily at Jarla and the soldiers. "See she doesn't go anywhere," ordered Jarla. As the door shut, Jarla turned back to Magister Perball.

"I must protest," said Magister Perball. "You cannot come barging in here like that. I pay my taxes. I am a citizen of this county. I will be treated with due respect."

"You are a citizen of this country," began Jarla deliberately. "It is the duty of all citizens to do their utmost to protect the state. You have not."

"I am just a poor magician. I pay my taxes."

"You have allowed Argent to use a magician's stone to defeat our forces. You have not offered to use your stone to counter theirs or to help in any way. That makes you a traitor."

"Magician's stone?" exclaimed Magister Perball. "That is just a legend, an old wives' tale. I give people advice, sell them lucky charms and read their fortunes."

Delvin was suddenly aware of a message being projected into his mind. *'There is no such thing as a magician's stone. You should forget what you have been told about it. You should now go, since nothing more could be gained by staying.*' He glanced towards the others and saw them start to turn away towards the door. Magister Perball must be using his magician's stone on them he thought. But why was he receiving it as a clear message when all the others were receiving it into their subconscious minds. The messages continued. *'You have forgotten why you came. You will leave now. Magister Perball is a loyal citizen of Hengel.'* Jarla was looking slightly puzzled and began to thank Magister Perball for seeing them.

Delvin, who had been looking as blank as the others while it dawned on him what was happening, took two steps forward, and struck Magister Perball on the chin with a right hook that sent the magician tumbling over the arm of his chair to end up in a pile on the floor. Delvin followed up quickly, and before Magister Perball had time to regain his senses, he quickly rummaged through his pockets. Then noticing a chain around Magister Perball's neck, Delvin pulled his gown open to reveal a crystal hanging on the chain. Delvin grabbed the crystal and gave a huge tug. Magister Perball's head was pulled up, and as the chain broke his head fell back and banged on the floor.

"Here is his magician's stone," said Delvin triumphantly holding it up.

The others had been looking puzzled by his actions and two of the troupers were already moving to stop him attacking the magician. But with his words their memory seemed to return.

"For a moment I couldn't remember why we had come," said Jarla.

"He used his stone on you to make you forget and go away," grinned Delvin.

"Oh, he did, did he," said Jarla, her eyes flashing. "We will see about that. Pick him up." Magister Perball had been just starting to rise, but at Jarla's command, two troupers grabbed him by an arm each and hauled him to his feet. Jarla came up to him and placed a fingernail under his chin which she pushed inexorably upwards.

"You claim to be a citizen of Hengel, but you refuse to help when we get invaded. You try to deceive us with your magician's stone. Well let me tell you this." Magister Perball's head was now right back and Jarla's fingernail was biting into his flesh. "You are going to help. I will make sure you do. You will be fined five thousand gold royals for not helping earlier." Her fingernail bit deeper. "And, if you are ever slow in coming forward again, or show any disloyalty, you will discover how lenient I am being this time. Bring him and search the house for any more of these crystals." She extracted her nail and spun towards the door. Magister Perball collapsed between the two troupers who held him. Jarla strode from the room calling over her shoulder, "Bring him and that servant and woman as well. No word of this must get out. Come on."

Jarla marched through the front door and headed back up Silver Street to find General Gortly. Captain Mendip just had time to give the orders for his men to search the house and bring the prisoners.

Delvin still had Magister Perball's crystal and followed on behind with Maegar. They found General Gortly still supervising the construction of defences. Jarla strode up to him.

"General Gortly. I have brought Magister Perball. He is going to stop the guards falling asleep and stop them panicking. We need to talk to work out how to use him."

General Gortly turned from the defences and looked at the forlorn figure of Magister Perball with his bruised face and a trickle of blood running down his neck. He looked up at Jarla, his face turning red.

"Are you mad," he roared. "What do you think you are doing? Do you think some silly spells are going to help us? We are not children. This is a war. And do you realise." He pointed his finger at Jarla. "Do you realise what you have done? The Guild of Magicians controls its own sovereign country in the north. Attacking magicians could start another war, and that is one thing we do not want at the moment."

Magister Perball pulled himself together, "I protest in the strongest possible terms about what has been done to me. The

Guild will not allow this to go unanswered."

"Keep quiet," snapped Jarla, and she turned to General Gortly. "It is not a silly spell. Members of the Guild of Magicians have stones that they somehow use to project thoughts into people's minds. That was how Argent managed to take the bridge. They used a stone to distract our men."

"Those are just old wives' tales," said Magister Perball. "You don't really believe that."

"All right," said Jarla. "If it is just an old wives' tale, you won't mind us keeping your stone. I'm sure we will find out how to use it."

Magister Perball turned to General Gortly. "General I insist that anything these vandals have taken is returned and anything broken is repaired. It is an outrage the way they broke in."

Captain Berman stepped forward. "General, I believe Princess Jarla is correct. Magister Perball tried to use the stone on us to make us go away. Thoughts appeared in our minds."

"That's true sir," said Captain Mendip.

General Gortly slowly turned to Magister Perball. "So, you miserable scum, you are trying to pull the wool over my eyes. I want the truth… Now!" Magister Perball shrank back.

"You don't realise what you are asking. The Guild send assassins to kill anyone who discovers the secret."

"So, it's not only treachery, but murder too," growled General Gortly.

"I am only trying to warn you general."

"Well let me warn you. I'll give specific orders. If any one of the people listening here dies in a way that is at all suspicious, there will be instructions to put a crossbow bolt through your head. Does that relieve your fears about us getting assassinated?… The truth!"

Magister Perball looked wildly around at the implacable faces and his shoulders slumped. "Princess Jarla is right. The stone can be used to put thoughts into people's heads."

"Good. Now we are getting somewhere. You, you miserable

worm, are going to help us now. You are going to use your stone to put thoughts into Argent's soldiers' heads."

"The problem is," began Jarla, "how do we make sure he is helping us and not helping Argent."

"General, Princess Jarla," interupted Delvin. "I have an idea to make sure he doesn't double cross us."

Jarla and General Gortly turned to him.

"This had better be good," said Jarla.

Delvin explained his idea, and Jarla smiled.

General Gortly was smiling too. He turned to Jarla. "Princess Jarla, Berman, this is not the place to discuss this. Follow me and bring that rat." With that General Gortly began to stride off towards a building close by with two guards at the door.

When they reached the building, Jarla, General Gortly and the soldiers pulling along a reluctant Magister Perball all marched in, but the guards at the door shook their heads when Delvin and Maegar tried to follow, and as the door closed, they were left out in the street.

CHAPTER 20

Delvin and Maegar went back to where they had left the horse and cart. While Maegar sat in the cart looking disconsolate, Delvin unhitched the horses and took them to a water trough nearby, and then he fed his rabbit and gave it a run on a strip of grass.

After a little while a trooper came up to them.

"Master Delvin."

"Yes."

"I have been instructed to take you to the quartermaster and get you supplied with a list of items."

"I'll be right with you," replied Delvin as he caught his rabbit and returned her to her travelling box. He re-hitched the horses, and together with Maegar followed the trouper.

When they reached the quartermaster's, Delvin found the list was a long one. They were issued with three long black cloaks with huge hoods, several bags of travel rations, grain for the horses, water bottles, rope, two swords, three sleeping rolls, saddle bags to carry it all in and an extra horse plus two saddles. But the thing that worried Delvin the most was three bundles of clothes, that when Delvin opened them, he found were the uniforms of dead Argent soldiers.

"What's she up to?" he exclaimed when he saw what they were.

With the extra horse and the saddles, it looked like Jarla was intending to ditch the cart. So Delvin arranged with the quartermaster that it should be stored properly in the corner of the stables. He then checked through his belonging to see which he should leave with the cart and which he should take with him. He looked at Freda the rabbit who looked trustingly back at him.

"If I leave you here, you'll end up in the stew pot," he muttered as he put her travelling box next to his saddlebags and the other items he was taking.

By the time he had got everything packed and the horses brushed and fed it was late afternoon. Maegar had spent most of the afternoon just sitting around and saying nothing. Delvin was starting to feel fed up and left out. He was also hungry since it had been a long time since their breakfast on the road. His thoughts were interrupted by Jarla's voice.

"It will be dark soon. It's time we got ready. Have you got my uniforms there?"

"Yes, what are the uniforms for, and when's dinner?"

"I've already eaten, you'll just have to grab something. Come on, get changed into those uniforms."

"What are you planning to do? Why are we dressing as Argent soldiers?"

"However else do you think we are going to get through North Bridge."

"If we get caught, we will be executed as spies."

"You would. I would be ransomed. Come on, get on with it."

They put on the Argent soldier's uniforms. Delvin was relieved to find that the hole where the arrow had pierced it had been mended and the blood had been washed out. Jarla took one of the swords and gave the other to Maegar, who held it very nervously before fitting the scabbard to her belt. They then saddled the horses, strapped on the saddle bags and their other items, and put on the long black hooded cloaks.

"You are not taking that rabbit with you again," said Jarla exasperated.

"I am. If I go, she goes."

"Whoever heard of a solder with a rabbit?"

"You could say it was dinner. Anyway, she is coming."

Jarla turned and started to lead her horse out of the stable. Delvin grabbed a handful of the travel rations to munch as he followed her, with Maegar bringing up the rear.

It was getting dark by the time they reached the barricades. Delvin judged they were on the left-hand side of the bridge. There were squads of cavalry already waiting there, standing by their horses and talking in hushed whispers. All of them wearing cloaks over their uniforms. There were also three companies of foot soldiers behind the cavalry, some standing others sitting on anything to hand. As they came up to the barricade, an officer broke off from some men he was talking to.

"Princess Jarla? I'm Captain Trenton. My sergeant and I will be shielding you on the crossing."

"Good," said Jarla. "Look after our horses while we go to see General Gortly."

They handed the reins to the sergeant, and made their way back up the street to a narrow lane that led to the next street along. Delvin looked back as they were about to enter the lane, and noticed for the first time that one large section of the barricade was made thinner than the rest, and had ropes attached so that it could be pulled to one side. Jarla continued down the lane, turning left when she reached the North South Road and made her way to a large building immediately opposite the bridge. The soldier on the door started when he saw the uniforms, but recovered and saluted when he saw who it was.

Jarla marched up the stairs to an attic, where a narrow door led out onto a parapet around the building. The parapet was lined with archers. To one side stood General Gortly and the dishevelled figure of Magister Perball between two large troupers. There were also several lengths of rope and a large wicker basket.

"Ah Jarla," said the General. "It's almost dark, we are about to get ready. Would you like to brief our magician?"

"I would be delighted," said Jarla stepping forward so she stood in front of Magister Perball. "Your job is very simple. Some time tonight Argent will be attacking. Before doing so their magician's stone will be used to make our men fall asleep. Your first job is to detect when they start to use their magician's stone, and tell us so we can get ready for them. Then you must counteract their stone. Can you do that?" Magister Perball nodded. "Excellent. To make sure you are concentrating, there will be this rope round your neck." Jarla flicked her finger at one of the troopers who placed a noose around Magister Perball's neck. "The end of the rope is tied to this pipe here. You of course will be in this basket hanging over the wall on ropes held by these two gentlemen." She pointed to two of the troopers. "So, if you fail in counteracting Argent's stone, and the gentlemen fall asleep, down you go, until the rope around your neck stops your fall. Understand?"

Magister Perball was swallowing convulsively and his face had gone ashen. He nodded.

"Good. Argent will also use their stone to make our men frightened. Your second task is to counteract that as well. Understand?" Magister Perball nodded. "Your third task is to try to stop them seeing our men until they are on them, and you might as well try to stop them seeing you as well, though I'm not sure what they would make of seeing someone dangling in a basket, Understood?" Magister Perball nodded again. "Excellent. Now it's dark we begin. Tie him in the basket."

The two troopers lifted him into the basket and tied his hands to the sides.

"Delvin, the stone."

"Delvin?" exclaimed Magister Perball. "So that is why you were not affected. Well not for long Magister Delvin, not for long. The black magician is on your trail." He smirked a grin that contained no humour.

Slightly shaken by this outburst, Delvin stepped forward and handed Magister Perball's crystal to Jarla, who hung it round Magister Perball's neck beneath the noose. She turned to the troopers.

"Right, over the edge with him."

The two troopers picked up the basket and manhandled it over the parapet, keeping a firm grip on the ropes so that Magister Perball dangled just below the edge.

"Thank you general. Now we just have to wait. We'll return to the horses."

"Thank you, Princess. Good luck."

Jarla turned and led Delvin and Maegar back down the stairs and through the lanes to their horses.

CHAPTER 21

Time seemed to pass very slowly as they waited with the soldiers. Delvin thought about Magister Perball. He had said he would be able to detect when the stone in Argent was being used to make Hengel's sentries go to sleep. When Magister Perball had used his stone to try to get them to leave his house, he had heard it as a clear message. Did that mean if someone with a stone projected a thought to someone else with a stone, it came across as a clear message rather than in their subconscious? Maybe that was what had happened to him when he had had the sudden thought of falling barrels that had got him into all this trouble. Maybe the person with Argent's stone had been using it to influence people to knock the barrels off, and he had inadvertently picked the message up as well. Maybe the suggestion had been projected to a lot of people's minds, so there would be a good chance that one of them would knock one of the barrels down. An accident, even if it hadn't threatened the Royal family, would have cast a shadow over the festival and lowered people's morale. But if it had killed the duke as well, that would have thrown Hengel into chaos. It seemed that whoever was using the stone in Argent was not just confining what he did to the battle on the bridge, he was trying to subvert Hengel as well.

Delvin got up to stretch his legs. He was starting to feel stiff and tired. They had been up early and it had been a long day. He looked over to the others. Maegar was sitting on the curb with her head held between her hands. Jarla was looking restless. She had tied her black hair in a tight ponytail, so that from the front with her hood up, it looked as if she had a man's haircut.

"What will happen to Magister Perball?" asked Delvin.

"He has committed treason, the sentence for that is death. After the battle the soldiers will let go of the ropes holding up the basket."

"But he thought his life would be spared if he helped."

"He is being spared the much more unpleasant death that he would have had if he was sent back to my father."

Delvin was slightly shocked, particularly since he had suggested the use of the basket. But as he thought about it, he realised Magister Perball would always be a threat if he was let go. Particularly if he managed to keep hold of the crystal. It was likely he was responsible for the deaths of a large number of Hengel's soldiers by not helping earlier, and probably had even helped Argent.

A thought appeared in Delvin's mind. *'You are feeling sleepy.'* A moment later another thought came with an edge of panic to it. *'You are feeling wide awake.'* It had begun thought Delvin. The thoughts came thick and fast. *'You are falling asleep.' 'You are wide awake.' 'Look away from the bridge, nothing is happening.' 'Look towards the bridge. Something is there' 'You are tired.' 'You are wide awake.'*

A messenger came running up and gave a note to the officer in charge. He gave whispered orders to his men and the cavalry mounted their horses drawing their swords, their slightly curved cutting edges glinting in the moonlight. The foot soldiers got up from where they had been sitting, stretched and made themselves ready too. Two men positioned themselves by the ropes attached to the moveable part of the barricade. Jarla got to her feet and looked around. She signalled to Delvin to mount and turned to Maegar who was still sitting with her head in her hands. Jarla gave her a kick and Maegar jerked out of her dream, and at Jarla's whispered command got to her feet and mounted her horse.

The seconds ticked by and the sense of expectation grew. The messages were still coming thick and fast in Delvin's mind. *'You are sleeping. Nothing is happening on the bridge.' 'You are wide awake. Look at the bridge.'*

There was a sudden rushing, whistling, clicking noise and Delvin saw flights of arrows pour from every window and every parapet facing the bridge. There were yells and screams and the officer gave the order to pull back the barricade.

As soon as the barricade was back, the cavalry charged with the infantry pouring through behind. Delvin, Jarla, Maegar, Captain Trenton and his sergeant followed.

As Delvin reached the gap in the barricade, he could see Argent's soldiers near the bridge falling under the rain of arrows. A moment later the cavalry was upon them. A second force of cavalry coming from behind a barricade on the opposite side crashed into their other flank.

The whispers in Delvin's mind now changed. *'You are frightened. You must run or you will get killed.'* *'You are not afraid, you are winning.'*

Most of Argent's forward soldiers were lying dead or dying. The few remaining were running for the twin towers leading to the bridge with Hengel's cavalry charging through them cutting left and right.

When the cavalry reached the towers, they continued straight on under the arches, over the now repaired drawbridge and onto the bridge. Argent's soldiers who had been on the bridge moving forward for the attack on South Bridge, were now met by the men fleeing from the cavalry. The soldiers at the back, not realising what was happening continued to press forward, squashing those between who hardly had room to move. Hengel's cavalry ploughed into them, cutting and slashing and gradually pushing back the press.

Hengel's infantry had reached the first set of towers. Delvin could hear the clash of swords and screams as they fought their way up the stairs and onto the battlements.

On the bridge the cavalry had pressed Argent's soldiers back to the central towers. Some soldiers throwing themselves off the bridge and into the river rather than face the slashing swords. Delvin reached the first towers as the cavalry, with their horses' iron shod hooves flaying and their swords hacking, pushed

Argent's men back over the central drawbridge.

The drawbridges were quite long, both to improve the defence and to allow big ships through. Each of the drawbridges hung from a pair of beams that extended over the drawbridge and reached back into the towers. The beams were pivoted where they entered the towers and had huge counterweights attached to the other end. This meant that a single man pulling on a rope could raise or lower the drawbridge. However the drawbridge was now covered by a heaving mass of men and horses, and to lift the drawbridge would mean lifting them as well. Argent's men flung themselves onto the counterweight and the rope to try to raise the bridge, but to no avail. The weight of the men and horses was too great and held the drawbridge firmly in position.

The defenders on the battlements of the central towers kept up a steady stream of arrows at the attackers coming across the bridge, but as Hengel's infantry hacked their way up the stairs towards them, they had to turn to meet them.

Everything had happened so fast that Argent's officers in North Bridge had only just begun to realise what was happening. They yelled at their men to fall back, trying to stop more men pressing onto the bridge and making worse the crush of men who could now scarcely move. Their orders could hardly be heard above the noise of battle. In desperation an officer ordered a drummer to beat the retreat to try to get the men to move back.

On the bridge, Argent's hard-pressed men heard the retreat, and what little fight was in them disappeared. Now their only thought was how to get back and how to escape the swords and hooves of Hengel's cavalry. Some jumped off the parapet of the bridge into the river, others flung down their arms. A few tried to pretend they were dead, while the remainder joined the crush trying to escape from the bridge, only to be hacked down and join the piles of dead and wounded.

The cavalry had reached the final drawbridge. The crush was now so great that the defenders had no hope of raising it, so after a few desperate heaves they joined the mass of men trying to get away. Hengel's men poured into the last towers, meeting little resistance as they pounded up the stairs to the battlements.

Jarla led her group across the bridge. They picked their way through the heaped bodies of men and horses. The towers they passed under now all bore the blue and white flag of Hengel. As they crossed, fresh companies of infantry ran past them to join the battle now forming in the square in front of North Bridge's half of the bridge. The last towers had been quickly taken and Argent's army was now being pressed back across the square in front of the bridge and towards the streets of North Bridge itself.

Jarla turned to Delvin and Maegar. "Fling back your cloaks, draw your swords and pretend you are fighting."

Captain Trenton and his sergeant who had been riding with them, drew their swords too, and the next moment Delvin found himself parrying a cut from Captain Trenton.

"Whoever taught you to fight? Get your sword up!" yelled Captain Trenton.

Delvin did as he was told, and had to concentrate so hard in keeping even the practice strokes from Captain Trenton at bay, that he didn't notice that they were now on the edge of the main fighting, with Argent's soldiers only a few feet away. Captain Trenton and his sergeant pressed them into one of the side streets.

"Break off," shouted Jarla.

Captain Tenton and his sergeant wheeled away leaving Delvin slightly stunned. Jarla held Maegar's horse back as it tried to follow the soldiers.

"This way," called Jarla.

Delvin followed Jarla as she turned her horse down the side street, pulling Maegar's horse after her by its bridle. After a little way, Jarla led them into a narrow cobbled alley. The alley was deserted, the locals having locked and barred their doors hoping the fighting would not reach their houses. The alley was very dark, but Jarla rode confidently down it. A little way ahead after crossing a wider better lit road, she turned right and continued on.

"Do you know where this goes?" asked Delvin.

"It should lead to the town walls. If we turn right again before we get there, that should get us back on the main road to the gate."

The streets and alleys in this quarter of North Bridge were something of a maze. They did have to retrace their steps once after coming to a dead end. But after a few turns and trying to keep to the narrower streets, they came close to the town wall near the gate. They crossed over a main road, dodged around several running people, went down another alley and came out into North Bridge's main road leading to the gate.

Two large flaming torches illuminated the scene in front of the gate. A crowd of townspeople were arguing with the guards. There were several waggons waiting at the gates and others were arriving as they watched. The people were demanding to be let out of town, casting worried glances towards the sounds of battle coming from the far end of the street.

Jarla turned her horse towards the gate, passing a waggon filled with an odd variety of furniture and belongings and with the frightened faces of two children peeping from the back.

"Make way!" shouted Jarla as she rode her horse through the crowd. "Make way!" She reached the gates and turned to a guard who was arguing with a florid faced man. "Let us through, duke's messengers."

The guard looked up and saw the officer's uniforms. "I can't open up sir. I'd never get the gate closed again with all these people sir."

Jarla turned on him. "Would you delay the duke's messenger. If you can't deal with this rabble, I can." She drew her sword and turned towards the florid faced man who hastily stepped back, tripping over a handcart behind him as he did so.

"We mean no harm sir. We aren't no fighters. We're just trying to get away."

"Well get away from this gate. Now!" The man and those around him all stepped back as Jarla moved her horse threateningly towards them. Jarla turned her horse towards the guard.

"Open!"

"Yes sir," said the guard, and began to lift the great bar from across the gate. Jarla turned her horse towards the crowd again, and they shuffled back, none wanting to face her. The guard had the gate open, and Jarla turned to the others.

"Come on." The three spurred their horses through the gate leaving the guard to try and shut it before the townsfolk reached him.

It was quite dark beyond the town since the moon had gone behind a cloud. They slowed their horses down to a walk, and peered ahead trying to see where the road ended and the verge began. Once Maegar's horse stumbled as it stepped into a hole, and once a branch almost swept Delvin from his saddle. Jarla continued on until the sounds of battle had faded and all they could hear was the rustling of the trees, the clop of their hooves and the occasional lowing of a cow.

After what seemed to Delvin to be an age, Jarla stopped and peered to the side of the road.

"I think this is a rest shelter. Delvin, have a look."

Delvin climbed stiffly from his saddle and handed his horse's reins to Maegar who took them dully. He then stepped towards the dark outlines of the building. By feeling his way along the wall, he found a door. He banged on it shouting, "Anyone there?"

"Go in and check it out," snapped Jarla.

There was no reply to Delvin's shout, so he found the latch and opened the door. The room inside was pitch dark.

"I can't see anything."

"Take this tinderbox," said Jarla.

Delvin took the tinderbox, entered the building and struck the flint. Just in time he realised he had nothing to light once the tinder had burnt. He stepped back out to find some dried grass.

"Well?" demanded Jarla.

"I can't see much yet. I'm just getting some grass."

"Well, get on with it."

Delvin entered the building again and struck the flint. The tinder caught and Delvin lit his dried grass. The room was plain and empty with a dry mud floor and a fireplace in the centre of the wall opposite the door.

"There's no one here," called Delvin as he stepped over towards the fireplace where someone had already laid a fire. He pushed his burning grass under the kindling and the flames took hold. He stood back and looked around again. The door was large, big enough to lead a horse through. From the droppings on one side that was obviously what people did. There were no windows or any other features at all.

"I've got a fire going."

"So I see," said Jarla leading her horse in. "Right, horses that side, us this side. Get them unsaddled. We need to take off these Argent uniforms. We won't pass for soldiers in daylight. Then let's see if we can get some sleep."

They unsaddled the horses and gave them some grain and a quick rub down. Delvin gave Freda his rabbit some grain too. Maegar was still acting in almost a daze and Delvin had to help her with her saddle. They changed out of their Argent soldier's uniforms, took their sleeping rolls, and using their saddles as pillows made themselves as comfortable as they could. As they settled themselves down, Delvin turned to Jarla.

"Do you think Hengel have captured North Bridge?"

"Sheffs no. That would cause all sorts of problems. Argent would then raise another army to take it back and this war would never be over. The plan was that when they had secured the square in front of the bridge, they would fall back to the first set of towers. That would put us in a good bargaining position when we finally sort this lot out."

"Why was Argent trying to take South Bridge then?"

"That I don't know, and I wish I did. It doesn't seem right."

Delvin was still thinking about it as the flickering fire slowly died down and he eventually fell into an exhausted sleep.

CHAPTER 22

Delvin was woken by a kick in the ribs. Jarla was standing over him.

"Get some more firewood, and see if you can find a stream to water the horses."

Delvin rolled out of his bedding roll feeling hungry and stiff. Maegar had also just been woken and was groaning slightly as she got up.

"Come on, let's see if we can find a stream," said Delvin to Maegar.

Delvin led the way out into the early morning sun. There had been a heavy dew and the grass was wet. He looked around. The building they had spent the night in was a solid stone structure with a simple thatched roof, single chimney, no windows and a wide door made of crude wooden planks. It was set back a few yards from the road which ran along a small valley with low hills on one side and woods on the other. Behind the hut, the hill was fenced off from the road and some cows were grazing away to the left. On the other side of the road the trees in the wood were coming into leaf, and Delvin could see plenty of dead wood they could collect as firewood.

"Let's go to the top of that hill and see if we can see a stream anywhere," suggested Delvin. They climbed over the fence into the field and quickly reached the top of the hill. Ahead of them the hill fell away to another small valley with a stream at the bottom. Delvin looked to see if it crossed the road, but if it did, it did so out of sight. Just beyond was a farmhouse. Smoke was already rising from its chimney and they could see the farmer making his way to a shed at the back.

"We had better get the horses," said Delvin. They walked back to the traveller's rest shelter and led the horses out. They had to go a little way down the road to find a gate and then walked over the hill to the valley and stream beyond.

As the horses drank, Delvin turned to Maegar. "I'm hungry. Let's see if we can buy some breakfast at that farm."

"Have you any money?" asked Maegar.

"I think I should have enough."

They led the horses over to the farm and knocked on the door. It was opened by a large plump woman with a huge white apron and massive bare arms.

"What you be wanting at this time in the morning?"

"Have you any bread and ham you could sell us?" asked Delvin.

"Sell is it. Let's see your coin."

Delvin took a few copper bits from his pocket. He had taken some from his cache when he had got up.

"Coppers is it. Well, I can do you a good slice of ham in two slices of fresh bread for two coppers each."

"That would be splendid."

The woman nodded and went into her kitchen to return with two huge double slabs of bread, each with a thick slice of ham in the middle. Delvin handed over the coins.

"Thank you, they look lovely."

"Enjoy them, you both look like you need feeding up."

They ate their bread and ham as they walked back towards the road. As they neared the hill, a scream coming from the rest shelter stopped them in their tracks. A moment later they were running as quickly as they could back towards the shelter. As they came over the brow of the hill, they saw two women with a donkey laden with goods, almost running down the road, pulling the donkey after them. Delvin just caught their comments.

"...sucked the life out of that poor soldier...the Evil One...what is this land coming to?"

Delvin quickly swallowed down the last of his bread and ham and ran panting up to the shelter's door and pulled it open.

Inside Jarla was standing looking furious. One of the soldier's uniforms was laid out flat on the ground in front of her. She was wearing her long black cloak, with her black hair hanging free to her shoulders.

"What happened," gasped Delvin.

"Those peasants came in and told me I had to tidy up before I left, so I told them I would leave as much of them as I left of this soldier if they didn't get out. The idiots. Have you got the firewood?"

"No, not yet."

"Well get on with it then. We need to be on our way."

Delvin stepped out of the building as Meagar came up.

"What's happened?"

"Some locals told Jarla to tidy up. She got the better of the argument."

"What did she say?"

"She had one of the uniforms on the floor in front of her. I think she implied she had sucked the life out of him, and would do the same to them if they didn't get out."

"So that's what the scream was."

"We'd better get the firewood."

It took them only a few minutes to collect armloads of firewood from the woods which they stacked in the shelter. Jarla had already packed her bundles and was saddling her horse.

"Delvin bury the uniforms. We don't want to be caught with those. Maegar get packed and saddled."

Delvin did as he was asked, and before long the three were on the road heading away from North Bridge. They could make quicker progress in daylight, and they alternated between trotting and walking. After a short while they came to a fork in the road. An ancient signpost pointed right to Dandel and left to Argent.

"This way," said Jarla taking the left-hand road.

The country began to get flatter, and the fields of corn and lush pastures reminded Delvin of the farms he had grown up with at Byford. The farm buildings were slightly different, being timber framed rather than the whitewashed buildings of his home. But the smells were familiar, and Delvin felt more relaxed than he had been at any time since they set out.

They passed through the village of Thanley in the late morning, and stopped shortly after at a small stream to rest and water the horses. The sun was shining and the day was warm. Sitting on the grass eating their travel rations it was hard to believe that only the evening before they had been involved in the battle on the bridge, and that now they were in enemy territory.

Jarla was keen to get on, so they were soon on their way, and by mid afternoon the walls of Argent came in sight.

CHAPTER 23

As they rode down towards Argent, they got a good view of the city. Argent was built around a huge natural harbour. The point furthest towards the sea, rose up as a great rocky cliff over one hundred feet high and was surmounted by Argent Castle, the ancient stronghold of the Dukes of Argent. The dukes no longer lived there. They had long since built a palace on the edge of the city below the castle. The palace was built to resemble a fantasy castle with a series of towers and mock fortifications. It was painted pink which contrasted curiously with the dark grey of the stone walls and towers of the genuine fortifications of the castle on the cliff above. The city walls connected to the castle and ran round the landward side of the city, with regular towers and a deep ditch giving further protection. At the other end of the city wall was another fortification, the Harbour Fort. This was a lower building than Argent Castle. It had been built out into the sea so that its seaward walls rose straight up from the water of the bay.

The main city gate of Argent was massive. Two eighty-foot drum towers supported a drawbridge over the ditch. On the landward side of the ditch, two further towers with a short stretch of wall formed a barbican. The view of the barbican had become partly blocked by a number of buildings that had sprung up on the road leading into the city. As Delvin, Maegar and Jarla rode towards Argent there were at first a few houses, then these got closer together, until by the time they reached the barbican with its gates and portcullis, there was a row of thriving shops and the bustle of a busy street.

The guards at the gate seemed to be hardly examining the

people entering and leaving the city, and they got past them after just a brief disinterested look.

Delvin's first impression of Argent was the salty smell that got stronger as they rode down Dock Road towards the sea. The buildings too seemed subtly different from those of Hengel. Their gables were steeper with a greater use of timber framing.

"We need to find an inn near the palace," said Jarla heading off across the square in front of the ornate Guild Hall with its intricly carved portico held up by two barley-sugar shaped pillars. They passed the great temple into Royal Road and headed towards the palace and castle. The area near the palace turned out to be a district of large private houses and they had to turn back and head along the seafront before they found an inn.

The Argent Bay Inn was a large three-story inn with a courtyard behind. They left their horses with a groom and Jarla was about to stride in when Delvin tapped her on the shoulder. She stopped and glared at him as he stepped ahead.

The inside of the inn had been painted white which gave it a light airy feel. As they came through the door, the landlord, a small neat man, came out to greet them rubbing his hands together.

"Gentlemen, ma'am, how can I be of service?"

"Have you two rooms for the night?"

"Certainly, would you like a sea view? I have two lovely rooms looking out over the harbour."

"How much are they?"

"One gold royal per night for each room."

Delvin swallowed. "Have you something a little more economical?"

The expression on the landlord's face became less ingratiating.

"I do have two rooms at the back overlooking the yard. They are five carls per night each, payment in advance."

"Those will do, we would like to stay one night." Delvin turned to Jarla. "May I have my purse dear?"

Jarla scowling, handed him her purse and he counted out the

coins.

"Up the stairs, turn left, it's the two rooms at the end of the passage."

They followed the landlord's directions and found the two rooms. One was quite small with just a bed, chair and washstand. The other had two beds and a table with four chairs around it.

"We'll take this one," said Jarla indicating the larger room.

"Why couldn't we have a sea view?" said Maegar. "I like the sea."

"We don't want to stand out," said Delvin. "People take notice of people with money."

"And I'm paying," said Jarla. "My purse Delvin."

Delvin handed Jarla her purse turning to face her. "Why are we here in Argent? What are you hoping to do here?"

"We need to find Fionella so we can show she has not been kidnapped, and so stop this war. The last place she was seen was the palace here. So that's where we start."

"You're not planning to just walk into the palace, are you?"

"No," Jarla looked towards Delvin. "You are. The servants always know more than they are meant to, and you are going to find out what they know and what the gossip is."

"Why me?"

"Because you are the only person who can get in. I'd be recognised. That leaves you."

"But Maegar was a servant." He turned to Maegar. "Do you have any idea where Fionella went."

"No, but I didn't work in the palace. I was a cleaner in the castle. We used to come down to the palace occasionally, but we didn't mix much with the palace servants."

"How on earth do you expect me to get into the palace, let alone find out what the gossip is?"

"You are going to go to the servant's entrance and offer to put on a magic show for them. You can start talking to them once you get there."

"Just like that."

"Have you any better ideas?"

Delvin's mind raced as he tried to think of an alternative, and at the same time ran through the tricks he had with him that he could use in a magic show for the servants.

"Good that's settled," said Jarla. "You need to get a move on, or it will be too late. We'll be waiting for you here."

"You don't expect me to go there tonight?"

"Why not? We need to find Fionella as quickly as we can."

"I need to get prepared."

"Well get prepared, but don't take all night about it. Come on, move it."

Delvin took his things into the smaller room and sorted through them to find suitable tricks he could perform for the servants. After about ten minutes he had worked out what he could do and bundled up the props he would need. He went out into the passageway and knocked on Jarla's door.

"I've worked out some tricks. How do I get to the servant's quarters?"

"Maegar, you were a maid in the palace, show him the way."

Maegar came out of the room. Telling Delvin to follow her, she set off along the passage, down the stairs and out into the street. Delvin hurried to catch up.

"Who is the head of the servants in the palace?"

"Balinow is the High Steward. He's so stuck up you won't see him. He thinks he's part of the nobility. You'll probably see Botherwin. He runs the kitchens and the household servants. You want to be careful with him." Maegar smiled.

"Why, what's wrong with him?"

"Nothing really, you'll find out."

Maegar had turned off from the seafront and was heading through some narrow streets behind.

"Do I just knock on the door and ask to see Botherwin?"

"I don't know what you do. I don't remember anyone coming to be an entertainer for the servants before."

"Oh, Great!"

They had now come to the exclusive private houses and

Delvin stopped talking as he thought about what approach he might make. They skirted the edge of the palace, and going round a corner they came to a large double gate that stood open to the street. Delvin could see a courtyard inside painted in the same pink as the palace and with the same mock battlements along the top of the building. At the far side of the courtyard was a large door with steps leading up to it.

Maegar stopped before reaching the gate. "It's through there. Go to the big door and present yourself there. I'm not going any further, someone might recognise me. See you back at the inn." With that she was gone.

"Thank you," said Delvin to her retreating figure. He looked at the gate, squared his shoulders and stepped forward.

There was a gentleman sitting inside the gateway's arch. "What is your business?"

"Porvar the Great to see the honourable Magister Botherwin."

"What is your business with Magister Botherwin?"

Delvin looked down his nose at the doorman and touched his crystal, projecting the thought that he had better let him through.

"I have come to wish him good tidings. Show me the way!"

"You are meant to have proper business to come in here."

"Indeed. I have come to read his fortune, provide entertainment and enjoyment and bring good fortune to all. Ah...I can see something." Delvin stared intently at the doorman's face.

"What's that?"

"It's in your face. Did you know you have a dice player's face?"

"Dice player's face?"

"Yes, that's right. Do you play dice?"

"No. I play a bit of cards."

"Do you win?"

"Only sometimes. I usually lose."

"There you are. You should be playing dice. You have the face. You really do."

"I might try that. Thank you. Go on, go through. It's the big door on the other side." The doorman pointed towards the door on the other side of the courtyard.

Delvin walked across the courtyard. The door was panelled, with large iron studs and huge ornate hinges. More the front door of a nobleman's house than the entrance to the servant's quarters he thought. There was a big iron bell pull hanging down. Delvin took hold of it and gave it a heave. There was the far off sound of a bell ringing. After a moment the door opened and a maid looked out.

"What's your business sir?"

"Porvar the Great to see the honourable Magister Botherwin."

"Come in sir, I'll tell him you're here."

Delvin entered the building. Inside was a wide, stone-flagged passage with several doors leading off it. It was fairly dark since there were only two small windows by the door to give light.

"Could you wait here sir. I will tell Magister Botherwin you are here."

There was a leather covered armchair by the door and Delvin sat down and studied his surroundings. The passage was obviously the hub of the servant's quarters since people were constantly coming in through one door and going out through another.

"Can I be of assistance sir?" Delvin was woken from his daydream and turned to see an immaculately dressed man of medium height approaching his chair.

"Magister Botherwin?" said Delvin rising from his seat. "I am Porvar the Great. I came to visit your beautiful city and enjoy the sea air, and I found it so much to my liking that I thought I should do something in return. So I have come to you to offer my services in telling your fortunes, divining your futures, entertaining your colleagues, and bringing luck, diversions and pleasure. Porvar the Great at your service magister."

"And what may I ask would be the charge for all this?"

"No charge at all magister. I'm here in return for the pleasure your beautiful city has given me. If people wish to make a small contribution, my hat will be available. If any of your colleagues wish to buy any small lucky charm, I still have one or two left. But if you would like one, it will be my pleasure to bestow it upon you." Delvin brought one of his charms out of his pocket with a flourish.

Magister Botherwin put his hand on Delvin's arm and looked him up and down. Finally looking him directly in the eye with a slight smile on his lips, he said, "You do talk a load of rubbish... But a show would be fun." He gave Delvin's arm a squeeze. "We are serving dinner at present. The duke is not here of course, so it is only a small dinner, five or six courses. When it is cleared you may perform for us in the servant's hall. It will be in about an hour. You can wait in the servant's hall if you like. It is through there." He indicated a door on the right. "You could use my room if you want to get changed."

"Thank you," said Delvin. "I had better go to the hall, there are a few things I need to get ready."

"Right. I'll see you later. If you need anything, ask one of the maids." He turned and walked away down the passage leaving Delvin wondering what he had got himself into.

Pulling himself together, Delvin made his way to the servant's hall. The hall was full of bustle. There were four long tables, each with benches down both sides and armchairs at the head. Some servants were sitting at the tables eating their dinner, while others brought the dishes from the kitchen that was next door through a large arch. There were sideboards and shelves filled with plates and mugs around the side walls, and on the far wall was a large gold framed portrait of some long-past head steward.

Delvin made his way to a table where three maids were sitting giggling over their meal.

"My Ladies, may I join you? I am Porvar the Great, fortune teller and magician extraordinary. Magister Botherwin said I may partake of some refreshment before I perform for your entertainment. If I can combine that with the pleasure of your company, I will be a fortunate man."

"Oh, come on, sit down. What a to do," giggled one of the girls. "Hey, Petron, bring another plate and a mug of ale over here...

thanks."

"Are you really a magician?" asked the girl to Delvin's right.

"Indeed madam I am. Let me see your hand." Delvin took her hand in his. "Oh, what a line of love. You are very fortunate. I can see romance here. Do you have a special friend?"

He girl blushed nodding.

"I thought so. He is a lucky man to have a girl with such strong feelings and emotions."

A plate of sliced meat and vegetables arrived with a large mug of ale.

"My thanks sir. This looks magnificent. Tell me ladies, where in this wonderful palace do you work?"

"We clean the rooms."

"Do you do all the rooms?"

"Oh yes. We do any rooms we are sent to. We do the royal quarters sometimes."

"The royal quarters? They must be splendid."

"Oh they are sir, and if we see the duke or princess they are always very gracious."

"Magister Botherwin said they were away at present."

"That's right sir. The duke is at North Bridge directing the army. Did you hear, Hengel have taken the bridge? I don't know what will happen if they take North Bridge. They say more troops are being rushed down there. Whyever did Hengel kidnap Princess Fionella? It's terrible. Princess Fionella is so nice. To think of her in the hands of those horrible people."

"Did you help Princess Fionella to pack when she went to Hengel?"

"Oh no sir. That was her personal maid that did that."

"No it wasn't," said one of the other girls. "It was Eliana that did it. Kylene, that's her personal maid, disappeared a few weeks before."

"Disappeared?"

"Yes it was very strange. First Princess Fionella disappears. Then Kylene is rushing around like a mad thing packing trunks. Then she disappears too. About a week later Princess Fionella comes back again, but there is no sign of Kylene. There's been no sign since."

"Good riddance if you ask me."

"Oh, that's not kind."

"What happened to the trunks she packed?"

"They got sent somewhere. A haulier came in and took them."

"I would have thought they would have gone in a royal carriage," said Delvin.

"Oh no. Luggage often goes by the haulier. I think Botherwin has something going with Endel that runs it. He is a pretty boy."

"Ooo he is," the girls giggled.

"Botherwin has something going with him?" asked Delvin puzzled.

"Ohh, hadn't you noticed," grinned one of the girls. "You had better watch it. You're a pretty boy too." All three girls started laughing.

"Has he invited you up to his room yet?"

"Just to get changed."

"Is that what he said." The girls grinned.

"Have you arranged for a room here?"

"No, I was going back to my inn after I finished."

"The girls laughed again."

"The meal will finish in an hour, that will be half past eight. One hour for your performance. I bet Botherwin gets the gate shut before nine."

All three girls were enjoying themselves hugely.

"That's only for the palace staff surely?"

"Oh no. Once the gate is shut, no one goes in or out."

"No one?"

"No one at all. Oh, you should see your face!" All three girls started laughing again.

"You are kidding me."

"No we aren't. I think you are going to have a new magical experience."

"Thank you ladies. I think I'll be on my way."

"What, and disappoint Magister Botherwin. He's not a man to

disappoint. He'll have the palace guards after you."

"And that will be an even more magical experience." The three girls fell about laughing again. The one in the middle, a short girl with a big smile, round pink cheeks and curly brown hair, looked him in the eye.

"I could help you."

"You could?"

"Will you cover for me?" She turned to the other two who nodded grinning. "After you finish your performance, go through that end door there." She pointed to a green baize-covered door at the end of the hall. "Take the second door on the right down the passage. It's a store room. Wait for me there."

"Thank you. Can I give you some reward?"

"Oh, you'll reward me all right." All three girls started giggling again.

"We must be going. See you later."

"Wait, I don't know your name."

"Hanny. See you."

Delvin sat feeling slightly stunned. Was that what Meagar had meant when she had warned him to be careful with Botherwin. But at least he had got a lead on where Fionella might be. In the morning he would find Endel the haulier and see if he could discover where he had taken Fionella's baggage. Right now, he must tell a few fortunes, sell a few charms and get ready for his show. And then there would be Hanny…

Delvin got up from the table and approached a group of grooms finishing their meal.

"I am Porvar the Great, come to tell your fortunes and bring you luck. May I join you for a moment?" Delvin gradually worked his way around the room, and half an hour later had told six people their fortunes, sold five lucky charms and flirted with several girls and a footman. Maybe another of Botherwin's friends thought Delvin. Dinner by this time was coming to an end, so with the help of the footman he arranged the room, with two of the tables together at one end to act as a stage, and the chairs in rows facing it.

As soon as they had finished setting up the room, the chairs started filling up and there was an excited buzz in the air.

Magister Botherwin came in to see how things were progressing. "My dear Porvar, I see you have things organised. This is splendid. You seem to have everything ready." He looked around. "Is everyone here?... Come on Antone, come on... Right... all settled..." He raised his hand and a hush fell over the rows of servants. "Dear friends, it is with great pleasure that I introduce to you this evening a magician extraordinary," he looked at Delvin. "Porvar the Great!" The audience cheered.

Delvin bowed and climbed onto the stage. He performed his cups and balls trick using some of the mugs from the servant's hall. He cut a piece of rope, only for it to seem to come together again. He asked one of the maids to come up on stage and help him. Then he took another piece of rope and tied it round her waist. When he pulled the rope, it seemed to pass right through her. He finished by making a series of balls appear, disappear and change colour with bewildering speed.

He took his bow and indicated his hat on the side of the stage. As he expected he got more applause than coins, but a few people threw coppers into the hat. As he came down from the stage, a crowd of people surrounded him urging him to tell their fortunes. He picked up his hat and told the crowd he would move down the room to give the footmen a chance to rearrange the room. He then made his way down to the far end of the hall, and set himself down near the baize covered door that Hanny had indicated earlier.

For several minutes he sat there reading palms, telling fortunes and joking with the crowd of servants. Occasionally, as the crowd moved, he caught a glimpse of Botherwin who seemed to be waiting in the background.

Delvin stood up and gave a sweep of his arm. "Gentlemen and good ladies, I must wish you all good fortune for it is time for me to go... Farewell!" With that, he was up, out of his chair and through the door before anyone could move. He shut the door behind him and tore down the passage to the second door on the right which he yanked open, leapt inside and shut the door after him, panting from the sudden exertion.

Outside the door he could hear the delayed reaction from the crowd in the servant's hall. Someone had obviously opened the door into the passage to see where he had gone but had been too late to see him go through the second door. He could hear surprised voices. "He's disappeared!" "Vanished into thin air!" "...told me I would find a good wife..."

In the dark of the store room, Delvin felt his way to the wall behind where the door opened.

The voices were coming down the passage.

"He can't have just disappeared."

"He is a magician."

The door was suddenly flung open, and Delvin pressed himself against the wall so the open door shielded him from anyone's gaze.

"He's not in here."

"I told you, he's disappeared. He's a magician."

The door shut again, plunging the room into darkness and Delvin breathed a sigh of relief. In the brief light when the door had been opened, Delvin had seen that the store room contained some old tables and chairs, several boxes against the far wall and a large floor to ceiling cupboard against the wall to Delvin's right.

How had he got into this, he thought to himself. Jarla had made it all sound so easy. What would happen if Magister Botherwin found him? And how would he manage to get away in the morning?

He had no way of telling the time in the pitch dark, but it seemed a long while before the door suddenly opened. There was a quick shuffling as someone came in, and the door closed again.

"Are you there, Magister Porvar?" asked a soft voice.

"Is that you Hanny?"

He was answered by a giggle and the sound of steel on flint. There was a spark from a tinderbox, then a burst of light as the tinder caught. He saw Hanny's grinning face as she lit a candle.

"Ooo Magister Porvar," she said. "Let's see if we can make

ourselves comfortable. You'll find blankets in those cupboards. That should make the floor a bit softer…"

CHAPTER 24

Hanny sneaked Delvin out of the palace shortly after dawn. The first deliveries of milk and vegetables were arriving and Delvin was able to leave with the delivery drivers. He had a roll of hot bread in his pocket that Hanny had found for him. She gave him a lingering kiss on the lips and the injunction to take care and not to forget her. He gave her one of his charms. And as he left her, he touched his stone wishing happy thoughts into her mind.

It was with a light heart and a smile on his face that he set out to find the haulier called Endel. He tried first down at the docks, reasoning that ships needed hauliers to transport the goods they carried. There were several ships tied up at the quayside. The first one he came to was being unloaded and there was a large crane poised over its open hold. He asked a man leaning against a bollard if he had heard of a haulier called Endel, but the man just shook his head. The second man he asked was checking a pile of crates. He looked up at Delvin's query.

"Endel? Aye. Go down the quayside, down Portal Street, then second right. You'll find his yard down there. Watch those crates!" he shouted as a young man tried to wheel a cart too close to the pile of crates he was checking.

"Thanks," said Delvin setting off in the direction he had indicated.

Portal Street was full of warehouses and small businesses. Although it was still early, there was a bustle and hum about the place. Delvin took the second road on the right and found Endel's yard without difficulty.

A wide arch flanked by shuttered windows led through to a

yard in which two teams of horses were being harnessed up to huge waggons. Delvin strode in purposefully and approached a man holding the head of one of the lead horses.

"Can you direct me to Magister Endel?"

"Hold on a minute, whoa, whoa, calm down." The huge horse was moving restlessly. He turned to Delvin again. "Go through that door under the arch, you should find him through there."

Delvin thanked him and walked over to the door which was slightly ajar. He pushed it open and went through. Inside was a room obviously used as an office. On the wall opposite the door there were rows of shelves containing huge legers, and on the other side a desk was placed under the window to catch the light. A slim athletic looking man sat at the desk. He looked up from a pile of papers at Delvin's entrance.

"May I help you?"

"Are you Magister Endel?"

"I am. Who are you?"

"Hornold from the duke's tax office. I've come to make a spot check."

"I've paid my tax. What's this all about?"

"It's just routine, we're checking random businesses to make sure the tax they pay is correct."

"Have you any identification?"

A tingle of fear and doubt shot through Delvin as he thought fast. He looked the haulier in the eye, put his hand in his pocket and touched his crystal. He then projected the thought to Endel that he had seen his identification and that it was in order.

"May I see your ledgers for trips made in the last three months?"

"Certainly Magister Hornold. I'll get them for you." Endel got up, moved over to the shelves and took down a large ledger. "This one covers the last four months."

"Thank you," said Delvin taking the ledger and putting it on the desk. He began to do a quick calculation in his head. This was the sixth day since setting out with Jarla. The war had been going on for three weeks before that. Allow at least two weeks for Fionella to be at Hengel before the war was declared. Two weeks to train Meagar as Fionella. So, the trip to take the real Princess Fionella's baggage must have been at least two months ago. The entries showed the date, the person commissioning the trip, the destination, time spent and the price charged. Endel had done several trips for the Duke of Argent, but most seemed to be collecting goods from other countries and bringing them to the palace. Whatever did the Duke want with a stuffed lion thought Delvin. Then he came to an entry that looked promising. Five chests to be taken from the palace to a place called Anderal. Where was Anderal he wondered. It had been eleven weeks ago. He checked before and after it. It was the only one that fitted what he was looking for.

Delvin closed the ledger with a snap and looked up to find Endel hovering worriedly at his shoulder.

"Is everything all right Magister Hornold?"

"As far as I can see, it all seems to be in order. We will get back to you if we find any discrepancies. We are being much more careful and checking much more these days. Thank you for your time." Delvin bowed. Endel returned the bow and opened the door. Delvin went out, gave a last final bow and started back towards The Argent Bay Inn.

He was feeling pleased with his morning's work. He had found out where Fionella was likely to be, so now hopefully they could find her. He took the bread roll Hanny had given him out of his pocket and munched it happily as he made his way back towards the inn.

It was still quite early as he opened the inn door. Some guests were having their breakfast in the room at the front and a smell of cooking came from the kitchen.

Delvin made his way up the stairs and along the passage and knocked on Jarla's door. There was a slight pause.

"Who is it?"

"Delvin."

"Where have you been?... Enter."

Delvin opened the door and stepped inside. Everything went

black as something was thrown over his head. A heavy weight fell on him and he fell to the floor the weight bearing him down. He rapidly realised the weight was a man as his arms were pinned to his sides. Hands grabbed his wrists and pulled them behind him, and despite Delvin's struggles, expertly tied his wrists together. The man pulled him upright. As Delvin tried to regain his wits, light flooded back as the thing that had been thrown over his head was removed. The whole thing had taken only seconds.

"Where have you been? We've been stuck here since last night." Jarla was looking furiously at him from a chair across the room. Then Delvin noticed that her arms were tied behind the chair. He glanced across to the bed where Maegar lay trussed up. Whatever had happened? He turned his head quickly to see who his attacker was. Standing behind him was a tall gaunt looking man with long dark hair, dressed all in black. The cloak that he had thrown over Delvin was black as well.

"So, we meet at last young Delvin."

"Who are you?" asked Delvin, trying to sound calm as he manoeuvred himself so that his crystal would be touching his leg.

"You may well ask!" snapped Jarla. "He's had us trussed up since last night waiting for you to come back."

The man glanced at Jarla and she stopped talking. It seemed as though she had suddenly forgotten what she was going to say. The man turned to Delvin again.

"Where is Borlock's crystal?" A second voice seemed to come into Delvin's mind, telling him he wanted to tell this man where the crystal was, and that if he told him, all would be all right. A sudden realisation hit Delvin like a blow and a shiver of fear ran through him. This must be a magician sent by the Guild of Magicians to get Borlock's crystal back. What was it that Magister Perball had said? The Guild sent assassins to kill anyone who found out the secret of the crystals. He must make sure that whoever this man in black was, he didn't realise that Delvin knew the secret. Whatever else Delvin did, he must not try to project a thought to this man as it would just come out like a clear message and give him completely away.

"Borlock's crystal?" he replied looking puzzled.

"The crystal Borlock gave you when he died. You will have found it in his things." The voice in Delvin's head kept repeating that he should tell where the crystal was, and everything would be all right.

"There was a crystal with his money. Is that what you are looking for?"

"That's the one, where is it?"

"It's where I keep my money, sewn into my saddle."

"You will go and get it and bring it here."

The man went behind Delvin's back and untied his hands. The voice in Delvin's head changed. Now saying, *'You will go down to the stables and bring the saddle back here. You will talk to no one. You will bring the saddle back here.'*

"I shall be watching through the window. Don't try to run away and don't talk to anyone. I will be here with the ladies, and it will be very unfortunate for them if you disobey me."

The man casually took his knife from his belt and ran the point in an 's' down Maegar's face. With horror Delvin could very faintly hear the voice in his head saying to Maegar, *'You are paralyzed. You cannot move. The tip of this knife will burn like fire.'* Delvin could see Maegar's eyes staring in pain. He took a step towards the man who turned back towards him.

"All right," said Delvin. "I'll bring it back here."

"Good," said the man. "Remember, I will be watching from the window."

Delvin saw that there was a loaded crossbow leaning against the windowsill and gulped. The voice in Delvin's head was now talking to him again and not Maegar. *'You will go down to the stable. Bring back the saddle. Talk to no one.'*

Delvin, as if in a daze, went back through the door and down the passageway. How could he get out of this? His secret pouch was with his magic tricks and not in his saddle, and it contained his money and not his crystal. When the black magician saw there was nothing sewn into his saddle what would he do? How could he get Jarla and Maegar out and not let on he knew how the crystal worked? Would the black magician kill them all anyway? He must think of something.

He went down the stairs and out of the back door of the inn and into the stable yard. He desperately wanted to look up at the window to see if the man was watching him with his crossbow, but resisted as it might give him away. He went into the stables where the saddles were stored and reached up to get his down. Maybe he could put something in it. Suddenly a weight hit his shoulders and he was face down in the hay with an unseen figure yanking his wrists behind him and tying them together. "Not again," he thought.

"Don't struggle Master Delvin. Let me take your knife, then we will talk." Delvin felt expert fingers remove his knife, then he was roughly pushed into a sitting position.

"Grimbolt!" Delvin exclaimed.

"Captain Grybald to you. Now what's going on?"

Jumbled thoughts raced through Delvin's head. What should he tell Grimbolt? Then the thought struck him, maybe he could help, after all he was working for Hengel and Jarla's Father. He looked up at Grimbolt standing over him.

"I'm not absolutely sure what is happening, but Jarla and Maegar are being held captive by a man I think is a magician."

"You are a magician, so how do you fit in? And who is Maegar?"

"Maegar is the person you think is Princess Fionella. She is not really Fionella. She is a maid forced to impersonate her. I think the magician is after me."

"Why is he holding Princess Jarla and Maegar captive, and why should he be after you? You are a magician too."

"He's a member of the Guild of Magicians. I'm not."

"Right, let's get this straight. A magician who you say is after you, holds Princess Jarla and…Maegar captive, but lets you go… come on!"

"He thinks he has me under his influence. Have you been up

there?"

"No. I followed you here and was checking out the layout of the inn when I found this." Grimbolt pointed to what looked like a bundle at the back of the stables. Delvin turned his body so he could look at what Grimbolt was pointing to and recoiled in horror. It was the innkeeper. A line of blood snaked down his face in the same pattern that the black magician had run his knife down Maegar's face. But the thing that horrified Delvin most was the grimace of pain and terror, frozen into the innkeeper's face by death. The eyes stared and the mouth looked as if it wanted to scream but paralysis prevented it. What had the black magician done to him, and why had he done it? Delvin felt sick and looked white-faced at Grimbolt.

"Not a pretty sight Master Delvin. When I found that, I thought I had better observe a little longer. Then you came along. Now I want the full story. If he thinks he's got you under his influence, why aren't you?"

"Are you sure you really want to know? The Guild of Magicians kill people who know the secret."

"Oh yes. I want to know Master Delvin. Is that what happened to this man?" Grimbolt nodded towards the body of the innkeeper. "When you have told me, then I can decide if you are telling me the truth."

All the while the voice in Delvin's head had been pulsing, *'Bring the saddle upstairs. Talk to no one. Bring back the saddle.'*

Delvin realised that he was going to have to tell Grimbolt the whole story and he fervently hoped that he would believe it. Delvin took a deep breath and explained to Grimbolt about the crystals, how he came to have Borlock's crystal, and how Jarla didn't know he had it. Grimbolt smiled thinly at that with his slightly lopsided smile.

"So, this magician wants Borlock's crystal back? How long does it take to project a thought?"

"Not long, only a second or so."

"Ah ha. So we have a second." Grimbolt reached round and cut the cord binding Delvin's wrists. "Right, get that saddle down, you're expected back upstairs."

"Aren't you going to shoot him through the window," asked Delvin hopefully.

"No. He's standing too far back. I can't get a clear shot. When he comes to the window, he's looking down here. He'd see me. You're going to go up there."

"But," Delvin began. "There's nothing in the saddle."

"That doesn't worry me," said Grimbolt smiling thinly again.

Delvin lifted down the saddle swallowing convulsively. Now he didn't have time to sew anything into it. The voice in his head was getting more insistent now. *'Find the saddle quickly, or it will be bad for the ladies. Do not talk to anybody. Come upstairs now.'*

As Delvin went out of the stable into the yard carrying the saddle, the voice changed slightly. *'Bring the saddle upstairs. Talk to no one.'* Delvin again resisted the temptation to look up at the window, but he was sure he was being watched as he crossed the yard.

As Delvin entered the inn, a cook came out of the kitchen. "Why are you bringing that saddle in here. Can I help you?"

Delvin smiled, said nothing and carried on. The cook took a couple of steps after him, then thought better of it and returned to the kitchen.

As Delvin climbed the stairs, he wondered what Grimbolt was planning. Was he planning anything at all? Was he right to trust him? What else could he do? And most frighteningly, what would the black magician do when he found there was nothing hidden in the saddle?

He went down the passage, took a deep breath and knocked on the door.

"Enter."

He opened the door and went in. The magician stood by the window which was now open. As Delvin came in, he moved forward.

"Give me the saddle."

The voice in Delvin's head now changed again. *'Hand over the saddle then stand still.'* Delvin handed him the saddle,

"Where have you hidden it."

Delvin turned the saddle over and desperately pointed to the seam between the padding and the leather of the seat. How was he going to get out of this? The magician was going to find out that there was nothing there. The magician looked closely at the saddle and reached for his belt knife to cut into the seam. At that moment the door flew open and Grimbolt hurled himself across the room at the magician who was taken completely by surprise. The magician was still holding the saddle and was catapulted across the room. He tripped over backwards, catching the back of his legs on the window frame. As his arms flailed, he dropped the saddle, and before anybody could move his momentum had carried him through the window. There was a moment's silence then a crash as he landed in the yard. Delvin and Grimbolt rushed to the window and looked down. The magician was lying by a cart that had been left by the inn's wall. They could not see if he was seriously hurt, but he was certainly unconscious.

"Right, we need to be quick," said Grimbolt. "We must set this up to look right."

Jarla and Maegar seemed to have snapped out of their trance.

"Grimbolt!" said Jarla looking surprised.

"Good morning Princess Jarla."

"Get me untied. How did you find us?"

Grimbolt went over to Jarla and took out his knife to begin cutting the ropes that tied her to her chair. "It wasn't difficult. There were reports of a witch on the road from North Bridge. I thought, that sounds like Princess Jarla. I just followed on. First a vampire, now a witch. I'm longing to see if you can manage a werewolf to complete the set." He turned to Delvin. "Cut Maegar free."

Delvin did as he was asked, and soon both Jarla and Maegar were free and rubbing the circulation back into their wrists. Delvin was relieved to see that the black magician's knife had only left a scratch on Maegar's cheek, although it was looking red and sore.

"We have very little time," began Grimbolt. "You three get out fast. Wait for me at Thanley. I need to make this look like a robbery."

Jarla and Maegar were about to pick up their belongings when Grimbolt stopped them.

"This must look like a robbery. Your things need to look like they've been stolen by him." Grimbolt grabbed their belongings and threw them out of the window after the magician. "Fell as he was trying to escape with the loot. If he's dead, it explains it. If he's alive he'll have some explaining to do, particularly with that body in the stables." He smiled thinly again. "Go on. Out now. Go while I get the rest of this arranged."

Delvin quickly picked up his saddle and followed Jarla and Maegar out of the room.

As Jarla and Maegar went down the stairs, Delvin dashed into his room, grabbed his things and ran down the stairs after them.

There was nobody in the yard as they ran across it.

Although the cart was hiding the magician's body, Delvin knew it would not be long before it was found. They went into the stables and saddled their horses as quickly as they could. There did not seem to be any grooms around. Delvin presumed that either Grimbolt or the black magician had dealt with them earlier. He shivered.

They mounted their horses and without a backwards look, trotted out into the yard and the road beyond.

"We need to make for the city gate as quickly as we can said Jarla.

"Are we going to Thanley?" asked Maegar.

"Yes," replied Jarla. "Grimbolt got us out, that's the least we can do. We'll get rid of him there." She turned to Delvin. "Wherever were you last night? I remember we were waiting for you..."

Delvin remembered his comfortable night and grinned to himself.

"I think I have found out where Fionella is."

Jarla's head snapped round towards him. "Where?"

"Anderal," said Delvin smugly.

"Where's that?" asked Jarla

"I don't know," said Delvin feeling slightly crestfallen.

Maegar looked at them. "It's in the foothills of the Grandents, near the River Bolla. The duke has a hunting lodge there."

"Have you been there," demanded Jarla.

"I went there once when the duke needed extra servants since he was entertaining up there. It's a horrible place, very old. It's almost like a castle."

"How do you get there?"

"You go through Dandel, and there is a turn off on the Ablet Road."

Jarla turned to Delvin. "How did you find out she was in Anderal?"

Delvin explained to her what the three palace maids had said, omitting mention of the episode with Hanny. And then told her how he had visited the haulier Endel and looked through his records.

"Right," said Jarla. "We will go to Anderal after we have dealt with Grimbolt at Thanley."

CHAPTER 25

The three rode on in silence. At the city gates, the guards seemed as disinterested as they had been on their entrance. Jarla clicked her tongue and muttered about Argent incompetence. Delvin was glad of any slackness. They didn't want to be arrested as spies.

Beyond the gate they made quick time. The sun was now well up, and there were just a few clouds in an otherwise clear sky. It was quite warm with a gentle breeze and Delvin had begun to feel more relaxed, when Jarla's voice broke in.

"What was going on at the inn?"

"Going on?" said Delvin getting his thoughts back into focus.

"Yes, what was going on? I don't seem to be able to remember anything from when we were waiting for you to come back last night, to this morning when you came to the room…Maegar and I were tied up… It's starting to come back to me now… Sheffs! We were tied up all night!"

"That man in black was from the Guild of Magicians. That's why you couldn't remember anything. He'll have used his stone to stop you remembering"

"Why were we tied up?"

"He was waiting for me to come back."

"Did that worm Magister Perball in South Bridge get a message to the Guild of Magicians that we knew the secret of the magician's stone, so they sent somebody after us? I'd have cut his liver out if he hadn't already been hung. That's all we need, having a magician after us as well."

Delvin kept quiet. He had no wish to admit that he had a magician's stone. He thanked his stars that Jarla thought it was

Magister Perball who was behind the magician following them. He wondered if it was a good time to raise something that had been worrying him since they entered Argent.

"Jarla," he began. "Do you think it might be an idea to cut your fingernails? They are rather easily recognised. You don't want to be held hostage by the Duke of Argent, and they make it easier for that magician to..." He broke off at Jarla's furious look.

"No!"

"Just a thought," said Delvin meekly. But as he rode, he manoeuvred his crystal so it touched his leg, and began to project the thought that she would slip and break her fingernails.

After riding for just over an hour, they stopped by a stream that ran under a small bridge. Next to the bridge was a well beaten path down to the stream where travellers must have regularly watered their horses. The area was shaded by trees, so that now the day was warm they could rest out of the sun while their horses grazed. They took their horses down to the stream to drink, and then sat down on a fallen log for an early lunch. Delvin was the only one who still had his saddlebags, so they all ate some of the travel rations that he carried. Delvin let Freda the rabbit out for a run and gave her some food. After a short rest, Jarla stood up.

"Right, time to go. Go and get the horses."

Delvin and Maegar went to retrieve the horses who were nibbling at a bush nearby. They heard a crash behind them and turned to see Jarla face down on the ground cursing.

"Are you alright?" asked Maegar looking concerned.

"I just tripped over a root. Sheffs! I've broken my fingernails."

Delvin looked guiltily away and made out he was busy with the horses as Maegar went to help Jarla up.

As Delvin approached with the horses, Jarla had already got her knife out and was paring back what was left of her fingernails. They were now just an ordinary length rather than the knifelike claws they had been before.

"Get mounted," said Jarla grimly. Delvin and Maegar silently did so, and soon they were back on the road to Thanley.

CHAPTER 26

They reached Thanley about two hours later. Jarla hadn't spoken a word since their stop for lunch, and she was obviously not yet in the mood for company. She turned to Delvin and Maegar as they came to the first houses.

"You two wait here outside the village for Grimbolt. I'll go and get some supplies."

"I can do it if you prefer," started Delvin, before he was quelled by a look from Jarla. He shrugged and dismounted and Maegar followed suit. They found a shady patch beneath a tree where they could watch the road, and they sat down to wait.

A short while later, just as they were about to doze off, they jumped with fright as a figure leapt out of the woods behind them.

"You are not keeping much of a watch Magister Delvin. If I'd been a robber, you would be dead by now."

"Grimbolt, you scared me half to death," gasped Delvin.

"Captain Grybald if you please. Where is Princess Jarla?"

"She's gone to get some more supplies, she told us to wait for you here."

At that moment they heard shouts from the village. Amid the general noise they could make out a hysterical female voice.

"Witch, that's the witch!"

Grimbolt snapped round. "I think we had better see what's going on. I'll get my horse."

Delvin and Maegar hardly had time to untie their horses and mount before Grimbolt was back. Together they rode their horses into the village.

The village was built around a large pond. There was a square with a cross in the centre. One side of the square was open to the pond, the other three sides were faced by houses, shops and an ancient inn.

The square was now filled with people, some arguing and gesticulating wildly, others trying to calm them down, and yet others watching to see the excitement.

In the centre was Jarla with two large men holding her arms and looking at her warily. Another man was rolling around on the ground doubled up in pain and holding his crotch. A hysterical woman was alternately trying to give the man comfort and screaming at Jarla. A fat middle-aged man, who looked as if he thought himself important, was trying to stop another almost hysterical woman from clutching at his arm. He was wearing a long black fur-trimmed gown out of which his stomach protruded. His florid face was getting redder and redder as he tried to get control of the shouting people.

"What's happening here?" Grimbolt asked one of the bystanders.

"Mistress Evingdon and Mistress Ollid have accused that woman of being a witch. Mistress Ollid's husband tried to detain her for the magistrate, and you can see what happened to him." The man grinned.

The magistrate was at last starting to get some control.

"This lady accuses you of witchcraft. Are you a witch?"

"Of course not," snapped Jarla.

"Of course she denies it," screamed Mistress Evingdon. "You didn't see her standing with her claws out over the shrunken shell of that poor soldier."

"Claws?" asked the magistrate.

"Yes, claws on her hands. Take a look."

"I can't see any claws," said the magistrate.

"Oh…She must have cut them… She had claws. She killed that poor soldier."

"The woman's hysterical," flashed Jarla. "You can't believe a word she says."

"Mistress Evingdon is a truthful woman," began the

magistrate.

"And I saw her too," screamed Mistress Ollid. "And look what she has done to my poor Anton. Burn her!... Burn her!"

"She doesn't have claws," said the magistrate doubtfully.

"Burn her!" shouted Mistress Evingdon.

"We must try her properly first," said the magistrate coming to a decision. "How do you try a witch?" he asked turning to one of the men beside him.

"I heard you tie them up and throw them in the water. If they float, they are witches. If they sink, they are not."

"That sounds simple enough," said the magistrate.

"That's absolutely ridiculous," snorted Jarla. "If a person sinks, they drown. What are you here, barbarians or idiots?"

"I say," said the magistrate. "You must have some respect for the law. Get some rope. Tie her up. We will try her in the pond."

Two men ran off to find some rope, while the air of expectation in the crowd grew. Mistress Evingdon and Mistress Ollid were still screaming at the magistrate demanding that Jarla be burned, but he was studiously ignoring them, more intent in organising how the 'trial' would take place.

Delvin turned to Grimbolt. "What do we do?"

"There's too many people to charge in and use force. We'd have the whole country up after us...we wait." He lowered his voice and whispered in Delvin's ear. "Use your crystal to have her found innocent."

Delvin touched his crystal and began projecting thoughts to the crowd that Jarla was innocent, and that Mistresses Evingdon and Ollid were either making the story up or had mistaken Jarla for someone else.

The two men had returned with a length of rope, and under the direction of the magistrate Jarla's hands and feet were tied, though not before two of the helpers had received fierce kicks.

"Right," said the magistrate. "To the pond."

The little group moved over to the edge of the pond, with Jarla being carried by three men and struggling furiously.

"I think we might have to intervene in a minute," whispered

Grimbolt.

"We could say we were temple officials," suggested Delvin. "Then take her into custody, so we can take her for trial at the temple."

"That might work," muttered Grimbolt. "Will you be able to convince them?"

"I can try," whispered Delvin.

The men had reached the edge of the pond.

"Throw her out as far as you can," ordered the magistrate importantly. "One... Two... Thee... Out!"

Jarla flew through the air and hit the water with a resounding splash. There was a gasp from the crowd, a moment's silence, then the first ripple of laughter. The pond was not as deep as the men had thought, and Jarla was sitting on the bottom of the pond, her head clear of the water. Delvin turned to Grimbolt who was laughing.

"You are enjoying this aren't you?"

"Yes," said Grimbolt. "I haven't seen anything so good for a long time."

An argument was developing between Jarla and Mistresses Evingdon and Ollid.

"You've had your idiotic trial. I've sunk. I'm sitting on the bottom. That means I'm innocent. Now free me you fools."

"That's not a proper trial. It's not deep enough. Throw her in where it's deep."

The magistrate seemed undecided.

"Time to intervene" whispered Grimbolt. "See if you can get the crowd to free her. If that fails, we'll ride in as temple officials."

Delvin began to project thoughts to the crowd that Jarla was innocent and should be freed. Voices began to be raised urging the magistrate to let her go.

The magistrate, sensing the mood of the crowd, turned to them saying importantly. "I declare that having undergone trial for witchcraft, the lady is innocent."

There was a murmur from the crowd and a few people began

to drift away and go back to what they had been doing before all the excitement.

"Will you get me out of here," yelled Jarla.

Two of the men who had thrown her in, waded into the pond grinning broadly. "No kicking or you'll stay there," said one.

Suddenly there was a clattering of hooves, and a troop of cavalry cantered into the square, pulling up sharply as the remains of the crowd parted to give them room.

"What's going on here?" demanded the troop's leader.

"We have been trying a woman accused of witchcraft," said the magistrate importantly.

"Witchcraft? Is she local?"

"No. She's a stranger."

"In that case we will take charge of her. We are bringing in any suspicious people for questioning."

"Sheffs! That's done it," swore Grimbolt.

Two of the soldiers dismounted from their horses and helped pull Jarla ashore. They had her horse brought forward and tried to get her onto it without getting too wet or muddy, or too badly kicked. It was a difficult process since she was wet and slippery and in no mood to cooperate.

"Right," said Grimbolt. "We need to find out where they are taking her. It will obvious if we follow them. They'll be going either towards Argent or North Bridge. Delvin and Maegar, take the road towards North Bridge. I'll cover the road to Argent. Ride out now and do a slow canter. If the soldiers are going that way, they'll pass you since they will be going quicker. If they haven't passed you by the time you get to the next inn. Wait for me there. If they do pass you, follow them, see where they are going, and wait for me at an inn near where they take her. Now go!"

Grimbolt turned his horse and was gone. Delvin and Maegar looked at each other, then headed out of Thanley the other way. As they left the village Maegar looked back over her shoulder to see if anyone was following. Delvin quickly told her not to, though he was very tempted to do the same thing himself. They rode on, keeping a steady pace for what seemed a long time.

There were few travellers on the road and they ignored them as they cantered along, straining their ears to hear the thump of hooves behind them. Delvin would normally have enjoyed doing a steady canter down the road, but this was no pleasure. They must somehow get Jarla back before the soldiers realised who they had captured. If they realised that, they would all be in trouble. He had just decided that the soldiers must have gone the other way when he heard the first rumblings. The noise increased, and moments later the troop of soldiers began to stream past them. Delvin kept his gaze fixed ahead, and hoped Maegar and Jarla would not give away that they knew each other. As Jarla came past, Delvin could see that her hands were tied to the saddle's pommel. She flashed a ferocious glance at Delvin, but was past before she could actually say anything.

When the soldiers were well past them, Delvin shouted to Maegar. "We need to go a bit faster." They speeded up, still slightly falling behind but managing to keep the troop in view. Soon however, the twists and turns of the road and the low hills began to block their view, and before long the soldiers were out of sight on the road ahead. Delvin realised that the troop of soldiers would soon slow down to a trot to give their horses a rest. If he and Maegar kept cantering they might bump into them round a corner. It would then look obvious that they were following them. He took a deep breath. They would have to slow down and hope the soldiers were also slowing down ahead. He shouted across to Maegar to slow to a trot, and they both reined back. The horses were breathing quite hard and it was clear that they would have had to slow down soon anyway.

Delvin kept worrying he would lose them and was tempted to go speeding after them, but he was determined to wait until the horses were properly rested. After what again seemed an age, he called across to Maegar and they started cantering again.

They passed an inn with benches set out around the lawn in front, and Delvin thought how much more pleasant it would have been sitting in the sun waiting for Grimbolt, rather than trying to follow Jarla and the troop of soldiers. He guessed they must soon be nearing the fork in the road. It was important they were not too far behind there, since they needed to know if the soldiers turned north to Dandel, or south to South Bridge. He urged Maegar on a bit faster and kept hoping the soldiers had taken a break the same length as his.

The fork came into view round the next corner and there was still no sign of the soldiers. Which way had they gone? He was tempted to send Maegar one way and take the other himself, but he decided they must stay together.

"Which way?" asked Maegar.

"We'll try the road to North Bridge," he replied grimly

They set off down the road to North Bridge, picking up speed in the hope of catching a glimpse of the soldiers. Delvin saw a farmer ahead driving a herd of cows. His dog was running back and forth, keeping the cows on the road and making sure they didn't stop to eat the grass verges. They had to rein in as they got closer.

"Did a troop of cavalry just pass this way?"

"Aye, they did. Just this minute."

"Thanks!"

Delvin felt a surge of relief that he had not lost them and manoeuvred his horse past the cows as quickly as he could. If they were only just ahead, he decided they had better not go too fast. They again trotted for a few minutes before breaking back into a steady canter.

The hedges on either side of the road made it difficult to see much. And with the road still winding between low hills it was rare they could see more than thirty paces ahead.

They slowed to a trot again, and when the horses were rested, they again began to canter. As they rounded the next corner, they came into the rear of a troop of cavalry. Delvin reined in quickly, and was about to signal to Maegar to stop when he realised to his horror that this was not the troop they had originally been following. There were too many of them, and they wore blue uniforms rather than the red ones of the other troop. His heart sank. This must be the troop that the farmer had seen, and the troop he was after must have gone north to Dandel.

The troop was moving quite slowly, and Delvin had just decided that they should turn round and try the road to Dandel when he saw that the head of the column was turning off the road into a field. A few paces further on it became apparent that the field contained a sizable camp. There were three rows of tents and long picket lines of horses. As Delvin watched the troop move into the field, he saw a movement that made him signal to Maegar to slow down. They both slowed to a sedate walk, and as their horses ambled past the camp, he saw that his first glace had not been mistaken. A figure was being bundled by two soldiers towards an old farm building that looked like it was being used as the troop's headquarters. There was a yell as the figure's foot caught someone's shin. That's Jarla, thought Delvin. They walked their horses on past the camp trying to appear unconcerned.

"We need to find an inn," said Delvin. No sooner than he had spoken, they came to an inn around the next bend. That's probably why the camp is here, thought Delvin, so the officers can visit the inn. He thought about carrying on to find an inn with less of a chance of being full of soldiers, but decided against it. All the inns on the road to North Bridge would probably have camps by them. Argent would be assembling their forces in case Hengel took North Bridge and then try to break out towards the city of Argent itself.

They rode into the inn's yard. Before handing their horses over to a stable boy, Delvin checked his rabbit Freda. She seemed to have been unaffected by the ride and sat calmly snuffling. He then removed his bundle of tricks that contained his secret cache of coins. Jarla had had her purse with her when she got captured, and Grimbolt had not offered him anything so he was going to need some money.

Having made sure their horses were properly stabled and looked after, they made their way into the inn.

The inn was an old rambling building that looked as if it had gone through many changes over the years. The roof was thatched with a row of first floor windows poking through. The walls were slightly crooked with small black-framed windows set irregularly in them.

It was only mid-afternoon, but as they entered the inn's common room, they saw that there were already several uniformed soldiers drinking by the bar.

"Magisters, how may I help you?" The plump innkeeper greeted them warmly, a large smile on his round face as he rubbed his hands together in anticipation.

"We need a room and stabling for our horses. How much would that be?"

"Is that two horses magisters?"

"It is."

"That will be one carl eight bits each." The innkeeper rubbed his hands again.

"All right," said Delvin handing over the money. "I hope that includes grain for the horses."

"Oh it does indeed magisters. I'll show you to your room." The innkeeper led the way up a dark and narrow flight of stairs, and along an even darker passage to a low door. He opened the door.

"Your room magisters."

Delvin had to duck under the low beam over the doorway, but inside the room seemed cosy and comfortable. There were two beds set against the wall to their right, and the ceiling opposite the door sloped down so that it almost met the floor. Set in the middle of the sloping ceiling was a small window that stood open to let in the air. There were also two wooden chairs and a washstand.

"Couldn't you have ordered two rooms?" grumbled Maegar as Delvin shut the door.

"That would have looked very odd," replied Delvin.

"Well don't you dare try anything."

Delvin didn't bother to answer, but went over to the window to look out. The window was one of the ones they had seen poking through the thatch and looked out on the road they had been travelling down.

"We can keep a watch for Grimbolt through the window," said Delvin. "That way we can keep out of the soldier's way."

Delvin made himself comfortable by the window while Maegar lay down on one of the beds. He thought it might be a long wait since Grimbolt would need to check all the inns on the way. After about half an hour he was starting to get bored. He had seen several farmers, two merchants and a number of soldiers, but no sign of Grimbolt. Then he suddenly pulled back from the window in fright. Riding down the road on a large black horse, all in black with his black cloak flapping in the breeze, was the magician that Delvin had last seen lying in the inn's yard in Argent. His face was bruised, he had a black eye and he was looking furious. He heard the magician dismount and open the door to the inn. Was he going to stay at the inn too? Then a voice came into his head. *'Delvin, Maegar, Jarla. Shout hello. Jump up and show yourself.'*

Delvin leapt towards the bed, and managed to fling himself over Maegar and clamp his hand over her mouth just as she opened it to shout. Maegar struggled underneath him, biting the hand pressed over her mouth and scratching at his face with her hands.

"Stop it. I'm not trying to do anything to you," whispered Delvin, desperately trying to protect himself with his one free hand. "It's the magician. The one from Argent. I think he is trying to find us by making us shout out and show we are here."

Maegar stopped struggling and Delvin whispered urgently. "I'm going to remove my hand, don't shout." He took his hand away from Maegar's mouth and sat back, ready to pounce again if she started to shout or yell.

"You filthy pig," hissed Maegar. "I've heard excuses in my time, but that beats all. If you touch me again, I'll have your eyes out. You are not going to stay in this room with me. You either get yourself another room or you sleep in the stables."

"I was not trying to do anything," insisted Delvin, now starting to get angry. "That magician has just ridden in and was trying to get us to call out to show whether or not we were here."

"Well, where is he now then?"

"I hope he is about to ride on. If he has decided to stay here, we are stuck."

Delvin sidled up to the window and glanced down. The magician's black horse was still tied to a fence in front of the inn.

"His horse is still out at the front." Maegar came up to the window and looked out. Delvin pulled her back.

"Don't stand too close to the window, he might see you."

"Get your hands off me."

"Well stand back then…He's coming out. Don't let him see you."

They both peered cautiously out of the window. The magician strode to his horse, untied it, mounted and turned towards North Bridge.

"All right, so he was here," said Maegar reluctantly. Delvin looked back up the road in the other direction.

"Oh sheffs!" he swore. Grimbolt was coming down the road.

Maegar had seen him too. "Can we stop him?" she whispered anxiously.

Delvin leaned out of the window holding a hand in front of him in a stop gesture, hoping Grimbolt would see it and hoping the magician would not turn and look back. To Delvin's relief, Grimbolt reined in his horse looking quizzically up at the inn.

Delvin looked back towards the magician to see if he was out of sight and a chill went down is spine. A beggar by the roadside had tried to approach him. The magician had stopped his horse and was looking down at the beggar. The beggar was clutching his throat and then began to stagger this way and that. His face became red, his eyes staring, and even from the distance away that Delvin was, he could hear the gurgle as the man desperately tried to breath. He fell to his knees, mouth wide, swollen tongue hanging out, then pitched forward with a final desperate gurgle. The black magician looked up from the now still body and proceeded down the road.

Shaken, Delvin pulled himself back into the room and turned to Maegar. "I'll go down and check if the coast is clear for

Grimbolt."

Maegar simply nodded as Delvin slipped out of the room and down the stairs. He didn't use the inn's front door, since he couldn't creep carefully out of that without drawing attention to himself from the soldiers in the bar. He went through the kitchen door into the stable yard and then moved round the side of the building. As he came out to the road he looked carefully out in the direction of North Bridge. There was no longer any sign of the magician. He breathed a sigh of relief and turned towards Grimbolt who was sitting patiently on his horse twenty paces up the road. He beckoned to Grimbolt to come forward.

As Grimbolt drew level he looked down. "What was that all about Master Delvin."

Delvin explained quickly about the magician and Grimbolt nodded his bald head.

"You said the message he projected, was for you, Maegar and Jarla to shout out and show yourselves. That means he doesn't know Princess Jarla has been captured and he is looking for three people. Good. If he had asked if two men and a woman were staying here, he would have been told they weren't. That gives us some time. Do you know where Princess Jarla is?"

"I think she is being held in the old farm building in the camp up the road."

As Grimbolt dismounted and led his horse through to the stables, Delvin began to recount his trip and how they had tried to follow the soldiers without being seen. Grimbolt waved him to silence.

"Finish upstairs. Too many ears."

When Grimbolt was satisfied that his horse was being properly looked after, they made their way back into the inn and up to their room.

"Good afternoon Mistress Maegar."

"Good afternoon Captain Grybald."

Grimbolt smiled at the use of his correct name.

"Right. Tell me what happened." Delvin and Maegar recounted the details of their chase from Thanley while Grimbolt listened intently. When they had finished, he smiled.

"You did well. We'll have to try to get her out tonight. We'll go in after they have gone to sleep. We'll see what time the soldiers here go back to the camp then give it another hour or two."

"You can't leave her there all that time," said Maegar looking shocked. "You don't know what they might do to her."

"We can't ride into a fully armed camp in broad daylight. It will be difficult enough when they are asleep."

"You are a magician. Can't you make yourself invisible or something?"

"Invisible. That would be very difficult even for a magician to do," said Delvin. But as he said it, his mind began to race as he started to think of the possibilities. Even with his stone, getting people to look the other way would not be easy and he suspected someone would notice them before they had got very far.

"It may be difficult, but can you do it?" persisted Maegar.

"Let me think," said Delvin… In a magic trick, if he was trying to stop the audience from seeing something, he would try to disguise it as something else and misdirect them so they would look the other way. Could he do that here, so they would in effect become invisible? What could they be disguised as, and how could he misdirect the soldiers? Having his stone, he might just be able to do it. He just might be able to make them invisible.

CHAPTER 27

Delvin and Grimbolt walked towards the camp. They had left Maegar back at the inn. After they had gone a few paces beyond the inn, Delvin nodded to Grimbolt who nodded back. It was time to start.

First the misdirection thought Delvin. He must make sure that the soldiers in the camp were preoccupied when they got there. He touched his stone and began to project his thoughts very tightly towards the camp. He projected the noises of battle. First very faint and in the distance, with shouts, screams and the clash of steel. Then gradually louder, as if it was coming closer. He held it there as they continued down the road towards the camp.

As they rounded the last corner and the camp came into view, the effect of his projection became evident. The camp was in turmoil. The cavalry were mounting their horses and forming up, and a detachment of infantry were already marching towards the entrance.

In the field on the other side of the road from the camp several cows grazed contentedly. Delvin and Grimbolt went up to the field's gate, and Delvin projected the thought to the cows that there was a field of really lush juicy grass on the other side of the road. He was careful not to use words. Back in the inn at Shappley, it had been feelings that had worked with the dog, not words. The cows began to walk towards the gate. Delvin and Grimbolt leaned on the gate sucking straws, watching the turmoil in the camp and the infantry marching out. Delvin began to project the thought that he and Grimbolt were farmers that everyone had seen before.

They were ready. They had their misdirection. They had their disguise. Could they walk invisibly into the camp? A cow nudged Delvin's back. It wanted the lush grass over the road.

Delvin undid the gate, and together with the cows he and Grimbolt ambled over the road into the camp. All the time Delvin continued to project the noises of battle to the soldiers, being careful not to project too far afield in case the magician in black was to pick it up.

The guards on the gate were so intent on what was happening that they hardly looked at them, except to tell them to get the cows out of the way. The infantry were now in the road and the first troop of cavalry was trying to get past them with much shouting and cursing.

Delvin and Grimbolt walked up to the old stone farm building. It now looked deserted as the soldiers tried to join the battle that they thought was taking place down the road. As they reached the side door, they glanced quickly around to make sure they were not being observed and slipped inside. They were in a short passageway leading into a hall. With Grimbolt leading the way, they moved silently down the passageway into the hall. Grimbolt stopped suddenly and stepped back a pace. Then crept carefully forward again. Outside one of the doors leading off the hall, a figure was slumped. Grimbolt moved cautiously forward and gave it a push. The figure rolled over and lay in a growing pool of blood. It was a dead guard with his throat cut.

Grimbolt opened the door behind the guard and crept carefully in. Inside was another still figure. This one had his belt undone and his breeches around his knees.

"Good girl," whispered Grimbolt.

"What's that?"

"She's learnt the lesson well. Wait till his hands are occupied undoing his belt then hit him in the throat. Then when his hands come up to protect his throat, knee him where it hurts. Finished him off with his own knife by the looks of it."

Delvin felt sick.

"Come on," said Grimbolt. "She's done really well... Right, back to the hall, we need to follow where she has gone."

They stepped over the dead figure outside the door and went back into the hall. Grimbolt tried the first two doors, but no one was there. The third door led into the kitchen where they could see a third body, bleeding freely, lying slumped under the table.

"Good girl, taken from the back by surprise," whispered Grimbolt again.

"You sound as though you approve," said Delvin feeling even worse.

"Of course I do. I taught her."

"You taught her to do this?" said Delvin stunned.

"I was her tutor for two years. She grew out of her previous one." He grinned maliciously, then looked sharply at Delvin. "What did you expect her to do, lie back and be raped?"

Delvin couldn't think of an answer, but followed Grimbolt as he slowly opened the kitchen door and looked out into the yard beyond. The yard was quiet. Then Delvin saw another body lying in the shadows. Grimbolt had seen it too."

"She went that way."

They crossed to the body. There was a small door behind it leading from the yard. They opened the door carefully and peered through. The farm building was at the edge of the camp, and the door led out to a wood that lay behind the yard.

"She's gone into the woods. Good girl."

They crossed the short distance to the trees and began to make their way deeper into the wood, when a familiar voice hissed, "About time too."

"Good afternoon Princess Jarla, are you alright?"

"Yes Grimbolt, but no thanks to you."

"Captain Grybald if you please."

"What's going on, is there a battle?"

"No Princess. Just a diversion. They'll all start coming back soon, so we had better find somewhere to hide. When they find those bodies they'll come looking for you. Delvin, can you get those cows back in the field?"

"I'll try," Delvin replied.

As Grimbolt had been talking, Jarla had stepped into view from behind a large tree. Delvin was shocked by her appearance. Her arms and front were covered in blood, her lips were swollen, and one eye was partly closed by what looked to be the beginnings of a black eye. Together with her matted black hair and muddy torn clothes, she somehow looked very young and vulnerable, more like a street urchin than a princess.

"We need to find a stream. You can't go into the inn looking like that," said Grimbolt, leading the way deeper into the wood.

As they moved away from the camp, Delvin projected thoughts back to the cows that the lush grass was now in the field they had just left. He hoped it would work. If the cows were back in their field there would be nothing to show they had been there.

They did not find a stream, but they did find a small pond in the wood and Jarla was able to wash the blood and the worst of the mud off herself. They then changed direction and began to head back towards the road. Grimbolt did not want to hide in the wood, since that was where the trail of bodies led and would be the first place to be searched. They reached the road out of sight of the camp, and crossed to the other side which was bordered by a dry-stone wall. A little way to their right was a small copse with a hedge running away from it forming the boundary of a large field.

"That will do," said Grimbolt leading the way into the copse. There was a small depression in the centre of it, bordered by a fallen tree trunk and some bushes. Grimbolt gathered some branches and undergrowth and led them into the depression, where he told them to lie down. He then placed the branches and undergrowth over them. He turned to Delvin.

"Is this good enough for you to make sure they can't see us?"

"It should do," he replied.

"That's not going to stop them," said Jarla looking annoyed. "After they've checked the wood, they'll look here, and those few sticks won't stop them seeing us,"

"I think it will Princess Jarla." But before Jarla could retort they heard the sound of soldiers, and Grimbolt signalled silence. Delvin touched his stone and began to project the idea that there was just a pile of rubbish under the branches, while all three held their breath.

"I don't think she can have got this far," said a voice.

"We need to check." Two soldiers climbed the wall, one walking down the field, the other making his way towards the copse.

"I can't see anything."

"I'll just check over here." The soldier came over to the copse and looked around as Delvin continued projecting the thought that just rubbish lay under the branches.

"Nothing here."

"Whatever happened to her?"

"Someone said she was a witch."

"Witches don't cut people's throats and we would have found her."

"Unless she changed herself into something."

"That's werewolves that do that."

"You don't think she was do you?"

"You've done it," whispered Grimbolt grinning as the voices faded away. "The full set. Vampire, witch and werewolf."

Jarla scowled at him.

CHAPTER 28

They waited in the depression until it was dark. During the first hour they several times heard the sound of soldiers searching, but after that they just heard the occasional traveller on the road. Eventually Grimbolt stood up pulling the branches away from them.

"Time for us to get back to the inn."

Delvin and Jarla stood up as well and stretched their stiff legs. It was starting to get chilly and Jarla was looking cold, never having got dry from her ducking earlier. They climbed back over the dry-stone wall onto the road, and carefully made their way back towards the camp and the inn, with Delvin continually projecting thoughts that they were just three farm labourers.

When they reached the camp, all seemed quiet again. There was a row of camp fires between the tents, and they could see soldiers sitting around them. Delvin saw the guard at the entrance, and projected the thought to him that someone on the far side of the camp had a very pretty girl with him whose dress had come undone. As they walked by, the guard stared across the camp away from the road.

When they were past, they all felt easier and a short while later the inn came in sight.

"Delvin, take Princess Jarla in the back entrance up to the room. I'm going in the front to book a room for myself. That will keep the landlord busy while you get up there. I'll then go into the common room and order my meal. You and Maegar can come down when you are ready. Princess Jarla, we'll have to sneak your food up to you. If the soldiers in the bar see you, they'll have a fit. All right everyone?" They nodded in agreement.

When they reached the inn, Delvin and Jarla made their way round the side of the building, and Delvin led the way through the side door up to the room. A maid was coming out of the kitchen as they went past. Delvin touched his stone and projected the thought that she was seeing two guards going upstairs to their rooms. When he reached the room, he knocked on the door.

"Come in," called Maegar.

As they entered, Maegar jumped off the bed and came towards them. "Where have you been? I was so worried. I thought you had been caught and they would be coming for me. Jarla whatever has happened? Come over here into the light and let me see."

Delvin quickly explained what had happened, while Maegar sat Jarla down by the washstand, and by the light of the room's candles began to help her get cleaned up.

"I'll come down and join you in the common room when I've got Jarla organised and into bed. She's freezing cold. What were you doing letting her sit around in wet clothes like that?"

Delvin thought better of saying it was either that or being captured by the soldiers. He let himself out of the room and made his way downstairs and into the common room.

Grimbolt was already there, sitting at a table by the wall with a tankard of ale in front of him. There was a group of soldiers by the bar, and some of the other tables were occupied by locals and travellers. Despite it being early summer, a fire burned in the grate that gave the room a flickering light that augmented the candles on the tables.

Delvin made his way over to Grimbolt's table and sat down.

"Maegar will be down soon, she's helping Jarla get fixed up."

Grimbolt nodded. "I've got myself a room. You'll share with me. They can have your room."

A serving girl came over and Delvin ordered a tankard of ale.

Grimbolt looked across to the soldiers and smiled. "She's stirred up a hornet's nest there, There's talk about witchcraft, werewolves the lot."

"Well, I hope it doesn't spread," replied Delvin with feeling. "Or we'll get that black magician back again. Do you know anything about the Guild of Magicians?"

Grimbolt sat back reflectively. "I know the duke is worried about their power and influence. They have their own country, Norden, north of Argent. Very few people live up there now. There used to be diamond mines up there, but they closed about forty years ago. It's really just a long peninsular and a row of islands stretching out north of the Gulf of Ablet. It acts like a reef with the winds and currents of the Northern Ocean blowing up against it. They say there can be huge waves on one side of the peninsular with calm waters on the other. Very few people go there since there is only rocks and grass. There are no big cities. Rostin is the only town, and that's quite small. It has a fishing harbour and the magician's castle but not much else. Otherwise, there's just a few hamlets. When I was a boy, that land used to be part of Argent and there wasn't a Guild of Magicians, just a few travelling conjurers. Then magicians who said they belonged to the Guild started to appear in the big cities, and they started to do rather well. About ten years ago, the Courts in every country received a declaration that the northern part of Argent was now an independent state that they called Norden. We all waited for the Duke of Argent to march an army up there and hang the lot of them. But it didn't seem to happen. There were people in Argent who said something must be done. But then that stopped." Grimbolt sat back thinking. "I bet they used their stones to shut them up. Anyway, after that they started investing in all sorts of things, which usually seemed to work out well for them." He sat back looking reflectively into his beer. "I wonder if they used their stones to make sure their investments went well... So that's the position. They have their own country that few people go to, and I don't think those who do go are really welcome... And they are starting to become something of a problem. And now there's this war with Argent that they seem to be involved in." He looked at Delvin. "I don't really know if I should be telling you all this since you are a magician too."

Delvin smiled. "Though not a member of the Guild."

"True," said Grimbolt. "That makes you rather unique."

At that moment Maegar appeared in the doorway and Delvin beckoned her over.

"How is she?" he whispered.

"She'll be all right, just tired and cold."

The serving girl came over and Grimbolt ordered another round of ale and cold meat and bread for the three of them. Delvin would have liked the broth that he could see someone at the next table eating, but he couldn't think how he could smuggle it up to Jarla without it looking obvious.

The cold meat turned out to be ham and beef and each of them had a small loaf of bread. Grimbolt took one of the loaves, split it in half, filled it with meat and put it out of sight. They then tucked in to the remainder.

"What happens tomorrow?" asked Maegar.

"I shall be taking you back to Hengel," replied Grimbolt. "My orders were to bring Princess Fionella back, which now means you." He looked at Maegar. "With if possible, Princess Jarla and the magician Delvin."

"What about the real Fionella? Jarla is trying to find her to get this war stopped."

"You can't have a royal princess dashing around a country that we are at war with. Now that we hold the bridge at South Bridge, Argent will agree to peace. There is no need to find Princess Fionella."

"I don't know about that," said Delvin. "This whole war was a set up. If they agree to peace, it will just be to gain time before they make another attempt."

"That's as maybe," said Grimbolt. "But I have my orders." They fell silent as they finished their meal. Delvin was depressed at the prospect of returning before they had accomplished what they had set out to do.

Maegar drank the last of her ale. "Give me the bread and meat. I'll take it up to Jarla and see you in the morning."

Grimbolt gave her the loaf and she got up and left to go upstairs.

"Well Magister Delvin, we had better stay down here a bit longer. We might pick up a bit more information. Do you play cards?"

"A bit," replied Delvin, thinking that he did not so much play cards as use them for card tricks.

"Good," said Grimbolt taking a pack from his pocket. "We won't play for money since you claim you haven't got any. Though I do wonder how you booked your room without any money." He smiled his thin lopsided smile and Delvin blushed. Grimbolt dealt the cards and they began to play. Grimbolt was obviously an experienced player and he was soon well in the lead.

"I think you are too good for me Grimbolt," said Delvin looking at the pile of points that Grimbolt has amassed.

"Captain Grybald, if you please Magister Delvin. It's just beginner's luck. You'll start winning soon."

As they were not playing for money, Delvin wondered if he could use some of his card slights to help him. He nicked the edge of one of the cards to help him notice it from the back when it came up again. But the more he tried cheating, the more he seemed to lose. By now he had made nicks on several cards. At last the cards seemed to have fallen right for him. He had an excellent hand, and from the nicks on Grimbolt's cards, he knew that Grimbolt had a good hand too, but not as good as his. Now he would get him, he thought. He bet a large imaginary sum. Grimbolt replied doubling it. Delvin doubled again. He would get back all his losses. Even if they were playing for imaginary sums and not real money, Delvin hated the idea of losing. Grimbolt doubled once more and saw him. When they displayed their cards Delvin's mouth fell open. The cards Grimbolt held were not those Delvin had thought. Delvin had lost again and Grimbolt sat back in his chair grinning.

"I enjoyed that. The trouble with cheating Magister Delvin is that I am an even better cheat than you are," he laughed.

"I wish I knew how you did it, Captain Grybald. I thought I was good with cards, but I can't touch you." They both laughed.

CHAPTER 29

Delvin woke at dawn. There was only one bed in Grimbolt's room, so Delvin had made himself as comfortable as he could on the floor. As he stretched his stiff limbs, he saw that Grimbolt was already up and shaving himself at the washstand.

"Good morning Magister Delvin."

"Good morning Captain Grybald."

"When you are shaved, we'll wake the ladies. If we make an early start, we can be in Hengel by nightfall."

Delvin didn't reply. He thought he would to wait to hear what Jarla had to say. Although he would like to go back, he also wanted to complete what they had begun.

Delvin shaved and straightened his clothes, and then they made their way along to the other room. Grimbolt knocked on the door calling out, "Good morning ladies. Time to rise."

"Come in, we are already up," came the reply. Grimbolt opened the door and they went in. Jarla and Maegar were both dressed and Maegar was packing away the last of her things. Jarla was looking much better, though her clothes looked rather the worst for wear. She glanced at Grimbolt.

"Maegar tells me you intend to take us back to Hengel."

"That's right Princess Jarla. My orders are to take Princess Fionella, which now means Maegar, back to Hengel. And we can't have royal princesses dashing around a country we are at war with."

"Do you realise what we are trying to do here? We are trying to stop this idiotic war. Take Maegar back by all means. But I will not be coming with you. Good as you are, even you would not be able to smuggle three people, two of them refusing to go with you, through enemy territory and back to Hengel."

"Magister Delvin, will you come with me back to Hengel?" asked Grimbolt.

"I'm sorry Captain Grybald. I think we should finish what we set out to do."

Jarla gave Delvin a brief smile. "Delvin and I will stay, Grimbolt. We will need two horses, so you and Maegar will need to share one, unless you can buy or hire one here."

"I have my orders Princess Jarla."

"Your orders are I believe, to return Princess Fionella to Hengel, and if possible, Delvin and I. Well in the case of Delvin and I, it is not possible. So you will be obeying your orders."

"You will be the death of me Princess Jarla. All right... Magister Delvin, you look after her. Make sure she doesn't do anything too stupid."

"I do not need looking after," snapped Jarla. "Right. Breakfast, then we need to get going."

They ate a hurried breakfast. Grimbolt bringing Jarla's breakfast up to the room while Delvin gave his rabbit her morning feed. Then Delvin and Jarla saddled their horses and set off on the road to Dandel. Grimbolt had given Jarla some coin since she had lost her purse when she was captured.

As they passed the soldier's camp, Delvin projected the thought that a merchant and his lady were riding by. But he hardly needed to have bothered since no one in the camp paid them any attention.

They rode on through the early morning. When they reached the fork, where previously they had turned left to Argent, they now bore right on the road to Dandel. The low hills and undulating countryside gradually gave way to flatter land. The farms were now given over to wheat, and the green stems of the growing crops stretched away in neat fields in all directions. There were farms and small communities dotted between the fields, with an occasional windmill where an enterprising man had decided the wheat should be ground near where it was grown.

Before long they were able to see the town of Dandel in the distance, rising up from the green fields all around. As they approached, they could make out more details. Although Dandel had a wall surrounding it, it was a much smaller town than North Bridge and South Bridge. Its wall was quite low, and there were no towers at regular intervals like those that protected the walls of larger towns. Its only tower was its gatehouse, which was a square construction with a pitched roof. It looked more like a tall house with an arch going through it than a defensive tower. As they came to the gate, they found that the local watch was as rudimentary as the defences. An elderly man in a worn and patched uniform chatted amiably with the travellers passing through. He obviously knew most of them, greeting them as friends, and when Delvin and Jarla approached, he smiled jovially at them.

"Good day my friends. Where are you headed?"

"To the North," replied Jarla.

"Have a good journey." And they were through.

Dandel itself was a town of mainly undistinguished buildings. There were a few inns to cater for passing travellers, but its main feature and reason for its existence, was its bridge over the River Bolla. Dandel was the first point where the Bolla could be crossed as it flowed sluggishly across the plain, and a bridge had existed there for centuries. The original bridge had gradually grown more elaborate over the ages, with bits being added to it until the present structure had finally evolved. The bridge was wide, two carts could pass abreast on it, and several buildings had been erected on the bridge itself. There were a number of shops, and in the centre of the bridge there was a large inn, The Royal Bridge, which arched over the road and overhung the river on either side.

Delvin looked up in interest as they rode over the bridge and under the inn, but they did not have time to stop and admire. They continued on and out through the Northern gate, which again was watched over by a man who looked as if he was long retired from more strenuous work.

As they left the town behind, Jarla turned to Delvin.

"This is the Ablet Road. Maegar said you turn off this road towards the Grandents. Keep your eyes open."

The first two lanes leading off the road led to small hamlets. One track looked promising, so they set off down it, only to find after about ten minutes that it only led to a mill. It was past midday, so they stopped in the shade of some trees to rest, eat some travel rations and water the horses at a nearby stream.

"Do you think we should ask someone where Anderal is?" Asked Delvin.

"No. We must not leave any clues we are looking for it. We'll find it," replied Jarla.

After only a brief stop, they remounted and continued on. After one more false trail, this time leading to a small cluster of houses hidden from the road by a small wood, they came to another road leading off into the distance.

"We'll try this one, I can't see where it goes," said Jarla.

"Probably another mill, we haven't seen one for a while," replied Delvin, turning his horse after Jarla's down the lane. After five minutes they could see a farm ahead, hidden from the road by a shallow depression.

"Looks like a farm, we'll try the next one." Jarla began to turn her horse,

"Hold on, I think the road continues on past the farm," called Delvin.

Jarla turned back and peered ahead. "We'll check it."

As they rode on, they saw the road did indeed continue past the farm and wind its way towards the Grandent mountains, looming in the distance. They passed two more farms and went over a narrow bridge, all the time expecting the road to end and to find themselves retracing their steps.

The mountains grew closer and the flat plain began to give way to low hills. There was the occasional small farmhouse. The wide green expanses of wheat were replaced by sheep in small fields, bounded by dry stone walls, some with large boulders rearing up out of the grass.

They came to a fast-flowing river running through a narrow gorge. A substantial stone bridge had been built over it, taking the road ever closer to the mountains. Delvin and Jarla looked at each other, knowing that such a bridge would only have been built if the road led to somewhere important. They crossed the bridge and the landscape began to change, with rocks, trees and patches of stubby grass. As the hills grew steeper and the trees thicker the lane wound this way and that, gradually climbing higher into the foothills of the mountains.

They had been traveling down the road for over two hours, and had long since left behind the farms and other signs of habitation, when they saw ahead, between the trees and rocks, what at first looked like a castle.

"That must be Anderal," said Jarla." We had better keep of sight."

They guided their horses off the road and found a spot of grass sheltered from view by huge rocks. After checking the spot could not be seen from the road, they dismounted and tethered the horses where they would have plenty of grass to eat. They then carefully made their way through the rocks and trees towards Anderal.

When they got closer, they could see Anderal more clearly. There was one very old square tower with a corner turret, narrow arrow slits and crenellations that had obviously been built for defence. The rest of Anderal had wide windows and the battlements were ornamental. It was built as a square with the old tower at one corner, and the lower, more recent buildings, surrounding a small courtyard in the centre. The lane they had been following wound up to it and entered the courtyard through an arch, now blocked by a massive and closed door.

"What do we do now?" asked Delvin.

"We need to find out where Fionella is being held," replied Jarla. "I can see two sides from here. You make your way round to the other side and keep watch from there. If you see Fionella, see where she goes then re-join me here. If you don't see her, come back at sundown."

Delvin nodded and carefully made his way round to the other side of the building. It took him some time, since he needed to keep out of sight, and the ground was rocky with steep slopes and small ravines, much of it covered in dense forest. He eventually found himself a good vantage point at the top of a small cliff where he could see the far side of Anderal, and he set himself down to watch. He was well above the highest of the lower buildings, and so could look down over them and see part of the courtyard below. An occasional soldier or servant crossed the courtyard, but apart from that, the building was quiet. He peered at the windows, but the rooms inside were dark, and he doubted he would see anybody unless they put their face right up to the glass. He watched the building for well over an hour. No one left, and no one came up the road towards it.

Just as he was starting to get bored, the door in the corner turret of the old tower opened, and a figure in a blue dress with long blond hair came out onto the battlements. Delvin was suddenly all attention. The figure walked backwards and forwards several times, before finally looking all around, and then going back through the door and out of sight.

Delvin waited breathlessly to see if there would be any further sign of her, but there was nothing. After ten minutes he decided to make his way back to Jarla, who must also have seen her on top of the tower.

"Where have you been?" demanded Jarla when he eventually got back to her.

"I was waiting to see if I could see where she went."

"And did you?"

"No. She's either still in the tower, or has gone somewhere out of sight of where I could see."

"Right. So we know she is in there. Now we need to get her out."

"How are you going to do that?" asked Delvin.

"You could knock on the door as a travelling magician," mused Jarla.

"Out here in the middle of nowhere?" replied Delvin. "They'd realise something was up instantly."

"I wonder if she ever goes outside the gates. That would give us a chance to get to her."

"Do you really think she'll just go out for a walk? I think the duke is holding her here. That gate would be open otherwise."

"Right. We have to break in then," said Jarla decisively.

Together they looked dubiously at Anderal. The windows may have looked wide, but they were high up from the ground. And even if they could have climbed up, which Delvin doubted, the windows had stone tracery, and the gaps between them looked too narrow to squeeze through.

It was now starting to get dark, and glows began to appear from some of the windows as candles and torches were lit. As they looked at the top of the old tower, a glow appeared through the arrow slits.

"Whatever way we manage to get in," said Jarla, nodding towards the tower. "That's the place to start looking for her."

"I have an idea," said Delvin suddenly grinning.

CHAPTER 30

It was well past midnight, and as they stood beside the main gate in the dark, Delvin and Jarla hoped that most of Anderal would be asleep. Freda the rabbit's travelling box lay open on the ground at Delvin's feet, and he held a branch in his hand.

"Right. Let's try it," whispered Jarla.

Delvin began to scratch the big gate with the branch, using small jerky movements, so that he hoped it would sound like an animal trying to get in. At the same time, he touched his stone and projected a thought to the gatekeeper that there was a dog outside, and that he should open the gate to let it in.

After a few moments, Delvin heard the bolt scrape back and the gate began to open. Delvin immediately projected the feeling to Freda the rabbit, that there was some lovely grass just where the gate was opening. Freda lolloped happily along towards it.

"Sheffs, it's a rabbit. I thought you were a dog. Come here."

The rabbit lolloped a few paces further away from the gate. As the guard stepped out after the rabbit, Jarla took one step forward and hit him over the back of his head with a stone. The guard fell where he had stood.

"You've trained it well."

"I need to for some of my tricks," dissembled Delvin as he scooped Freda up and put her back into her travelling box.

Jarla checked the guard and expertly tied his hands and feet. She stuffed an old rag into his mouth which she bound round with another piece of cloth to keep it in place and to stop him crying out when he came to.

They passed through the gate and shut it behind them. In the pale moonlight, they made their way across the courtyard to the old tower in the corner. A faint flickering glow came from the arrow slits near the top.

At the base of the tower was an iron-studded door. On trying the round ring-handle, Delvin was relieved to find it was not locked. he pushed it open as gently as he could, but the squeak of the hinges made him catch his breath and listen in case it had roused anyone. Inside it seemed pitch black. It was only when the door was fully open and a little moonlight shone in, that they were able to see a spiral staircase leading upwards in the far corner of the room.

They shut the door behind them in case anyone awoke and investigated why it was open, and carefully felt their way across the room to the stairs. Delvin heard Jarla strike her shin on something and stifle an exclamation. On reaching the stairs, Jarla led the way upwards. After what seemed a long climb in the dark, Delvin noticed a flickering glow ahead. Jarla had seen it too and was moving even more carefully.

As the stairs came round the next bend, they could see the entrance to the tower's top floor. A short passage led off the stairway, lit by a torch set in a sconce on the wall. A guard stood outside two doors that led off the passage.

Jarla pulled back quickly when she saw the guard and signalled to Delvin. He opened his rabbit box, and Freda hopped up the stairs as Delvin projected his thoughts to her.

"Sheffs, what are you doing up her?" they heard the guard exclaim.

They could hear the guard moving towards the stairs, and Delvin sent the idea to Freda that she should continue on up the spiral stairs.

The guard came through the stair's entrance, his gaze following the rabbit as she hopped up towards the battlements above. He was concentrating on the rabbit, looking up the spiral stairs and so had his back to Jarla, who struck him on the back of his head with her stone. The guard fell back, and Delvin only just caught him and saved him from crashing down the stairs to the floors below. Together with Jarla, he hauled him back to the passageway, where Jarla tied and gagged him while Delvin retrieved Freda, who by this time had reached the roof.

Delvin looked at Jarla who took a deep breath whispering, "We'll try this door first." Jarla opened the door as quietly as she could. It was dark in the room, the only light coming from the torch in the passage behind them.

"Bring the torch," whispered Jarla.

Delvin took the torch from the sconce and followed Jarla into the room. The room was richly furnished with tapestries on the walls and rugs on the floor. A large canopied bed occupied one wall with another wall taken up by an elaborate wardrobe. In the bed lay a sleeping figure, her blond hair, glowing in the torchlight, was spread on the pillow on either side of her head. She looked remarkably like Maegar had done before Jarla had cut her hair, and in the soft light with her face relaxed by sleep, she looked very young.

"Is that Fionella?" whispered Delvin.

"I think so."

Jarla moved over to the bed, and had just put her hand on Fionella's shoulder, when a door connecting to the next room burst open.

"What are you doing to my daughter?" hissed a grey-haired bearded man striding into the room. "Let go of her at once!"

"Father," said the girl waking in alarm. "What's going on?"

"That is what I intend to find out," said the man. "What the sheffs are you doing here?"

Delvin was struck dumb with horror. Maybe this wasn't Anderal after all. Jarla too seemed shocked to silence. Her face white as she stared at the man.

"I think there may have been a mistake sir," mumbled Delvin, desperately trying to think of an excuse for being in this girl's bedroom.

"You are right there has been a mistake," growled the man. "Firstly, I am not sir, I am 'Your Grace'. Secondly, the penalty for raping the Duke of Argent's daughter is death."

The words Delvin was going to say died in his throat. They

were at Anderal, but the Duke of Argent was here too. He must have taken a break after the battle on the bridge to come and see his daughter.

"We are not trying to rape your daughter, Your Grace," said Jarla, finding her voice at last.

"And who might you be?"

"We thought your daughter was in trouble."

"I said, who are you?"

Jarla hesitated and Delvin closed his eyes. If Jarla told him who she was, he would think they had come to kidnap or kill Fionella. After all, the duke had set up the war with Hengel on the excuse that Hengel had kidnapped her. And what a bargaining pawn Jarla would make.

"I am the Princess Jarla of Hengel." Delvin's legs seemed to turn to jelly.

"You are what?" He stepped closer and peered at her in the flickering light, his beard sticking out belligerently. "Sheffs, you are... And what may I ask are you doing here?"

"It's a long story Your Grace."

"I am all ears." He folded his arms across his stout chest and fixed her with his eyes.

"When you declared war on Hengel..."

"When I declared war?" The duke's eyes seemed to almost pop out of his head, and his chest expanded as he sucked in a deep breath. Delvin could see his face turning red.

"Yes, Your Grace," continued Jarla. "When you declared war on Hengel..."

"I did not declare war on Hengel!"

"You... I am sorry Your Grace, when Argent declared war on Hengel..."

"Whatever are you saying," exploded the duke. "Is there a war between Argent and Hengel?"

Jarla suddenly looked puzzled.

"You don't know there is a war between Argent and Hengel?" Then realisation hit her. "Are you and Princess Fionella being held captive Your Grace?"

"Of course we are. Whatever do you think we are doing here, and what may I ask is this war being fought over?" asked the duke very deliberately.

"You accused… Someone accused Hengel of kidnapping your daughter the Princess Fionella when she came on a visit to Hengel. I was hoping to bring her back to show that she hadn't been kidnapped, and so stop the war."

"So that's what they are up to." The duke turned away and paced across the room. He turned back to Jarla.

"How did you get in here?"

"We broke in, Your Grace."

"And the guards?"

"They are tied up, Your Grace."

"So you can get out again?"

"Yes, Your Grace."

He turned to his daughter who was sitting up in bed.

"Fionella, get dressed as quickly as you can."

"You," he pointed to Delvin. "Come with me and help me get dressed too." He turned to Jarla. "We must get this stopped." He spun on his heel and strode back to the other room with Delvin following behind.

The duke's room was even more richly decorated than Fionella's had been. In the flickering light of a single candle, massive pieces of ornate furniture cast grotesque shadows across the room which was dominated by a huge bed surmounted by an enormous carved crown.

Delvin was still trying to catch up with what had happened.

"Do you know who is holding you captive, Your Grace."

"I haven't the slightest idea. I can't remember a single thing about how I got here."

It must be the magicians thought Delvin. They must have kidnapped the duke and princess. They had certainly substituted Maegar for Fionella. Maybe they had done the same with the duke, and either their nominee, or more likely a magician, was acting as the Duke of Argent.

The duke had got an ornate gown out of the wardrobe and was

about to put it on.

"Your Grace," began Delvin. "I suggest you wear plain riding clothes. A gown as splendid as that will stand out, and we need to get you away from here without people noticing. Perhaps you could bring that with you for when you are restored to your position."

"Is that why Princess Jarla looks like that?" said the duke turning to Delvin.

"Partly Your Grace, but she also had a slight accident."

The duke turned back to his wardrobe and removed some leather riding breeches and a coat. They were far better quality than those worn by any but the highest nobility, but thought Delvin, they were probably the plainest things the duke possessed.

When the duke was dressed with his other clothes and essential items packed in a small bag, they returned to the other room.

Jarla, like Delvin, must have insisted that Fionella wear riding gear, since she was dressed in breeches and a jacket, very fashionably cut and made from a pale grey cloth, but hopefully not instantly recognisable as being the clothes of a princess. Jarla was just finishing tying Fionella's hair back so that it could fit under a cap.

"Are you ready my dear?" asked the duke.

"Yes father," Fionella picked up a small bag similar to the duke's.

The duke nodded to Jarla, "Lead the way."

They crept out of the room. Jarla insisting that they return the torch to the sconce, since the light of a torch moving down the stairs and across the courtyard would arouse suspicion.

As they stepped over the guard in the passage, Fionella deliberately trod on his hand. Jarla raised an eyebrow.

"I didn't like him. He said nasty things to me."

Without the torch to light the way, they had to step very carefully down the stairs, with one hand on the wall and feeling for each step with their feet. They reached the bottom without mishap, and felt their way across the room to the door into the courtyard. After the dark of the stairs and the room at the bottom of the tower, the courtyard in the moonlight seemed bright to Delvin, and as he came out of the tower door, he felt exposed and certain someone would see them.

"The stables are this way," whispered the duke.

Jarla shook her head. "The noise of the horse's hooves will wake everybody. We have two horses tethered outside. We can share those."

The duke looked at her a moment and nodded. They crossed the courtyard, keeping where possible to the shadows. When they reached the main gate, they pushed it open, passed through, and then closed it behind themselves.

Delvin felt easier outside Anderal, and as they slowly made their way back to the horses in the moonlight, his spirits began to lift. The horses were where they had been left. Jarla and Delvin quickly saddled them and led them to where the duke and princess were waiting.

"My daughter can ride behind me," said the duke taking Delvin's horse and mounting it. Delvin gave Fionella a leg up to get behind her father, and then turned to Jarla who had already mounted her horse.

"Get up behind," she commanded. Delvin scrambled up behind Jarla, holding onto his rabbit box as best he could, and they set off down the road towards the Dandel Ablet Road.

CHAPTER 31

They rode in silence, guiding their horses as carefully as they could down the road. When the moon was out, they could see well enough to keep up a steady trot, but when the moon went behind a cloud, they had to reduce their pace down to a walk. All the time they were listening for the sounds of pursuit. If anyone found the bound and gagged guards, they would be sure to check the duke and princess, then they would come down the road since it was the only way to get to and from Anderal. Their only chance was to get to Dandel before the pursuit reached them. Then they could hide out during the day and make their way to North Bridge when the coast was clear. The duke was determined to go to North Bridge rather than Argent, since that was where the imposter was directing Argent's armies.

Delvin found himself speculating when the change of guards would take place, since that was when the chase would begin. He tried to think of thoughts he could project back to slow things down, but no ideas came to mind. If he got them to look around outside Anderal first, they would quickly find where the horses had been tethered and come after them just the same. He worked out that if the change of guards was not until dawn, they might have reached the main road by then, and it would take the pursuers some time to catch up with them. They might just do it.

They reached the Dandel Ablet Road just as the first streaks of dawn began to light the sky, and still there was no sign of them being followed. The horses were looking tired from having to carry double their normal burden, but there was no time to rest them as they turned towards Dandel.

By the time they had reached the town gates the horses were

looking spent, so they dismounted while they waited with the farmers and traders queuing to take their produce into the town or over the bridge.

Delvin was very stiff and sore from having to sit behind the saddle, and from the way Fionella was moving carefully, she obviously felt the same way. As they reached the gatekeeper, the duke and Fionella positioned themselves so that the horses shielded them from the gatekeeper's gaze.

"Travellers bound for Argent," announced Delvin, and the gatekeeper waved them through without Delvin having to use his stone in any way. As they made their way through the town, still leading their tired horses, Jarla suggested they stop at a small, poor looking inn by the main road.

"I'm not staying there," said the duke, eyeing it with distaste.

Jarla did not seem to want to argue the point, so they carried on towards the river. On reaching the bridge, the duke looked up at the inn sign hanging out over the roadway.

"The Royal Bridge, that sounds suitable," he announced and turned to Delvin. "Book rooms for us there."

"Have you some money, Your Grace," asked Delvin.

"I don't carry money," replied the duke.

"Jarla?"

Jarla fished in her purse, and brought out some of the money she had been given by Grimbolt and handed it to Delvin.

As Delvin entered the inn, he checked the money Jarla had given him. There were three gold royals and four silver carls. There were not many people taking breakfast in the inn's common room. A narrow-faced man with slightly sunken cheeks came up to him.

"May I help magister?"

"I need four rooms and stabling for two horses," said Delvin. A smile came across the man's face.

"Certainly magister. The stables are on the right, just over the bridge towards Argent."

"How much will it be?" asked Delvin.

"Half a gold royal for each room and two carls for

the stabling." The smile on the landlord's face was looking particularly ingratiating.

Delvin looked around the few customers in the common room and raised an eyebrow.

"But for you magister, as you are taking four rooms, I will not charge you for the stabling."

"With grain for the horses?"

"But of course, magister."

"All right." Delvin handed over two gold royals which the innkeeper deftly pocketed.

"Thank you, magister. You will have our best rooms. They are over the river on the other side of the road. Come, I will show them to you."

Delvin followed the innkeeper back out of the front door and across the road, where he got quizzical looks from Jarla and the duke, and in through a door on the other side. Delvin saw that the inn spanned the road, like a tunnel, with the common room on one side of the road, and a passage with four bedrooms leading off on the other. Both the common room and the bedrooms jutting right out over the river. The rooms themselves were simply furnished, with a bed, a washstand, a chair and a rug on the floor.

Delvin thanked the innkeeper and was given two tokens for the stables before he went back to join the others.

"We have four rooms through there," he pointed to the door. I'll get the horses stabled and re-join you in a minute."

Delvin led the two horses to the inn's stables, and made sure they were being properly looked after before making his way back to the rooms. He was annoyed to find that the duke and Fionella had left their bags for him to bring in, and he toyed with the idea of leaving them with the horses, but thought better of it.

He left the bags in the passageway, and knocked on the first door but it was empty. He found everyone in the second room he tried. They had brought two extra chairs in and were seated around the window looking out over the river.

"Bring my bags in here," said the duke. "Princess Fionella is next door and Princess Jarla at the end. Then you can bring us some breakfast."

Delvin went back out feeling annoyed. He picked up the duke's bag and grinned. It was almost identical to Fionella's. He put the duke's bag in Fionella's room, his own in the remaining room, before returning to the duke's room with Fionella's bag.

The three were still talking by the window, and hardly looked at Delvin as he placed the bag by the bed. He then let himself out to find breakfast. He crossed back over the road to the common room, where he ordered breakfast for four and a tray.

When the four cups of hot leaf and the four small loaves of bread came, Delvin thanked the waiter, paid him and took the tray back over the road to their rooms. He opened the door to the duke's room with his arm, and put the tray down on the floor in front of them while he looked around for somewhere to sit. He was brought up by the duke's voice.

"Go and buy two more horses. We can't continue to ride two to a horse any longer."

"I will need some money," said Delvin taken aback. He wanted to have his breakfast.

Jarla looked in her purse. "I have four more gold royals. We will probably need those in North Bridge. How much have you got?"

"I have one royal and two carls left from the money you gave me."

"No. How much of your money have you got?"

Delvin opened his mouth to deny having any, but was interrupted by Jarla. "You couldn't have booked that room by the camp without any money, so I know you have some. Have you enough to buy two horses?"

"Not good ones."

"Since you will be riding one and Princess Fionella the other, I suggest you make them as good as you can." Jarla turned away dismissing him.

Delvin was tempted to sit down and have some breakfast with them regardless of their dismissal. But he thought better of it, and returned to the common room where he ordered his own breakfast and sat eating it annoyed at their attitude towards him. As he was finishing his bread and the slice of meat he had ordered as well, the door of the inn burst open and three soldiers strode in, looking this way and that around the common room. The gaunt faced landlord came running up to them.

"Magisters, may I be of help?"

"Have two or more travellers just booked in here?"

Delvin rapidly touched his stone and projected the thought to the landlord that only one single man had booked in that morning.

"Only one man on his own magisters. He is eating his breakfast over there." The landlord pointed to Delvin.

The soldiers took a few steps towards Delvin and looked him up and down. "That's not him. Let them know at the guard house if any do book in." With that the soldiers turned, and were out of the inn before Delvin could take another sip of his hot leaf. Delvin was not sure how long or how well the thought he had projected to the landlord would hold. He decided he would need to keep an eye on him to make sure he didn't have a sudden return of his memory and go and fetch the soldiers.

Delvin finished his breakfast and returned to his room to retrieve his pouch of coins that he was now hiding in the lining of his bundle. He opened the pouch and counted the coins. There were twenty-three gold royals, seventeen silver carls and eleven copper bits. Even a fairly poor horse would cost ten or more royals, and then there was the saddle and bridle to buy. It would take all his money unless he bought some broken-down old beast. If there was a chase, he would be on the broken-down old beast and would be the one to get captured. He shivered. Then he had an idea and grinned to himself. The soldiers would be looking for two or more riders. If they were all mounted on good horses, they would be exactly what the soldiers would be looking for. They wouldn't have a chance of getting through the town gate, never mind getting to North Bridge. He smiled to himself as he set off into town to try and find what he needed.

CHAPTER 32

Delvin returned to the inn towards midday and knocked on the door of the duke's room but there was no reply. After waiting a few moments, he opened the door and peered in. The duke was fast asleep on the bed and the others had apparently gone back to their rooms. Delvin was feeling very tired himself since he had had no sleep the previous night, so he quietly closed the door and went to his own room, where before long, he too was asleep.

When Delvin awoke it was evening. Shadows were lengthening and the sky was beginning to darken. He quickly shook the sleep from his head and straightened his clothes before making his way to the duke's room. He knocked on the door and was bid to enter. Jarla and Fionella were already there, though they too looked as if they had only recently awoken. The duke turned to Delvin.

"Bring us some dinner and then go and fetch the horses. With luck we will be in North Bridge well before morning."

"Your Grace," began Delvin. "There are soldiers out looking for us. If we travel at night, we will be immediately suspicious. They probably have checkpoints on all the roads. We need to travel in the daytime when there are other travellers about as well."

"We got here with no difficulty, and we travelled at night then."

"Yes, Your Grace, but they were not looking for us last night."

The duke turned to Jarla. "What is your opinion Princess Jarla?"

"Delvin has a point. But if there are no check points, less people are likely to see us at night."

"We go tonight," said the duke firmly.

"There's another problem, Your Grace," persisted Delvin.

"What is it?" said the duke irritably.

"The town gates shut at dusk. Even if we leave this minute, we may well be too late. And there are sure to be soldiers watching there."

"Shut? I've been through the gates later than this."

"Yes, Your Grace. But you are the duke. The gates shut for ordinary folk at dusk."

"So, what do you suggest?" The duke sounded annoyed.

"That we wait till morning, Your Grace."

"It looks like we may have to," interposed Jarla.

"Bring us some dinner while we discuss it." The duke waved Delvin out of the room.

Delvin had to restrain himself from slamming the door behind him as he left the room. He made his way across the road to the common room and ordered three portions of the roast chicken and vegetables, with a bottle of wine and three glasses. He did not make the same mistake as he had that morning of ordering four meals, since he knew he would not be invited to join the others. The meal made further inroads into his diminishing money supply, and he fervently hoped they would get to North Bridge without incident, or he would have nothing left.

He carried the meal on its tray back over the road to the duke's room, where as expected, he was waved away after he had placed it before them. He returned to the common room where he ordered the same meal for himself, but with ale rather than wine.

When he had finished, he returned to his room. He had thought of knocking again on the duke's door, in the hope of being asked to join in their planning. But he suspected they would just tell him to clear away their plates, and he didn't feel like doing that.

Some while later, Delvin heard the other doors down the passage open and close. They must be returning to their rooms, he thought, to get some sleep before tomorrow. He lay down on his own bed, but having slept all afternoon, he found he could now not get to sleep. After tossing and turning for what seemed like an age, he decided to get some fresh air to see if that might do the trick.

He got out of bed, put on his boots and went out onto the roadway of the bridge. The town was quiet with few lights showing. The section of the bridge next to the inn had no shops or buildings on it, just a parapet over which Delvin could see the river glittering in the moonlight as it flowed under the bridge beneath his feet.

At first Delvin thought he was alone, but then he saw that another figure, difficult to see in the shadows of the building, was also looking over the parapet into the water below.

"Were you not able to sleep either?" asked Jarla.

"No. I must have slept too long this afternoon."

There was a short silence.

"That was a good idea to use your rabbit to distract the guards."

Delvin looked towards Jarla and caught the flash of a smile.

"Thanks." He replied.

They watched the river again in silence. Delvin was about to bid Jarla goodnight and return to his room, when a noise from the common room made him turn his head. Two figures were moving across the road towards their rooms. Delvin slipped into the shadow and looked across to Jarla to warn her, but she too had seen them and was watching intently.

One of the men turned to the other. Delvin just managed to catch his whisper. "Leave the women till last. We can have some fun with them before we drop them through the hatches."

Jarla signalled Delvin to follow, as she quietly made her way to the door to the bedroom passage through which the men had now gone. As they reached the door themselves, Delvin could dimly see that the men had now opened the door to the duke's room and were advancing on the figure in the bed.

Jarla did not hesitate. She took one step forward, and before the man could plunge his dagger into the sleeping form, she had stepped up behind him, whipped her arm under his and thrust her knife into his throat. The man let out a gurgling noise as he fell right across the duke's bed.

Delvin realised he was meant to be dealing with the other robber. He had his knife out of his belt, but the man turned quickly and dropped down into a knife fighter's stance.

Delvin knew he would be no match in a knife fight, so he touched his stone and projected a feeling of panic into the man's mind. That might stop him attacking too quickly he thought as he saw the whites of the man's eyes widen in fear. He wondered if he could make the man think he had been stabbed. Delvin lunged forward, projecting a feeling of pain at the point in the man's chest he was stabbing at. Although the blade stopped some two feet from its target, the man cried out clutching his chest and stepping back.

Jarla by this time had disengaged her knife from the first robber's throat and came up behind the man Delvin was fighting. With a sweep of her leg, she tripped him as he stepped back, then calmly dispatched him with another thrust to the throat.

She looked at Delvin quizzically as she wiped her knife and hands on the dead man's jacket.

"What's happening," came the voice of the duke, as he struggled out from under the body of the robber who had fallen on his bed.

"These two men were trying to rob us and murder us in our beds," replied Jarla. "They said something about hatches… I wonder." She stepped over to the rug and pulled it back. Beneath was a trap door, held in place with a bolt. "I think this inn needs a bit of investigating. Right, Delvin, get the candle lit so we can see what we have got."

Delvin went to the washstand, managed to find his tinderbox and lit the candle. In the improved light an extraordinary sight met his eyes. The duke, still wearing his riding clothes, was covered in blood from the dead robber who had fallen over his bed. Jarla too had blood across her clothes and arms. In fact he was the only one who seemed to have escaped the mess. Jarla had opened he trap door and was looking down into the river below.

"Right," said Jarla closing the trap door. "Let's see what these two have. We can use their clothes as well. Get them off."

While the duke sat staring, a look of horror on his face, Delvin and Jarla checked the purses and pockets of the two robbers and stripped them of their clothing.

"Five royals, eight carls and some coppers," said Jarla, pocketing the money. "Right. Let's get rid of them. Open the hatch."

Delvin obediently opened the trap door and helped Jarla manhandle the two corpses through it, and into the river below.

Jarla went over to the washstand, took off her jacket and began to wash her arms and the jacket in the water.

"Delvin, bring the water from your room in here. We need to try to get things cleaned up before the morning."

The duke had got up from the bed, but was still staring around incredulously as Delvin slipped out to get the jug of water and bowl from his room. When he returned, the duke was standing by the washstand, and was starting to wash the worst of the blood from himself. Jarla was checking through the clothing they had taken from the dead robbers.

"These might be useful to disguise you, Your Grace… and Princess Fionella. I think this one might fit her."

"But it's filthy," objected the duke.

"I should be able to get the worst of the blood off." Jarla took the garment over to the washstand. "Delvin, take this dirty water and swill the blood up off the floor. Here, use this." She threw him a piece of clothing from one of the robbers that she had been using to sponge blood off the other clothes.

Delvin did as he was asked, and before long they had the room looking reasonably normal again.

"Shouldn't we tell the landlord and raise the town watch?" said the duke, beginning to recover from his shock.

"The landlord probably sent them and the watch are probably looking for us," said Jarla dryly. "We'll wait until morning and then be gone. I suggest we all try to get some sleep." The duke dully agreed, and a short while later Jarla and Delvin left for their own rooms, but only after Jarla had shown the duke how to put a chair underneath his door handle.

When Delvin got back to his room, the reaction from what had happened suddenly hit him and he felt sick and shaky. He jammed his chair under his door handle, lay down on his bed, and tried to get to sleep. Although his mind had been racing, the incident had left him drained, and before long he was sleeping soundly.

When Delvin woke, he took a moment to orient himself, then he jumped quickly out of his bed. Dawn was just breaking, and the first sounds could be heard from the town coming to life. Good, he thought. I've just enough time to get ready.

He put on his boots and straightened his clothes. He was unable to wash or shave since his water had been used in the clean up during the night. Grabbing his belongings, he removed the chair from his door and went out into the passageway. He was about to knock on the duke's door, but thought better of it after the night's happenings, and knocked on Jarla's instead.

"Yes."

"It's Delvin. Could you make sure that you and Fionella don't leave your rooms till I return. It's important."

"What are you up to?"

"I'll be back soon."

Delvin was off, out of the door and into the road before Jarla could ask any more questions. With a smile on his face and a jaunty step, he made his way off the bridge and into the town.

CHAPTER 33

A little while later, Delvin knocked on the duke's door, waited a moment till he heard 'enter' and went in. Jarla and Fionella were in the room with the duke.

"Princesses," he began. "Please could you remain here. Your Grace, please could you help me with the coffins."

"Coffins?" exclaimed Jarla and the duke together.

"I have hired a hearse. It is the perfect way to smuggle us out of Dandel and into North Bridge. That attack last night worked perfectly for us. Before that happened, I had been wondering how to get the princesses into the coffins. I had thought we might have had to do it in a back street."

"In a coffin," exploded Jarla. Fionella's jaw dropped.

"That's right. The soldiers will be looking for a young lady and a gentleman," he nodded to the duke. "And maybe some helpers. They won't be looking for two men driving a hearse."

"No!" said Jarla.

"After last night's attack, we tell the landlord something terrible has happened and two of us have been robbed and murdered. We say we are taking their bodies back to their families in North Bridge, and that we will inform the town watch on the way. The landlord will think his men have run off after the robbery, and so won't do anything. The last thing he wants is to have the town watch asking him awkward questions. It will work perfectly. If the soldiers check up on our story of taking the bodies to North Bridge, it will all check out." Delvin smiled around the room at the stony faces around him.

"Well," said Delvin. "How else do you think we should get to North Bridge?"

"I thought we were going to ride," said Fionella quietly.

"And how far do you think we would get with the soldiers looking out for us?" replied Delvin. "I doubt we would get past the town gate."

"It's more likely to work than riding," said Jarla grimly.

"Do you think so?" said the duke uncertainly.

"Unfortunately, yes," replied Jarla.

"Right. We shall do it," commanded the duke. "Where is the hearse?"

"Parked outside with our horses, and with the coffins in the back."

"You presumed rather a lot," said Jarla coldly.

"I didn't have enough money for decent horses. It was the best I could think of."

"You had better bring in the coffins," muttered Jarla.

The duke and Delvin went out to the hearse. The horses, the ones Delvin and Jarla had ridden to Anderal, were tied to a rail by the door. They now had black plumes on their heads and looked rested and ready to go. They carried the coffins into the duke's room, where with great reluctance, Jarla and Fionella lay down in them, and Delvin placed on the lids.

"I'm only going to screw the lids on lightly," said Delvin. "So that you can get enough air to breath."

"Screw them on…don't you dare," came the muffled reply. But it was too late, as Delvin deftly put the screws in the holes.

Having fastened the lids, Delvin and the Duke crossed the road to the common room where they demanded to see the landlord. He came running with genuine consternation on his face, probably thought Delvin, because he thought they should be dead. They then complained loudly and vociferously about the poor security, the town, how people should be able to sleep soundly in their beds without being murdered, low moral standards, the town watch, the ruffians who were attracted to his inn and about the world in general where this sort of outrage could happen. The duke worked himself up into an impressive rage, and when Delvin, secretly grinning, added a complaint about a duke who could let this happen in his realm, his anger became even greater. The landlord had been unable to get a word in with the tirade coming at him. And when Delvin announced that they were taking the bodies of their colleagues back to North Bridge, and would never enter his door again, he looked positively relieved, only to turn white again when the duke told him to expect a visit from the town watch, as they would inform them of what happened as they left.

"Come outside," said Delvin, "You can help us with the bodies."

They marched the white-faced landlord across the road, where he started at the sight of the hearse. If he thought the undertaker had got there quickly, he didn't dare say a thing. Delvin opened the door to the duke's room and they strode in. The landlord came to a sudden halt as he was faced with two coffins.

"Right," said Delvin. "You take the front. I'll take the back." Together they picked up the first coffin, took it out and loaded it into the back of the hearse. They then went back and got the second.

"I'm not staying in this evil place a moment longer," announced the duke as he climbed into the driving seat. Delvin had already untied the horses and climbed up beside him. The duke flicked the reins and they were off, leaving the landlord standing in the road staring after them.

Delvin had saved the black jerkins worn by the robbers the night before. Now he handed one to the duke and put on the other himself. They drove off the bridge and through the streets of Dandel, sitting as straight in their seats as they could and with solemn expressions on their faces. The people they passed stopped in respect, removing their hats and bowing their heads.

When they reached the gates, as Delvin had suspected, the old gateman was now joined by a large squad of soldiers, who were carefully checking every person passing through the gates. A queue had built up, both entering and leaving the town. Some traders and merchants mouthed silent abuse as they were made to dismount and their carts and carriages were examined.

As it came to Delvin's turn, he touched his stone and projected the thought that the coffins might contain the bodies of people who had died of a terrible contagious disease. The soldier stepped back quickly and waved them through.

Once out of the gates they made steady progress, farm workers stopping work and removing their hats as they passed.

Just before they reached the fork in the road to Argent, they came to a checkpoint. A farmer was arguing with the soldier's captain who was insisting his load of hay be searched. Delvin again projected the thought that they might be carrying bodies that had been the victims of a contagious disease, and the captain waved them through.

The road now began to seem more familiar, and before long they passed the camp where Jarla had been taken as a prisoner and the inn where they had left Grimbolt and Maegar. Delvin began to relax. Now all they had to do was to get through the gate into North Bridge.

As they came round a bend in the road, Delvin's breath caught in his throat as he saw ahead a figure coming towards them, dressed in black with a black cloak and riding a black horse. A shiver of fear ran through him as a voice in his head whispered, *'Delvin, Maegar, Jarla. Shout hello. Jump up and show yourself.'* It was the black magician. He was still hunting for them. As Delvin desperately wondered what to do, he faintly heard a muffled 'hello' from Jarla's coffin followed by a bump. She must have tried to jump up he thought. Lucky the lid was screwed on, he grinned to himself. No more noises came from the coffin, and Delvin wondered if Jarla had stunned herself when she had tried to sit up.

The black magician rode past. He had been too far away to hear Jarla's muffled shout, and he did not recognise Delvin with his day's growth of beard. When he was past Delvin let out a long breath and steeled himself to keep looking ahead, and not look back over his shoulder to see if the black magician had turned and was now following. No one overtook them and Delvin heard no hoof beats behind. So after a while he was able to relax again.

They reached North Bridge by mid-afternoon. Again there was a queue at the gate as a squad of soldiers checked everyone entering the town. Delvin did not think he should try the contagious disease idea again, since the soldiers would not like disease brought into the town. Instead he tried the idea of bodies horribly mutilated in an accident, and the thought that as they had been on the road for a while, there should not be any delay in taking them to their families and getting them buried. The soldiers questioned them a bit longer than those at Dandel and at the checkpoint. But they didn't want to look in the coffins, helped by suggestions of dread and of feeling sick, put into their minds by Delvin. After a moment or two, they stood back and waved them through into North Bridge.

Once inside the town, Delvin asked the duke to turn off the main street, and they started to look for a quiet alley where they could let the princesses out of the coffins. Eventually Delvin saw the entrance to a yard that looked deserted. One of its gates was shut, the other swung gently on its hinges. There was a house by the yard that seemed shut up. He asked the duke to pull up, and he climbed down and knocked on the door. There was no reply. Had there been one, he would have simply asked for directions.

"This will do," he called up to the duke. "I'll open the gate and we can bring the hearse in here." The duke drove the hearse into the yard and Delvin shut the gate behind them. He then climbed into the back and removed the screws from the coffin lids.

Jarla sat up. She was white faced and held her head. "If you dare do anything like that to me again Delvin, I'll rip your heart out."

"It got us here without problems, didn't it?" he replied smiling.

"What do we do now?" asked Fionella, stretching as she climbed out of the coffin and off the back of the hearse.

"We go to the Governor's House and get the imposter arrested," said the duke.

"We need to be careful," said Jarla. "If we just march in, we'll be the ones to get arrested, and this time they won't just hold us captive. We need to check things out first. I suggest we book into an inn, then Delvin can go and find out what is going on."

"A good idea Princess Jarla," said the duke. "We shall find an inn."

"If I may make a suggestion," said Delvin. "There are soldiers looking for us everywhere. They are sure to be checking the inns. If the four of us book in, we will be immediately suspicious. I suggest just Your Grace and I book in, getting two rooms. Then we come back here for you." He nodded at the princesses. "You act as two women we have just picked up and who we take back to our rooms."

"You've made me act as a dead body, now you want me to be a whore," hissed Fionella furiously.

"Better to act as a whore than to be arrested and disappear," said Delvin dryly.

"Disappear?" gulped Fionella.

"You've escaped once. If you are captured, they won't risk it again. You'll simply disappear, and I'm not talking magic."

Fionella turned white.

"You have your father to cuddle up to," said Jarla to Fionella. She eyed Delvin with distaste. "I'm left with him."

"Right. I need some money," said Delvin smiling sweetly at Jarla. She frowned back at him, but handed him four royals and two carls.

Delvin and the duke unhitched the horses, and retrieved their saddles that he had hidden in the back of the hearse. They soon had their horses saddled and ready, and they trotted into the town leaving the princesses in the yard. They had tied their bags across the saddles, and Delvin had propped Freda's travelling box on the saddle in front of him.

A number of the main streets were filled with soldiers, and the whole part of the town near the bridge was blocked off due to the war. They eventually found a small inn in a side road near the Governor's House. There they were able to book two rooms for four carls each, with stabling another two carls. They made their way on foot back towards the yard where the princesses were waiting. As they passed the shops in the main street, Delvin suddenly stopped.

"Wait here a moment."

"What is it?" said the duke.

"Have you ever seen whores in riding clothes, or the sort of clothes your daughter has?"

"I don't..."

"I won't be a moment." Delvin quickly turned and entered a lady's clothes shop they were passing. He had never bought lady's clothes before but had a good idea of what he was looking for. He picked out two garishly coloured dresses, but when the shopkeeper asked him for the size, he was for a moment lost for words.

"A little smaller than yourself mistress," he replied blushing.

"In that case magister, perhaps the ones over here." It was some minutes later that an embarrassed Delvin, with a parcel under his arm, re-joined the duke. He had not realised the complexities of lady's clothes and undergarments.

They made their way back to the yard where Jarla and Fionella were waiting, leaning against the hearse.

"Have you found somewhere suitable?" asked Fionella.

"I hope so my dear," replied the duke.

"Right. Let's go," said Jarla.

"I have some dresses for you." said Delvin apologetically.

"Dresses?" said Jarla fixing him with a stare.

"Ladies we might pick up would not be in riding clothes," said Delvin quickly.

"Whores you mean," growled Jarla flexing her fingers.

"I've got you some clothes that I thought might be more appropriate."

"Whores' dresses," said Jarla taking a step towards him.

"I like dresses, what are whores' dresses like?" asked Fionella.

"You don't want to know," said Jarla.

"I think Delvin could be right," said the duke.

"Show them to us," said Jarla very slowly.

Delvin gulped, and opening the parcel held up the dresses.

"Sheffs!" exclaimed Jarla, eyeing the bright colours and low-cut tops.

"Ohh!" gasped Fionella.

"You expect us to wear those?" whispered Jarla dangerously.

"We've got to look the part," said Delvin getting increasingly more desperate.

"Can I have the red and blue one," interrupted Fionella.

"You can have them both for all I care," growled Jarla advancing on Delvin, who backed away quickly.

"Come on, let's try them on," said Fionella. Jarla turned, and was about to make a sharp remark to Fionella, when she saw the worried look on the duke's face and pulled herself together.

"Give it to me," she snapped at Delvin. He handed her a yellow and black dress and gave the red and blue one to Fionella. Then he backed away quickly.

"Where can we get changed?" asked Fionella.

"That outhouse doesn't look locked," said Delvin running quickly over to it and trying the door. To his relief the door opened. The outhouse was used for storing logs and there was plenty of space inside. Still scowling at him, Jarla followed Fionella into the outhouse as Delvin stepped quickly out of their way.

When they eventually emerged, it was apparent that Delvin's idea of dress sizes had not been completely accurate. While Jarla's dress hung off her, not being quite the right shape for her muscular body, Fionella's was tight, with her bosom bursting out of the low neckline.

"I hope you are satisfied," said Jarla giving Delvin an angry look.

"I think they look really nice," replied Delvin with a gulp.

"You would" growled Jarla. "Let's get organised and on our way." She packed up her riding clothes and other things and stalked out of the yard. The duke moved quickly to get ahead so that he could show them the way to the inn with Fionella rushing to catch him up. Delvin hurried along behind, shutting the gate after them.

Fionella seemed happy, and when she had caught up with her father she clung to his arm, leaning against him, and occasionally whispering in his ear.

Jarla on the other hand simply glared at Delvin. But as soon as they came into the main street, she wrapped her arm around him and fixed a smile on her face. Delvin put his arm around her, feeling the firm muscles of her body under the thin dress. A sharp pain in his side made him gasp, and he looked down. Jarla had dug her nails through his shirt and into his side. Although the nails on her forefingers had not had time to grow back, she had sharpened the others. A voice whispered in his ear. "If you don't watch where you put your hand, that will just be for starters."

He looked into Jarla's face, and she smiled sweetly back at him.

CHAPTER 34

They reached their rooms in the inn without further incident. One room faced the road, and the other was across the corridor facing the stable yard at the back.

"I shall have this room," announced the duke opening the door to the room at the front. "Fionella, Princess Jarla, you have the room at the back."

"Do I share with Your Grace," asked Delvin. The duke looked at him distastefully.

"I suppose so."

Delvin dropped his things in a corner of the room. There was only one bed, and he was sure the duke would take that. That did not leave much for him to sleep on, since the only other furniture in the room consisted of a washstand, a single wooden chair and a tall cupboard. There was not even a rug on the floor. Oh well thought Delvin, resigning himself to an uncomfortable night.

Jarla and Fionella came into the room having left their things in the other bedroom. The duke turned to Delvin.

"I will dine here with the princesses. It will be unsafe for them to go into the common room. Don't take too long, we haven't eaten all day and I'm hungry." He turned back to the princesses, dismissing Delvin as he did so.

Well, thought Delvin, of all the… He left the room, went down the stairs and out of the side door of the inn. Before looking for food for the duke and princesses, he went into the stables and checked that Freda his rabbit was being properly looked after. He opened her box and gave her a short run, before putting her back in again and going out to find the market. Delvin reasoned that if he ordered meals for four at the inn, it would draw attention to them having only booked rooms for two. A little while later he returned with two loaves of bread, some cheese, a meat pie, some apples and a bottle of wine. The wine had a cork, and Delvin grinned to himself as he thought of the duke trying to get the cork out of the bottle without a corkscrew.

Delvin placed the food on the floor in front of the duke, and was just leaving when the duke turned to him.

"Keep your ears open in the common room and see if you can find out what is going on. Also, go over to the Governor's House and see if you can find out anything there. Report back here."

Delvin was tempted to reply 'Yes sir' with a salute, but instead simply smiled and nodded as he closed the door behind him.

Delvin made his way down to the common room, where he ordered his dinner of a thick meat stew with bread and cabbage, and a mug of ale. Having finished his food, he sat back and sipped the remainder of his ale, trying to overhear the conversations of other people nearby. The people closest to him were a husband and wife talking about their children. At another table, a man with his hair slicked back was giving his friends a lurid account of his amorous conquests. Not much to interest the duke here thought Delvin as he finished his ale and rose from the table. He made his way out of the inn and towards the Governor's House. The duke had pointed out where it was when they had found the inn earlier.

The Governor's House stood alone. It was a square building, with pillars on either side of the door supporting an ornate portico. Mock battlements surrounded the roof with four large chimneys rising behind them. A flag bearing the silver and red of Argent fluttered from a flag post that stuck out over the door. The building faced a small square and two soldiers guarded the entrance. As Delvin watched, a continuous stream of people went in and out of the front door, many of them soldiers, some of them wearing impressive uniforms.

Delvin turned and walked down the side of the building. As he walked, his magician's stone was touching his leg. He began hear in his mind a voice, repeating itself continuously, *'I am the Duke of Argent. I am the Duke of Argent.'* So, thought Delvin, a magician was impersonating the duke, and he needed to keep continually deluding people. Delvin continued on behind the building noting the activity around the servant's entrance, and then on round the building on the other side. There was no easy way in. And even if he got in, he had no idea how they could deal with the magician who had taken the duke's place.

Another voice suddenly entered his mind, *'Delvin, Maegar, Jarla. Shout hello. Jump up and show yourself.'* A shiver of fear ran through him, the black magician must be here. He looked around, but could see no-one. What if the magician found Jarla at their inn? Should he go back and warn them? Or could that just lead the magician there? No. He must continue what he was doing.

Slightly shaken, Delvin went into a bar across the road and ordered himself an ale. As he sat sipping it, he tried to think of a way to get the duke into the Governor's House. But he had no inspiration. His thoughts were interrupted by a soft voice in his ear.

"A copper for your thoughts." He turned to see the smiling face of a woman a few years older than him. She had short dark hair, a large chin and a slightly crooked mouth that gave her face a character that was enhanced by her dancing eyes.

"All very boring," said Delvin smiling back, and desperately trying to think of something he could say which would not incriminate himself.

"I'm sure not," said the woman sitting down next to him.

"I was thinking that I've been in North Bridge for four hours, and I haven't yet seen a pretty girl...until now," he added grinning.

"What a load of flannel," said the woman laughing. "Buy me a drink and tell me some more. My name's Aggie. What's yours?"

"Delvin," he replied. He signalled to the barman and ordered Aggie a drink.

"Well, what's a handsome man like you doing in North

Bridge?"

"Looking for work," said Delvin. "I'm a children's entertainer, and there are too many of them in Argent. I thought I'd come here and see if it's any better in North Bridge. What do you do?"

"I work at the Governor's House. I'm in charge of the maids there." Delvin's attention sharpened.

"I would have thought you would still be working, serving dinner."

"I've just finished. Two of my girls are clearing up but I've finished for the night. Have you managed to find any work in your four hours?"

"I've mainly been looking around, trying to get the feel of the place to see if I want to stay here."

"And do you?"

"The people seem friendly," he grinned.

"Where are you staying?" She asked.

"I'll probably see if I can find a cheap room at an inn somewhere," said Delvin, thinking of the hard floor in the duke's room.

"I may be able to find you somewhere."

"That would be great," Delvin smiled.

They chatted together companionably over several more drinks, until the customers began to drift away. Aggie got up and stretched.

"I must be getting back, are you coming?" Delvin nodded smiling.

Aggie made her way out of the bar and down the side of the Governor's House. As they reached the tradesmen's entrance at the back, she signalled for Delvin to be quiet, then looked both ways before sneaking him through the door. Once inside, she quickly led the way up the backstairs to a small room on the top floor. As she shut the door behind them, she turned to Delvin and grinned. Delvin grinned back. He was meant to be reporting back to the duke, but this was much more interesting.

Later, as Delvin lay on the narrow bed listening to the snoring of Aggie beside him, he thought back on the activities of the day.

Suddenly he was wide awake. When Aggie had brought him up to her room, he hadn't heard the voice in his head despite the stone touching his leg. Of course, the magician had to go to sleep some time.

He very carefully got out of bed making sure he didn't wake Aggie. He put on his breeches, shirt and stockings, and quietly crept out of the room.

The Governor's House was sleeping as he slowly made his way down the stairs, stopping and listening every time a floorboard or stair creaked beneath him. When he reached the first floor, he could dimly see a narrow corridor leading both left and right with doors leading off it. This will be the servant's passage he thought, and the rooms on the side where the servant's stairs are will be the linen rooms and sewing rooms. He looked at the single large door on the other side of the passage, took a deep breath, and opened it a fraction so he could peep through. He stepped back rapidly and quietly pulled the door shut again. There was a guard stationed in the wide passage on the other side of the door. Delvin breathed a sigh of relief that the guard hadn't been looking in his direction and so had not seen him.

In the brief glimpse Delvin had got of the passage, he had seen three ornate doors leading off it. Maybe these are the bedrooms he thought. Maybe this is where the magician is sleeping. But how could he get past the guard?

He quickly dismissed the idea of using his stone to tell the guard to go to sleep, or go on a patrol around the building. Since if the magician was touching his stone when he had gone to sleep, the voice in his head would wake him up. Even if he tried to really focus his thoughts on the guard, there would probably be some spill over. But how about feelings? Feelings wouldn't come out as a voice. Would the magician get a spill over of a feeling he projected?

Another thought struck him. A command had the same effect whether it was a shout or a whisper. But a feeling or emotion had a much lesser effect when it was weak. So because any spill over of a feeling would be weak it would have little effect, and almost certainly wouldn't be enough to wake the magician. Even so he would have to really focus on the guard so any spill over would be minimised.

Delvin began to focus his thoughts. This was going to be like projecting feelings and ideas to animals he thought with a grin. He began projecting the feeling to the guard that he desperately needed to relieve himself. He then slipped through one of the doors in the passage, which as he expected, turned out to be a linen room, leaving its door slightly ajar.

Moments later, the door from the bedroom passage burst open and the guard rushed through and headed down the passage. As soon as he had gone Delvin was out of the linen room, across the passage and through the door into the wide passage beyond. Delvin knew he had to be quick since it would not be long before the guard was back.

He opened the first door and there was a smell of perfume and soap. He could dimly see an elaborate washstand and a huge tub. He quickly shut the door.

On opening the next door, there was a smell of roses and perfume. The canopy over the bed made it look like a bower from some fantastic garden. A sleeping woman lay on the bed. He quietly closed the door.

It must be the other one thought Delvin. He moved to the third door and carefully opened it. A squeak of the hinges froze him to the spot. Whatever am I doing here? He thought. I was only meant to be scouting out the building. He stood stock still, hardly daring to breath, but the building still slept. He edged through the narrow opening of the door into the room, not want to risk more squeaks by pushing it further open.

A candle burned low on a table by the huge ornate bed. In its flickering light the carvings on the bedposts looked like strange creatures climbing up to the great canopy above. Three couches surrounded the now empty fireplace and Delvin could see a stocking, and other items of clothing strewn across them. As he carefully approached the bed, he could see two figures lying on it. Closest to him a middle-aged man lay on his back. As he snored, his thin beard twitched and his large belly rose and fell. On the other side, a naked young woman lay face down, her tousled brown hair covering her face. There were what looked to be stripes on her back, and as Delvin drew closer, he saw with sudden shock that they were weals, and that her wrists were also marked.

Delvin looked closely at the man. His hands were out of the covers. He was not holding his magician's stone. It was not on a ring. He was not wearing it round his neck. Maybe it was in a drawer of his bedside table. He was about to check when he saw that the woman was not asleep and was looking at him with fear in her eyes. He put a finger to his lips, and she gave an almost imperceptible nod of her head. He was going to have to chance it, thought Delvin. He touched his stone and projected thoughts of reassurance to the woman, who visibly relaxed. He put his hand in his pocket and brought out his stone, pointed to it, and then to the sleeping man, projecting the thought *'Where is it?'* to the woman. She pointed to the pillow under the man's head, and mouthed through lips that Delvin now saw were swollen and bruised, 'Under there.' Delvin mouthed 'thank you', and bending down, carefully tried pushing his hand under the pillow.

His fingers touched something hard, when suddenly the man jerked awake his eyes snapping open. Without thinking Delvin projected *'Sleep'*. The man fell back on his pillow as if poleaxed. Delvin's heart was beating so fast he had to pause a moment to compose himself. Then he gripped the thing under the pillow and pulled it out. It was a crystal like his own.

Delvin stood up, and again mouthed 'thank you' to the young woman, but she too had fallen asleep. He then crept back to the door and sidled out of the room. He tried to prevent the door squeaking when he closed it by lifting up its handle. But it didn't work, and in the silence the squeak seemed loud enough to wake the dead. Delvin didn't wait. He was across the passage, through the door and back into the linen room as fast as he could, again leaving the door slightly ajar.

He was only just in time. Through the door's gap he saw the

guard come unsteadily back down the passage. In the dim light his face looked white and he wore a pained expression. He went back through the door into the bedroom passage and closed it behind him.

Delvin breathed a sigh of relief. He slipped out of the linen room, and moving as quickly and as silently as he could, crossed the passage to the servant's staircase and climbed the stairs back to Aggie's room. Once there, he quickly undressed and got back into bed. Aggie rolled over in her sleep and then lay still again. Delvin thought about the young woman in the magician's bed, or girl, for that was what she really was, and hoped she would be all right. He would need to wake early in the morning he thought, as he drifted off to sleep.

CHAPTER 35

It was still dark when Delvin awoke. Through the small window he could see the first lightning of the sky that preceded the dawn. He stretched and began to climb out of bed. Aggie put out an arm and whispered, "Come back."

"I must go," said Delvin kissing her on the cheek. "If I wait any longer the household will be up and I'll get you into trouble."

Aggie swung her feet off the bed running her hands through her hair and yawning. "I'll see you out."

They both dressed quickly and Aggie then led Delvin down the back stairs and out to the servant's entrance.

"Keep in touch," she said.

"I will," he replied kissing her on the lips, though both knew it was unlikely they would see each other again.

Delvin made his way through the breaking dawn back to the inn where the duke and princesses were sleeping. He had his hands in his breeches pockets and could feel the two magician's stones against his fingers.

When he reached the inn, the servants had only just got up and he had to wait for them to open the door to let him in. He ran up the stairs and let himself into the duke's room. The duke was lying on his back asleep in the bed, snoring. Delvin shook his shoulder gently.

"Your Grace, I've been scouting out the Governor's House. If we go there now and you say you've been at a secret meeting in the town, you can get in and get rid of the imposter."

"Eh, what?" "Secret meeting in the town," said the duke coming awake. "Get rid of the imposter. What if he is there, and he uses his magician's stone that Princess Jarla has been telling me about."

"He won't Your Grace. He hasn't got it with him."

"Hasn't got it?"

"No Your Grace. I'll go and wake the princesses."

Delvin quickly backed out of the room before the duke asked any more awkward questions, and knocked on the door of the princesses' room.

"Yes?" said a sleepy voice.

"The duke asks you get to dressed. We are going to the Governor's House to get rid of the imposter. Fionella should wear her dress...her good dress."

There was a pause.

"Delvin?"

"Yes, Princess Jarla?"

"Wait there a moment. I want to talk to you."

Delvin waited outside the door. A short while later the door opened and Fionella came out. She hadn't had time to brush her hair and her dress was on crooked. She glared at Delvin as she made her way across the passage to the duke's room.

"Right. Come in now." said Jarla.

Jarla stood there in her riding gear, feet slightly apart, and fixed him with her stare.

"What's all this about going to the Governor's House? The magician there has a stone. We will just get arrested."

"He hasn't got his stone with him."

"How do you know?"

"I met this girl in a bar," dissembled Delvin.

"Don't tell me, she told you he hadn't got his stone. You'll have to do better than that. Tell me."

"I stole it from him."

Jarla's eyes widened. "You stole it?"

"Yes. I stole it from him while he slept."

"You did... Hand it over." Jarla held out her hand.

"But..."

"Hand it over... Now."

Delvin put his hand in his pocket and touched the crystal,

projecting the thought to Jarla that she would forget the conversation they had just had, and that he did not have the stone.

"Right," said Jarla turning away. "We must go to the Governor's House." She strode out of the door with Delvin in her wake.

A short while later they made their way down the stairs. The duke now wore a magnificent robe and a chain of state that he had brought with him, and Fionella wore a deep blue dress. The inn's servants gasped and bowed as he swept past. As they marched down the road towards the Governor's House, the few people they passed moved out of their way and bowed as they went by.

They reached the Governor's House and the guards at the door snapped to attention, opening the door as they approached. Inside was a scene of confusion, people were running around, and they could hear shouting and loud voices. A man in knee breeches and a ruff ran up to the duke.

"Your Grace. I'm so glad you are safe. The most dreadful things have been happening. There is a dead man in your bed with a knife through his heart. And we couldn't find you. We thought you had been kidnapped. And the Lady Carolina is going hysterical." He looked up the staircase apprehensively. "We can't control her. She's shouting about imposters, thieves and magicians. I can't understand her."

"Lady Carolina?" began the duke.

Jarla interrupted. "The duke has been at a secret meeting. Bring the Lady Carolina down, and anyone else involved, and we will talk to them."

There was a crash from upstairs and a shout. "She's knocked the lamp over." Another voice. "Get a bucket!" There was another crash. "No, my Lady, don't do that!" A crash. "Get some water quick!" A wisp of smoke came down the stairs.

The man they were talking to, who Delvin thought must be the butler or major domo, stood shocked and looked up the stairs.

Jarla stepped forward. "Your Grace, Princess, wait outside. Delvin follow me."

She ran quickly up the smoky stairs with Delvin on her heels to be met with a scene of devastation in the room above. The lady that Delvin had seen asleep under the bower last night was hurling cushions, chairs, linen, anything she could lay her hand on, onto an ever-growing fire on the duke's bed. Delvin could see the body of the magician with a knife protruding from his chest in the midst of the growing inferno.

The servants were running around in confusion, some trying to throw water on the flames, others trying to restrain the lady as she shouted, "They will not have it! They will not find it!" as she threw more fuel onto the fire.

Delvin could see no sign of the young woman who had been in the magician's bed the night before. She must have killed the magician he thought when she realised that he couldn't control her with his stone any longer. He hoped she had managed to get away safely.

Jarla, rapidly taking in what was happening, stepped over to a sideboard, picked up a small stone statue and struck the lady hard over the head. She staggered and fell at her feet.

"Take her outside and keep her under guard," commanded Jarla. "You." She pointed to one of the servants. "Evacuate the building of everyone not fighting the fire." She pointed to another. "You. Get down to the kitchen and bring all the buckets you can find. The rest of you form a chain."

The smoke was now getting thick, and although Jarla soon had a chain organised passing buckets of water up to the fire it was obvious that they were fighting a losing battle, and they soon had to retreat down the stairs.

As Jarla and Delvin emerged outside, coughing from the smoke, they could see that the fire had now taken hold. One corner of the building was now well alight, and soldiers were running to help the servants fight the blaze.

The duke and Fionella were standing in the road looking up at the burning building.

"I don't understand," began the duke, "Who is this Lady Carolina?"

"That we will soon find out," said Jarla grimly. "Is there somewhere we can go?"

"There's the army headquarters," said the duke.

Jarla turned to the servants who were holding the still stunned Lady Carolina. "Follow us. Lead the way Your Grace."

As they turned to go, the guard captain saw them leaving and ran over with four of his men to escort them and clear a path through the growing crowd of onlookers.

The army headquarters building was attached to a small barracks only two streets away from the Governor's House. The guards at the door snapped to attention as they approached. One of the guards opened the door, and they went in and found themselves in a wide hall. There was a desk at one side at which sat a duty officer who leapt up as they came in, desperately trying to straighten his uniform.

"Your Grace," he began starting to salute, then turned it into a bow.

"We need a room," said Jarla. "And we do not wish to be disturbed."

"This way Your Grace," said the officer, rushing to open the door of a room at one side of the hall. The room had a table with several chairs around it. There was a large fireplace to one side and a window that opened out onto the barracks parade ground.

Jarla turned to the two servants who were still supporting Lady Carolina. "Sit her there then leave us."

The servants propped Lady Carolina in one of the chairs, bowed to the duke and backed out of the door. The door closed behind them, leaving in the room only the duke, Fionella, Jarla, Delvin and Lady Carolina. Lady Carolina was now starting to recover though she was still very white faced.

"Who are you?" demanded Jarla.

"Lady Carolina," she said defiantly.

"There's no Lady Carolina," said the duke.

"I was created Lady Carolina by the Duke of Argent, and

when..."

"I did not give you that title," interrupted the duke. The woman looked momentarily stunned. She had not realised until then that she was facing the real duke.

"Where are you from?" asked Jarla. "And why were you setting fire to the bedroom? Was it because when you found your imposter friend dead and couldn't find his magician's stone, you were determined no one else would find it?"

The woman's eyes flashed and she looked defiantly at the duke. "You can do what you like with me. Enjoy yourself while you can. The magicians will avenge me. With their stones they can destroy you just like that." She snapped her fingers. "Yes. I was making sure the stone was destroyed. With no stones you haven't got a chance." She turned to Jarla. "And when we take over, I hope I have the pleasure of dealing with you personally."

Before Jarla or the duke could retort, they were interrupted by a knock on the door.

"Who is that? I said we should not be interrupted," said the duke testily. Delvin opened the door, and a splendidly uniformed man marched in with his plumed hat tucked neatly under his arm.

"Your Grace," he bowed. "I hope I do not interrupt, but I thought you would wish to know that our attack has started."

The duke looked startled. "Our atta..."

"Give us the details," interrupted Jarla.

"As planned Your Grace, the infantry are pressing forward and the cavalry are standing by in reserve."

"Your Grace," Jarla turned to the duke. "The attack must be stopped and we must call a truce."

"We must indeed," agreed the duke.

The soldier looked horror struck. "We can't stop in mid attack Your Grace. They will think we are retreating. We will be defeated. They could take North Bridge."

"We must do this together Your Grace." Jarla set her jaw determinedly. "I'll try to stop Hengel's forces. You stop Argent's. We will need horses." She was already striding out of the room.

"You," she addressed the startled duty officer. "Bring four horses round to the front of the building now."

"My Lady," he began, looking flushed. "We have no horses here. This is an infantry barracks, and the officers have their horses with them...the attack...my Lady."

"Sheffs," Jarla spun to face the duke. "There are two horses at the inn. Delvin will fetch those. We will also need a white flag... And maybe some of these soldiers can try and find some other horses from somewhere." She turned to Delvin. "Go on, hurry up. Get the horses."

Delvin turned and ran out of the building and down the road as quickly as he could.

He had to slow down as he neared the Governors House since the road was full of onlookers watching the blaze, and squads of cavalry were attempting to move up to the battle that was developing on the bridge. Past the Governors House Delvin dodged a cart and eventually reached the inn and dashed into the yard. The stable door was shut, and breathing hard from the exertion Delvin pulled it open, to be brought up short by a horrific scene.

The black magician stood above the innkeeper, whose eyes stared in terror and agony as the magician's knife cut through his face.

The black magician spun towards the door, and the innkeeper collapsed back screaming, his hands coming up to his face as the magician's attention left him.

"Master Delvin," breathed the black magician.

Delvin grabbed for his stone and touched it only just in time, as the thought hit him, *'You cannot move. You are paralysed.'* Delvin did move. Clutching his stone, he turned and ran. He could hear the black magician coming after him.

Without thinking, he ran towards the road that led to the main square in front of the bridge. The road ahead was blocked with infantry and a first aid station, and he could hear ahead the screams, yells and clash of steel as the battle in the square ahead developed.

An image of himself suddenly came into his mind, and over the noise of the battle a message spoke in his mind, 'Look around you. Point to this man.' Several people turned and pointed at him. Even some of the infantry, looking grimly towards the square, turned back and pointed.

Delvin turned left, left again, then right, trying to escape the black magician. But peoples' faces and fingers followed him. He could see the corner of the temple ahead with its twisted columns and domes. There were more soldiers here. Some of the soldiers and the civilians who hadn't left the battle area, turned and pointed as they answered the message that kept repeating, 'Look around you. Point to this man.'

He turned left down the side of the temple, faces and fingers still following. Glancing back over his shoulder, he could see the black magician coming after him, crossbow in hand, cloak billowing behind, and eyes firmly fixed on him as the passer-by's fingers kept pointing him out.

Delvin turned right down the back of the temple, heading for the river. He tried to dodge and hide behind carts and horses to see if he could escape the black magician that way, but still the faces turned his way, pointing out where he was.

He ran over the next crossroads glancing to his left as he did so. In front of the Army Headquarters he could see Jarla and the Duke of Argent, now mounted and starting to ride towards the square with several soldiers. They must have managed to find some horses. He felt a quick surge of relief that the horses he had been fetching were not needed.

In idea struck him. Could he use them to block the view of where he went? But how could he stop people pointing him out? If he tried countering the black magician's message, the messages might not coincide so people might still point to him. If he sent a different message, the black magician would counter it. What else could he use? He needed to distract the people around him so they wouldn't point him out.

As Jarla and the Duke crossed the road behind him he turned left, hidden from the black magician's view by the duke's party.

Now for the distraction, he thought. He projected the idea to all animals that there was delicious food near where he was. It should distract people from seeing him, he thought, and if the black magician caught up with him, perhaps he could use them to help him escape. Dogs started running from houses, cats jumped from roofs. People started looking at the animals rather than him as the animals milled around.

Delvin knew the back magician would not be held up for long. He needed to get out of sight as quickly as possible. He turned right towards the river, continuing to project the feeling to animals that there was delicious food near where he was. He reached the road that ran along the river's edge and ran across it. A low wall bordered the river. Delvin looked over it. Great wooden beams, laid edge to edge and embedded in the river bottom formed the quayside to which boats could be moored. To Delvin's relief, a small boat was tied to an iron ring about five paces to his right.

Delvin ran toward to where the boat was moored and vaulted over the wall, almost missing the boat in his hurry to get below the quay wall and out of sight of the onlookers, who might soon stop being distracted by the animals. His fingers fumbled with the painter tying the boat to the quayside. As it came free the boat swung out into the river, caught by the strongly flowing water and almost pitching him in. He grabbed for an oar, trying to get some control of the boat as it drifted towards the great bridge.

Delvin was no boatman and the boat lurched as he dipped the oar in the water. What if he got washed out to sea he thought? He would be in real trouble then. The bridge was getting closer. Could he catch on to it as he went by and possibly hide under it?

He dipped the oar into the water again and the boat swung round, veering towards the quayside. He was below the square now and the noise of the battle in the square above was deafening. Stray arrows hissed overhead and a body suddenly toppled over the parapet, an arrow through its chest, sightless eyes staring as it hit the water, and then sinking under the weight of its armour.

Another small boat was moored ahead, and Delvin's boat crashed into it almost knocking the oar from his hand. Delvin grabbed the boat and held onto it with all his might. The boat swung round towards the quay wall. His uncontrolled drifting had brought him close to the bridge. He needed to control the boat and get it under the bridge without being washed downstream.

He had an idea, if he held onto the quayside, he should be able to control the boat better. He let go of the other boat and grabbed the wooden beams of the quayside. Then hand over hand he edged the boat down the quay wall towards the drawbridge tower. Another body fell just behind him and almost made him lose his grip.

The prow of the boat bumped into the base of the tower. The stone on the tower was worn, and the mortar had been washed out by the river and time. Delvin grabbed the stones and edged the boat round to try to get under the great drawbridge. He could hear, even over the noise of battle, the tramp of feet on the drawbridge above and the shouts of the sergeants, "Get a move on. Close ranks."

He held his breath as he edged around the great tower. Would there be somewhere he could hide from the black magician. He let out a sigh of relief as he saw there was a narrow stone ledge between the two drawbridge towers. The curve of the two huge towers shielding it from view from the quayside.

An iron ring was set in the stone by the ledge and Delvin gratefully grabbed it. He tied the boat's painter to it and then scrambled carefully up onto the ledge itself.

The sound of boots on the drawbridge above sounded even louder now, as though magnified by the towers and the river. The ledge was narrow, and the height from it to the drawbridge was insufficient for him to stand up. But as Delvin sat back crouching on the ledge, he at least felt safe.

He let out a big sigh. Above his head the tramp of feet continued. Officers shouting, "Left, right. Come on, get a move on, they are going to attack again. We need to get all our men across."

Across the fast-flowing water he could see the piers supporting the landing of the drawbridge and the first span of the bridge. Wooden beams had been driven into the riverbed to make a large diamond shaped base around which the river flowed. The base had been filled with stone and rubble to make a rough platform, from the centre of which rose the stone landing for the drawbridge. There was movement on the base as several rats sniffed the air expectantly.

Delvin suddenly froze in fear as the black magician stepped out from behind the stone landing opposite. He was picking his way carefully over the uneven surface of the diamond shaped base, holding his crossbow in one hand, and the painter of a small boat in the other. The rats, still sniffing the air, scurried to get out of his way. He looked coldly across the short stretch of water at Delvin.

"We meet again Master Delvin."

Delvin wondered desperately what he could do. If he jumped into his boat and drifted downstream, the black magician would either follow him, or shoot him with the crossbow.

The black magician looked up at the drawbridge. A loop of rope hung down on one side, almost spanning the river before it disappeared out of sight somewhere above Delvin's head. The black magician pulled his boat round the diamond-shaped base. Then dropping his crossbow into the boat, he reached out with his free hand and grabbed the loop of rope. Very carefully he stepped into his boat, dropping the painter and grasping the loop of rope, so that he now held it with both hands. Then hand over hand he began to pull the boat across the gap towards Delvin.

Delvin was almost paralysed with fear. What could he do? Could he cut the loop of rope with his knife? If he started trying to do that, the black magician would pick up his crossbow and shoot him. But what would the black magician do to him if he didn't.

The black magician was getting closer. There was now a cruel twist to his lips and his eyes seemed to be boring into Delvin.

"That was an interesting idea Master Delvin, to use animals to distract people," sneered the black magician. "But it seems to have backfired." He gave a cruel laugh. "The animals led me to you. They were all crowding on the quayside above where you were."

Delvin was horrified. His message to animals that there was delicious food near him had not worn off, and it had drawn the black magician to him. There were even rats under the bridge looking expectantly in his direction.

The black magician stopped pulling on the rope. He was now less than two paces away. Just too far for Delvin to reach him with his knife. Holding on to the rope with one hand, the black magician bent down into his boat, picked up his crossbow and pointed it at Delvin.

"Throw Borlock's crystal into my boat, very, very carefully. Come on now, we both know you've got it. Am I going to have to shoot crossbow bolts into you until you do as I say?"

Delvin put his hand in his pocket and took out the crystal he had taken from the fake Duke of Argent. The black magician obviously did not realise he had two crystals. Could he use that to his advantage? He tossed the false duke's crystal into the black magician's boat.

The black magician grinned cruelly and a message instantly appeared in Delvin's mind, *'You are paralysed. You cannot move. When my knife touches you, it will burn as though red hot.'* Delvin didn't move. The black magician dropped his crossbow and leaned forward to pick up the crystal. As he bent down, a message came into Delvin's mind, *"I have recovered Borlock's stone."* Then what seemed to be a reply. *'Good, return to Norden.'* The black magician crouched down to pick up the crystal from the bottom of the boat.

Now! thought Delvin. He projected the feeling to all animals that the black magician was the delicious food they had been looking for, and that he tasted wonderful. The effect was almost instantaneous. Rats leapt from the underside of the drawbridge, from the boat, from the stone base where Delvin crouched and from the drum towers, covering the back magician in a heaving mass of hungry, biting, clawing animals. More rats ran along the rope that the black magician had been pulling.

The black magician had been taken completely by surprise as he had been concentrating on picking up the crystal from the bottom of the boat. It was a second before he sent out a projection commanding the animals to stop attacking him. But as Delvin had discovered, animals didn't respond to projected words of command, they responded to feelings. So the rats continued to attack. It was a few moments before the black magician realised his mistake and began to send out the feeling that he tasted terrible. But as Delvin kept on projecting the feeling that the black magician tasted delicious, the two messages simply cancelled each other out. The rats had now got the taste of the magician and clung on, biting deeper and deeper.

The black magician had let go of the rope that was holding his boat in place, and it was now taken by the current and began to drift downstream. He had been leaning forward when the rats attacked and he now stood, covered in a seething furry mass, with great patches of red where rat's teeth had bitten into a vein or artery. The boat swayed dangerously as the current took it and as he tried beat off the rats. The beating became more frantic, and the boat lurched even further, until eventually the side of the boat tipped under the water and the boat capsized flinging the black magician into the river. The rats were still clinging on as the black magician disappeared under the water, his black robes weighing him down.

A feeling of relief swept over Delvin. The black magician was dead. Even better, the message he had sent to the Guild of Magicians that he had recovered Borlock's stone meant they would not be hunting him any longer. The fake duke's stone was at the bottom of the river which was a pity. But he still had Borlock's stone, and the only person who knew he had it was Grimbolt. All he had to do now was to get himself off his narrow ledge.

Delvin bent down, took hold of his boats painter and drew the boat towards him. Then very carefully he stepped into it. Holding onto the iron ring with one hand, he untied the painter with the other. The last thing he wanted to happen now was to get swept down the river towards the sea. Then as carefully as he could, he edged the boat around the tower.

He had just got as far as the quayside when his progress was arrested by a shout from above. "You there, what are you doing. Come on up. I have archers covering you."

Delvin looked up. An officer with a large moustache and flanked by archers was glaring at him.

"I'll just tie the boat up," called Delvin.

There was another iron ring set in the quay wall near where he was. He manoeuvred the boat to it and tied it up. He then stood up in the boat, and was immediately grabbed under the arms and hauled unceremoniously up and over the low wall and onto the edge of the square.

As he came over the wall, the full din of the battle hit him. Hengel's army had formed up in a tight formation and Argent's infantry were slowly pressing them back.

Two large wooden structures on wheels, covered in wet hides, were being pushed towards the bridge by rows of heaving men. Hengel's archers in the towers behind him were pouring arrows into them trying to slow their progress. Argent's archers were returning the fire in kind from every rooftop and window. The soldiers around Delvin had shields interlocked together to protect themselves from the arrows, and he suddenly felt very vulnerable in their midst.

"They are coming again," came a shout from his right. "The duke's leading them. It looks like this will be the big one."

Delvin was bewildered. Wasn't the duke trying to stop the battle? He strained to see what was going on, and saw the duke and Jarla pressing forward carrying a large white flag.

"He's carrying a flag of truce. He wants a truce," yelled Delvin. He grabbed his stone and began projecting a message towards the armies. *'Stop fighting. There's a truce. Stop fighting.'*

The duke and Jarla's progress had slowed, since the troops in the front line were far too involved in survival and death to notice anything other than their enemies in front.

"Truce!" The cry echoed back and forth as it was taken up by men down the line. The fighting began to stop. Men glaring distrustfully at enemies they had been trying to kill moments before.

"Stop those archers." Even over the cries and screams, and now the lessening clash of steel, Delvin could hear the duke's roar.

The arrows abruptly stopped, and an extraordinary quiet suddenly came over the battlefield. There were still the moans and cries of the wounded, but after the crash and noise of the fighting, the contrast seemed unnaturally quiet. All around there was a sense of unreality as though time had suddenly stopped. The men of both sides eyed each other warily, half expecting the battle to be re-joined at any moment.

A familiar stocky figure emerged from the tower by Delvin and was about to stride forward when he spotted Delvin between his captors.

"What the sheffs are you doing here," demanded General Gortley. "Don't tell me. This is Princess Jarla's doing."

"Yes General," replied Delvin.

"Come with me," growled General Gortly grimly, as he turned and began to stride through his troops towards the duke and Jarla.

"Princess Jarla," he roared. Heads turned at the bellow. "What the sheffs is this all about?"

"General Gortly, how nice to see you," replied Jarla.

"Get away from the battle this instant. This is not some picnic."

Jarla smiled sweetly. "May I introduce you to The Duke of Argent."

General Gortly hesitated in mid stride, and bit off the next remark he was about to make.

"Your Grace," continued Jarla. "May I introduce you to General Gortly, commanding Hengel's army."

"What are you up to?" growled General Gortly.

"We need to stop this war, and we are starting with a truce. Withdraw your men to the towers, and Argent will withdraw theirs to the other side of the square. Then get a message to my father, so we can sign a proper peace treaty." She turned to the duke. "Your Grace?"

"Men of Argent. Move back," shouted the duke.

General Gortly glared at Jarla. "Hengel back," he roared.

The two armies slowly separated, still looking suspiciously at each other.

"Would you care to dine with us General?" enquired the duke.

"Thank you, Your Grace, but I must await the arrival of the Duke of Hengel."

General Gortly bowed, never taking his eyes off Jarla and the Duke of Argent. The duke bowed back and turned his horse towards what looked like a group of generals who stood at the back of the square.

"Princess Jarla."

"Yes, General Gortly."

"You can take your pet magician with you." With that he gave Delvin a shove that propelled him across the lines and towards Jarla.

"Where have you been?" snapped Jarla angrily.

"The black magician was at the inn."

"I give you a simple task, and you mess it up." She turned her horse and went after the duke.

CHAPTER 36

Delvin followed the duke and Jarla back towards the Army Headquarters. Some of the town's citizens, beginning to realise that the war might be ending, peered at them from their doorways and windows. A few gave a thin cheer, still unsure if the war had really ended. When they reached the Army Headquarters, the duke and the others dismounted. Soldiers ran forward to take their horses.

Fionella had been watching for them from the window and ran out to greet them, flinging her arms around her father's neck. As they entered the building Jarla glanced up and noticed Delvin following behind. A smile crept into her face.

"We did well... Now bring our things from the inn." She turned back to the others.

Before Delvin could follow them into the Army Headquarters the door was closed behind them and Delvin was left outside. The guard on the door looked at him suspiciously, so he turned away and made his way to the inn to collect their bags. On checking the horses, he decided to leave them and his rabbit at the stables for the time being and paid the stable lad three copper bits to look after them until he returned.

He carried the bags back to the Army Headquarters, and approaching the guard announced importantly, "The baggage of Their Highnesses the Duke of Argent, Princess Fionella and Princess Jarla."

The guard looked suspicious but opened the door, and Delvin went in to be confronted by the duty officer at the desk.

"The baggage for Their Highnesses the Duke of Argent, Princess Fionella and Princess Jarla," he repeated.

"Put it in their rooms. You go up the stairs. It's the first three rooms on the right. Right hand side of the corridor." The officer made a note in a large book on his desk.

"Is my room up there too?" asked Delvin. The officer looked up from his book and eyed him pityingly. Then with an almost imperceptible shake of his head went back to his book.

Delvin waited a moment, then turned and trudged up the stairs to the rooms. Halfway up, he heard the duke's raised voice coming from the room they had been in earlier. "You let her escape? She was a traitor... What do you mean nobody told you to guard her..."

Oh dear, thought Delvin, not everything was going the duke's way.

When he had deposited the bags, he made his way downstairs and approached the duty officer again.

"Have the duke or Princess Jarla left any instructions for me?"

"Who are you?"

"Delvin."

The officer consulted his book. "No. I can't see anything."

"I had better go and ask them."

"I am sorry. I have instructions that they are not to be disturbed."

"Well, when can I see them?"

"If you are in the duke's party, you will be on the list for the dinner they are arranging tonight. I suggest you come back then."

"Can you get a message to them?"

"No. their instructions are that they are not to be disturbed."

Delvin let out a deep breath. "Right. I'll come back this evening."

Delvin spent the remainder of the day looking round North Bridge, but he frequently returned to the Army Headquarters expecting that Jarla or the duke would have asked for him. By evening there had been no summons, so he presented himself once again to the duty officer so he could join the party for dinner. A different officer was at the table, and he looked Delvin up and down in barely concealed disgust.

"The duke is having a private dinner."

"I'm in the duke's party."

"Your name?"

"Delvin."

The officer glanced at his book. "You are not on the list. Good day."

"But I must be."

"Good day," repeated the officer deliberately. Delvin turned and went back out onto the street. They couldn't have forgotten him, could they? He walked disconsolately back towards the smouldering ruins of the Governor's House. As he looked up at it, he stopped feeling sorry for himself and felt a pang of sorrow for Aggie. The Governor's House had been her job, and now she would have to find another one. He thought about the fire, and hoped she had got out of the building safely. On impulse, he went along to the bar where he had met Aggie the night before.

Delvin had just ordered himself an ale, when a voice in his ear said, "Hello handsome, fancy seeing you again." He turned smiling. Aggie had been sitting at a corner table where he hadn't seen her when he entered the bar. He bought her a drink and went to join her at her table. As they chatted, she told him that as her room in the Governor's House was destroyed, she was staying with her sister until she could find a new situation. Later that evening, giggling from the several drinks they had had, she sneaked Delvin in the back way of her sister's house.

He woke early in the morning, and was gone before Aggie's sister was up leaving no sign of his stay. Aggie crept back into bed after waving him good-bye.

Delvin's first task in the morning was to arrange for the return of the hearse to the undertakers in Dandel from whom he had hired it. When he had done that, he decided he was fed up with trying to help Jarla and the duke, and he would try to get over the river to South Bridge and back to Hengel. He returned to the inn and took out the horse that Jarla had been riding. After asking directions, he made his way to the horse dealers. He wanted to recover the money he had spent on hiring the hearse. He then returned to the inn to retrieve Freda and his own horse, and made his way to the square by the bridge to see if there was any way he could get across the river.

The square was a hive of activity. The marks of the previous day's battle had been largely removed, though Delvin noticed there were still squads of cavalry stationed in the side streets and archers lining the roofs. Several squads of workmen were swilling down the sections of cobbles where the fighting had been fiercest, overseen by officious looking men pointing out bits that needed more attention. A large tent was being erected in the entre of the square, and a military band was practicing the anthems of Hengel and Argent.

Delvin edged his horse around the workmen to try to reach the bridge. A self-important sergeant stopped him, telling him the bridge was closed, and would remain closed until a peace treaty had been signed. Delvin looked across at the bridge, and saw it was still lined with Hengel's soldiers, looking on suspiciously at the preparations in the square.

Just past noon, a party under the blue and white banner of Hengel could be seen advancing across the bridge. To meet them, the Duke of Argent, with Fionella and Jarla at his side, rode forward across the square under the silver and red banner of Argent.

The two parties met at the truce line. The Duke of Hengel embraced Jarla. He cut an extraordinary figure. The spikes of his hair were decorated with silver caps making his head look like a gigantic mace or starburst. Another figure came forward wearing an elaborate hat. With a start Delvin realised it was Maegar. So she had got back safely with Grimbolt, thought Delvin. She too embraced Jarla.

The two parties dismounted and made their way to the tent which was now decorated with flags and bunting. The dukes walked arm in arm. Princesses Jarla and Fionella chatted with Maegar as they followed behind. The band picked up the two countries anthems and a stream of servants made their way to the tent bearing a fantastic array of food. It looked as though it would be some time before anything else happened, so Delvin joined the crowd that was starting to disperse and made his way to a nearby inn that overlooked the square. There were still deep marks around the inn's windows showing where, until only the day before, they had been barricaded against possible attacks by Hengel.

It was late afternoon before the two dukes emerged from the tent, affably talking together. A small platform had been erected in the centre of the square and the dukes climbed onto it with the princesses and Maegar behind. The crowd had now gathered again and Delvin quickly finished his drink and joined them. He was not able to get close enough to hear what the dukes were saying, but it was greeted by a great cheer by those closest to the platform. The dukes embraced each other, then climbed down from the platform and began to make their way towards the bridge with the crowd following behind them.

Delvin ran back to the inn and retrieved his horse, and then joined the back of the crowd.

The royal party was making its stately way across Argent's side of the bridge. As they approached, Hengel's soldiers stood to attention, saluted, turned and marched off. After the two dukes had passed, Argent's soldiers replaced them.

Due to the huge crowd Delvin had not yet reached the bridge. He could see that a crowd had also formed in South Bridge on the other side of the river.

When the dukes reached the central drawbridge, they stood across the join between the two halves and embraced again. A great cheer arose from both sides of the river.

The royal party moved on towards South Bridge, walking calmly past Hengel's soldiers under their blue and white banners guarding Hengel's half of the bridge. Delvin looked up, and saw that the towers on the North Bridge side, now once again supported the silver and red flags of Argent.

The crowd had surged onto the bridge, eager to again be able to cross the river. As Delvin was swept along under the first towers, he could see the royal party had now left the bridge and was entering the town on the far side. After they had left the bridge, the South Bridge crowd surged forward. They too wanted to use the bridge again. There will be some party tonight thought Delvin.

When he finally got over the river, and manoeuvred his way through the spontaneous party that was taking place all around, Delvin made his way to the quartermaster's stables where he had left their cart. As he reached the building, a sudden feeling of apprehension came over him. What if the quartermaster did not recognise him, or if it was a different one on duty? He took a deep breath and went in.

"Ah, so you are back," said the quartermaster rising from behind his desk. A feeling of relief swept over Delvin.

"Yes. I've come to see if the cart's all right. I'm going to Hengel."

"Yes. It's all fine. I've been keeping an eye on it. Do you need anything out of it for the duke's party tonight, or do you just want to collect it in the morning?"

"I haven't been invited to the party."

"You haven't? Well, it's not every day that a war is ended. We're having a celebration in the sergeant's mess. Come along as my guest. I'll bet it will be more fun than the duke's party."

"Thanks. Are you sure?"

"Certainly. Get your horse stabled with the cart, then come back here. We'll walk over together."

"Thanks."

Delvin went out, and led his horse to the stables with a lighter feeling in his heart. It was really too late to set out for Hengel that night and Delvin felt he had earned a party.

When he had stabled his horse and fed Freda, he re-joined the quartermaster and they walked together over to the sergeant's mess.

The sergeant's mess turned out to be a long building under the shadow of the West Tower, the oldest building in South Bridge. By the time they arrived it was already starting to fill up. The other sergeants were happy to accept Delvin, and he sat down at a table by the wall and chatted amiably with a sergeant of the town's garrison. The duke had donated several casks of ale to celebrate the peace and soon it was flowing freely. Now that the war was over and the threat of death and disfigurement was removed, everyone was determined to have a good time.

Delvin remembered little of the latter part of the evening. His mug had continued to be refilled with ale. He remembered singing that had got louder, bawdier and more hilarious, and he dimly remembered being kissed by a large and busty lady. Someone had mentioned the big party at the Guild Hall, and Delvin remembered filling his mug with more ale and drinking it down in one swallow.

He awoke with his head hurting and his mouth dry and foul tasting. He gingerly raised his head, and saw he was lying on a pallet in what looked like a dormitory. The other pallets were occupied by soldiers, most of them still fully dressed though one or two had apparently been sufficiently sober to at least remove their boots.

He staggered to his feet, his head throbbing with every tiny movement and headed for the door. The door led into a hall, with stairs going down to a yard where Delvin found a pump. He put his head under it and pulled the handle. The cold water helped bring him awake. He took a deep drink of it and sat back, keeping his eyes shut from the glare of the sun.

A short while later, he heard someone else stagger from the building and make for the pump. It was one of the sergeants he had met last night and he waved a hand to him in greeting. When he too had doused his head, he guided Delvin to the kitchens where they got a cup of hot leaf and a roll.

Other sergeants gradually came in, and it was with some reluctance that Delvin finally took leave of his friends. It was with a lighter heart that he went to the stables to find his horse and the cart.

Delvin gave Freda a quick run while he checked over the cart's contents. It was all still there, including Maegar's dress and

Jarla's bundle. He checked his pocket. He still had his magician's stone and hadn't lost it in the revels of the night before.

Delvin hitched his horse up to the cart, looked in to say goodbye to the quartermaster, climbed into the cart, and headed the horse towards the Hengel Road.

With the new peace treaty and the parties of the night before, there were no guards checking travellers at South Bridge's gate. Delvin passed through into the flat farm lands beyond.

Just past noon, Delvin stopped by a steam to rest the horse and take a break. He still had some of the travel rations left and sat eating them in the warm sunshine. He was beginning to feel much better as the excesses of the previous night started to wear off. Having finished his meal, he set off again towards Hengel.

A short while later he heard a pounding behind him. Looking over his shoulder, he saw a large party cantering up the road. They were riding far faster than him so he looked for a place he could pull off to let them pass. He had only just got the cart off the road and onto the verge, when the cavalcade rode past. First came two columns of cavalry, their breast plates and helmets gleaming in the sun. Then came a figure that Delvin immediately recognised as the Duke of Hengel. The extraordinary points of his hair bending back in the wind, each tipped by a streamer that flowed back behind him. Riding closely behind him was Jarla. Now changed from her dirty riding gear into one of striking red. As she rode past Delvin, she glanced down at him. She gave a quick start of recognition and a fleeting smile as she cantered on. There were several other mounted figures and a carriage pulled by four horses that Delvin suspected carried Maegar. The rear of the party was made up of two more columns of cavalry.

Delvin steered his cart back onto the road. The fields were starting to give way to trees, and before long he was driving through a forest with trees stretching away on both sides of the road. After a while the road emerged from the forest, and Delvin could see in the distance the walls and towers of Hengel rising from the surrounding countryside.

The check by the guards at the great gate was only perfunctory, and as Delvin entered Hengel he could see celebrations were in full progress. The streets were decked with bunting, and enterprising traders had set up stalls and sideshows in the main streets and squares.

As Delvin made his way through the city, he could hear cheers and clapping coming from the square in front of the Castle. It sounded as if there was a huge crowd with someone addressing them. Delvin turned his horse away from the crowds, making his way through the back streets towards Mistress Wilshaw's. He pulled up outside the familiar house and got down from the cart, wondering if Mistress Wilshaw had re-let the room, or indeed if she would have him back at all.

He knocked on the door with a feeling of trepidation, and a moment later the door opened.

"Ooo! Master Delvin, where have you been? I never thought I would see you again when those soldiers came. They are not still looking for you, are they?"

Delvin shook his head.

"I was going to re-let your room, but Master Greg said to wait a bit longer. Ooo, have you heard, the war is over? Now you get your things in, and you can come down and have a nice cup of hot leaf and tell me what you have been doing."

A familiar face appeared at the top of the stairs.

"Greg."

"Delvin."

Greg ran down the stairs and embraced his friend.

"Where have you been Delvin?"

"It's a long story. Can you look after a horse and cart at the stables where you work until I can sell them?"

"Sure, let me help you with your things." Together they quickly emptied the cart and took the things up to the room that they shared. Then they drove the horse and cart over to Greg's stables, where Delvin brushed the horse down while Greg found it some feed.

As they walked back, Delvin gave his friend an outline of what had happened.

"You should be a storyteller," laughed Greg. "I've never heard such a load of make believe in all my life."

"It's true," insisted Delvin laughing as well.

When they reached Mistress Wilshaw's, a familiar figure was waiting for them.

"Magister Delvin, Princess Jarla sent me to get her and Maegar's dresses," Grimbolt smiled at him. Greg's mouth fell open.

"Captain Grybald!" said Delvin in surprise. "I'll just bring them down."

He ran up to his room, and came back down with Jarla's bundle and Maegar's dress.

"Here they are." He handed them over to Grimbolt.

"Thank you, Magister Delvin. I did mention to Princess Jarla that she should reimburse you for your expenses."

"You did?"

"She gave me this, and hopes it covers what you spent." Grimbolt grinned as he handed over a heavy purse.

"Thank you, Captain Grybald," said Delvin taken aback. "Please would you thank Princess Jarla for me."

"I will Magister Delvin. There was something I wanted to ask you. Can we go somewhere private?"

"I am sure we can. May we use the parlour, Mistress Wilshaw?" Mistress Wilshaw nodded, for once lost for words.

They went into the parlour and shut the door behind them, leaving Greg and Mistress Wilshaw still staring in astonishment.

"Magister Delvin," began Grimbolt. "Is the black magician still after you?"

Delvin explained what had happened in North Bridge, and Grimbolt nodded in approval.

"I have been wondering." Said Delvin. "What happened to Magister Perball's stone after he was executed?"

"Ahh," said Grimbolt his voice becoming serious. "An officer was detailed to take it to Hengel for safe keeping. He never made it. His body was found with a crossbow bolt in his back. The stone was missing. I have been thinking who could have done it. It couldn't have been that black magician, since he was in Argent going after you. My guess is it was Perball's assistant. I went looking for him after taking Maegar back. But he'd long gone."

"Oh," said Delvin. "I was hoping that stone could have been used by Hengel to stop anything like this happening again."

"It might have done," said Grimbolt. "But now Hengel has only one stone." He looked at Delvin meaningfully. "And... the magicians don't know about it." He smiled his lopsided smile and got up to leave.

"I'll be seeing you Magister Delvin."

"I'll be seeing you Captain Grybald."

"Call me Grimbolt," said Grimbolt with a grin.

"Call me Delvin," said Delvin grinning back.

The two clasped hands.

Look out for

The Three Card Trick

Book 2 of Illusions of Power

Printed in Great Britain
by Amazon